Fairy Tales for the Disillusioned

ODDLY MODERN FAIRY TALES
Jack Zipes, *Series Editor*

Oddly Modern Fairy Tales is a series dedicated to publishing unusual literary fairy tales produced mainly during the first half of the twentieth century. International in scope, the series includes new translations, surprising and unexpected tales by well-known writers and artists, and uncanny stories by gifted yet neglected authors. Postmodern before their time, the tales in *Oddly Modern Fairy Tales* transformed the genre and still strike a chord.

Kurt Schwitters *Lucky Hans and Other Merz Fairy Tales*

Béla Balázs *The Cloak of Dreams: Chinese Fairy Tales*

Peter Davies, editor *The Fairies Return: Or, New Tales for Old*

Naomi Mitchison *The Fourth Pig*

Walter de la Mare *Told Again: Old Tales Told Again*

Gretchen Schultz and Lewis Seifert, editors *Fairy Tales for the Disillusioned: Enchanted Stories from the French Decadent Tradition*

FAIRY TALES FOR THE DISILLUSIONED

Enchanted Stories from the French Decadent Tradition

EDITED AND TRANSLATED BY

GRETCHEN SCHULTZ & LEWIS SEIFERT

PRINCETON UNIVERSITY PRESS
Princeton and Oxford

press.princeton.edu
Jacket art: Ornamental flower pattern from Plate 38 of *Documents
Decoratifs*, 1902 (color litho), Alphonse Marie Mucha (1860–1939)/Mucha
Trust/Bridgeman Images

Library of Congress Cataloging-in-Publication Data

Names: Schultz, Gretchen, 1960- editor translator. | Seifert, Lewis Carl,
editor translator.
Title: Fairy tales for the disillusioned : enchanted stories from the French
decadent tradition / edited and translated by Gretchen Schultz and Lewis
Seifert.
Description: Princeton : Princeton University Press, 2016. | Series: Oddly
modern fairy tales | "The present volume contains thirty-five fairy tales by
nineteen writers, presented chronologically by author"—Introduction. |
Includes bibliographical references.
Identifiers: LCCN 2015051218 | ISBN 9780691161655
(hardcover : alk. paper)
Subjects: LCSH: Fairy tales—France. | French fiction—19th century—
Translations into English. | French fiction—20th century—Translations into
English. | Children's stories, French—Translations into English.

Classification: LCC PQ1278 .F35 2016 | DDC 843/.0208—dc23 LC
record available at https://lccn.loc.gov/2015051218

British Library Cataloging-in-Publication Data is available

This book has been composed in Adobe Jenson Pro & Caecilia LT Std

Printed on acid-free paper. ∞

Printed in the United States of America

1 3 5 7 9 10 8 6 4 2

For our sons,
Julian Schultz
and
Andrew and Patrick Gordon-Seifert

Contents

Illustrations

Translators' Note and Acknowledgments

The present volume contains thirty-six fairy tales by nineteen writers, presented chronologically by author. The process of choosing and translating them involved combing through around seventy collections of tales by nearly forty authors, some highly prolific writers of fairy tales, some who merely dabbled in them. Previous work on the decadent fairy tale facilitated the task of identifying many of these sources, in particular Jean de Palacio's *Perversions du merveilleux: Ma Mère l'Oye au tournant du siècle* (1993) and Nathalie Chatelain's dissertation, "Les Contes de fées en Europe à la fin du XIXe siècle" (2005). Francis Lacassin's anthology of French fairy tales from the seventeenth through the twentieth century, *Si les fées m'étaient contées* (2003), also provided difficult-to-find sources.

While we focused on writers associated with the decadent movement (including Jean Lorrain, Catulle Mendès, Rachilde) or at least with its preoccupations, not all those whose fairy tales we deemed worthy of inclusion would have accepted the "decadent" label. Some are more accurately numbered among the symbolists (Henri de Régnier, Marcel Schwob), and Charles Baudelaire preceded such distinctions. Alphonse Daudet was aligned with naturalism, decadence's antithesis. Others don't fit easily into such categories, while Guillaume Apollinaire and Claude Cahun follow them and are more typically associated with surrealism (Apollinaire as precursor).

What these tales share are their decadent themes: decline and degeneration, anxiety and distress associated with the incursion of the modern and the industrial, atypical gender expression and nonnormative sexuality. Many rewrite or unwrite traditional tales, foremost those by Charles Perrault, author of the *Tales of Mother Goose* and grandfather of the fairy tale.

The bulk of the tales included are newly translated by the editors; only four are taken from previous translations. Most of our selections have long been out of print even in the original French. We strove for fluid translations that captured both the archaic language of fairy tales and the startling incursions of the modern that the authors imposed upon that tradition. All translations pose obstacles unique to the text being rendered in a different language. The challenges we faced were commensurate with decadent literature's predilection for the baroque, the recherché, and the arcane. The specialized terminology employed by some authors in certain instances exceeded the limits of our own vocabulary. For example, Emile Bergerat's description of Cinderella's gown refers in technical language to no fewer than half a dozen different types of lace ("Cinderella Arrives by Automobile"). And Mendès's inventory of the esoteric dishes prepared to entice a young prince to eat includes such delicacies as "ragout of young monkey larded with Andean burnets" ("An Unsuitable Guest"). Rachilde's "The Mortis" is also virtuosic in its deployment of the technical lexicons of botany and entomology. But even more challenging than her vocabulary is her ornate and highly figurative prose, with its lengthy sentences and multiple subordinate clauses. These difficulties notwithstanding, the translations we offer here shatter preconceived notions of what the fairy tale is, even as they demonstrate the creative force of disillusionment.

This project would not have been possible without the encouragement of Jack Zipes, the series editor and eminent authority on fairy tales. We would also like to thank our editor, Anne Savarese, for her assistance and support, and the two anonymous reviewers whose comments and suggestions helped improve our introduction and translations. Finally, acknowledgment is due for the following translations: Anatole France, "The Seven Wives of Bluebeard" and "The Story of the Duchess of Cicogne and of Monsieur de Boulingrin," translated by D. B. Stewart in *The Seven Wives of Bluebeard and Other Marvelous Tales* (London: John Lane Company, 1920); Guillaume Apollinaire, "Cinderella Continued, or the Rat and the Six Lizards," translated by Iain White in *Spells of Enchantment*, edited by Jack Zipes (New York: Viking, 1991); and Jean Lorrain, "The Princess Mandosiane," anonymous translation in *The Parisian* 7.3 (1899).

Introduction

Fairies were dying off in the nineteenth century. . . . Their movements became languid in a fever of erudition and philosophy.
(Goyau 345)

The nineteenth century, arguably one of the most chaotic in France's history, was marked by perpetual revolution and regime change, cycling through two empires, two monarchies, and three republics. The fairy tales included in this volume were written by writers who participated in the decadent literary movement or whose work is indebted to the decadent aesthetic, a cynical and aesthetically driven reaction to this tumultuous century. Hundreds of "decadent" fairy tales appeared in France between 1870 and 1914, and our volume aims to introduce English-language readers to this enthralling and often troubling corpus.

In an important sense, these fairy tales are the continuation of a long-standing fascination with the genre known in French as the *conte de fées*. From the late seventeenth century until the Revolution, writers in France had written more than three hundred fairy tales, mostly for adult readers, that were influential far beyond the borders of metropolitan France, "the Hexagon." In the nineteenth century, the genre took on new life through rewritings and new tales by the likes of George Sand, translations of the fairy tales of the Brothers Grimm and Hans Christian Andersen, adaptations for opera and theater by Jacques Offenbach and Paul Dukas, and at the very end of the century in the films of Georges Méliès. All of these developments owed a great debt to the canonical status the *conte de fées* had acquired thanks especially to the burgeoning of children's literature at the time. Figures such as Puss 'n Boots, Cinderella, Little Red Riding Hood, and Sleeping Beauty—all characters featured by Charles Perrault in his *Stories or Tales of Yesteryear* (1697)—became ubiquitous cultural references because of the chapbooks, *images d'Epinal*,[1] children's books, and marionette plays that proliferated in nineteenth-century France. Alongside these literary and artistic developments were the efforts to collect and preserve oral folktales undertaken by folklorists.[2]

In France and elsewhere, fairy tales have often appeared in moments of cultural, social, or political crisis and transition, and decadent *contes de fées* were no exception.[3] Deeply indebted to the rich and variegated traditions of the *conte de fées* in nineteenth-century France, decadent writers also sought to depart from them in ways that responded to the political, social, and intellectual upheaval of their times. A European phenomenon, the decadent movement in France appeared during—and in reaction to—the Third Republic (1870–1940), which was born in the flames of the Franco-Prussian War of 1870–71 and of the short-lived Paris Commune (1871), a radical experiment in collective governance that was brutally quashed by the provisional government. Although constitutionally stable, the Third Republic witnessed a period of political, social, and religious contention. Historians have attributed a number of anxieties to the nation during this time, stemming from several social and geopolitical causes, including fallout from the devastating loss to the Germans, a rapidly evolving class structure, and the entrance of women into the workforce. Causing an influx of workers to cities, the Industrial Revolution fundamentally changed the economy and demographics and challenged class boundaries. The labor movement and demands from women's rights groups, including expanded education for girls and marriage reform, were perceived as threats on both the right and the left. In the political sphere, monarchists and their allies in the church continued to oppose the Republic, which, in return, stirred anticlerical sentiment. Republican secularism eventually culminated in the separation of church and state in 1905. Political divisions were often stark, as traditionalists sought a return to an order that no longer was possible, in opposition to defenders of the young Republic, who waved the banner of progress.

The nineteenth century was also an intellectually dynamic time. The philosophy of positivism, dating to the first part of the century and originating in the works of philosopher Auguste Comte, undergirded the rationalist affirmation of science and progress. Charles Darwin's theory of natural selection had a profound effect on the way people saw the physical and social world. Across Europe, innovation and discovery contributed to the extraordinary advances in industry, transportation, communications, and science. The expanding networks of railroads, automation, and electricity fueled the rise of industry. This period also saw enormous breakthroughs in medicine, such as Louis Pasteur's germ theory and work in immunology. Other developments include photography and X-rays, transatlantic ocean travel and automobiles, and the telegraph, all astounding innovations, many of which were on display at universal expositions in Paris and abroad at the end and turn of the century.

In the face of such innovation and change, observers toward the end of the nineteenth century noted the disparity between technological and broader social trends on one hand, and, on the other, the stereotypically unmechanized and yet magical world of fairy tales. According to historian and philosopher Ernest Renan, "the richness of the marvelous endures up until the incontrovertible advent of the scientific age" (*L'Avenir de la science* 263). It was frequently repeated that progress menaced the fairy, that "railways . . . put fairies to flight" (Goyau 18). Trends in literature during the second half of the century would also seem to have been inhospitable to the genre of the fairy tale. Naturalism, the hyperrealistic, scientific approach to fiction championed by Emile Zola, had no patience for irrationality, much less magic wands and talking animals. Its harsh and unblinking representations of the seamier aspects of contemporary France were anything but enchanting.[4]

In a different literary vein, one also the product of positivism and technological advancement, this period witnessed the development of science fiction as a genre. Although important precedents existed before the nineteenth century, inventions related to electricity and travel fueled writing that relied upon futuristic settings, unfamiliar worlds, or as-yet-unrealized technological inventions. The term "science fiction" was coined in the 1850s. Soon thereafter Jules Verne, considered one of the genre's founding fathers, began publishing books such as *Journey to the Center of the Earth* (1864) and *From the Earth to the Moon* (1865) to great acclaim from both general readers and members of the scientific community. Interestingly enough, one contemporary writer linked

Verne to the passing of fairies: "The good fairies of yesteryear are no longer among us.... There is only one remaining today: the fairy Electricity, whose godson Jules Verne might well have been" (quoted in Lemire 98). Jean Lorrain also lamented that "children of this generation read Jules Verne rather than Perrault" (*Princesses* 2). However, even Verne authored a story labeled as a fairy tale, called "The Rat Family" (1891), which was based on the premise of metempsychosis. Pierre Veber's "The Last Fairy" ironically invokes science fiction by representing a fairy who is dumbfounded and outdone by cutting-edge technology.

The fairy tale nonetheless thrived at the end of the century: one critic writes of an "invasion of fairies" around 1880 (Jullian 67). This burst in the production of fairy tales coincided with the decadent movement, the cynicism of which countered positivism in general and naturalism in particular. Beyond its literary and artistic manifestations, decadence could be called a philosophical position that took issue with the celebration of progress. As suggested by the word's Latin root, "to fall away from," the idea of decadence presupposed a world in decline rather than one moving forward. Although it was much more innovative and experimental than was the stylistic conservatism of naturalist fiction, decadent literature followed a logic that was *politically* conservative. Like monarchists and proponents of the church, decadent writers regretted the fall of the aristocracy and the rise of the bourgeoisie and working classes. Instead of seeing advancement in new technologies, they were frightened by modernization and appalled by democratization and ensuing changes in the social landscape. Philippe Jullian contends that this renewal in fairy tales "responds to the profound need for a change of scene; their magic wand is a protest against Edison's discoveries" (69–70).

In flight from the modern, decadent writers frequently looked back to classic fairy tales, which they recast with deliberately contemporary reinterpretations. They proposed sequels to classic tales, imagined new plots inspired by details from them, and blended magical fairy-tale settings with anachronistic elements. Several examples appear in this volume, including variations on Cinderella (Apollinaire, Bergerat, Cahun, Lemaître, Schwob), Sleeping Beauty (Fersen, France, Mendès), and Bluebeard (France, Lemaître, Schwob). Other tales borrow characters and weave them into their own plots, such as Renée Vivien's "Prince Charming" and Emile Bergerat's "28-Kilometer Boots," which takes elements from Perrault's "Little Thumbling." These examples confirm Jean de Palacio's contention that the tales of Charles Perrault had a particular resonance for decadent writers. Even prior to the decadent moment, Perrault's prominence among nineteenth-century writers was evidenced by such titles as Alphonse Daudet's *The Novel of Red Riding Hood* (1862) and Léo Lespès's *Perrault's Tales Continued* (1865). But there is a paradox in the decadent fairy tale's reliance on Perrault, who championed the "modern" notion of progress in the late seventeenth-century Quarrel of the Ancients and the Moderns, and whose fairy tales eschewed nostalgia for an aristocratic ethos found in many of the *contes de fées* by contemporaneous women writers.[5] And so, fin de siècle revisions were in no way constrained by respect for the master and, indeed, might better be called perversions rather than revisions.[6] Willy's "Fairy Tales for the Disillusioned," for instance, presents a parade of characters from Perrault's *Stories or Tales of Yesteryear* and allows such villains as the ogre of Little Thumbling, the wolf from Little Red Riding Hood, and Bluebeard himself to relate their own tales of woe, demonizing those who are victims in the original versions. Similarly, France's "The Seven Wives of Bluebeard" subtitled "according to authentic documents," contests the authority of Perrault's version altogether, as does Mendès in his "Dreaming Beauty." But the seriousness and naïveté that decadent writers attribute to Perrault stand in stark contrast to the mocking irony deployed by the narrative voice and the final morals of the *Stories or Tales of Yesteryear*. Their (mis) reading of Perrault is yet a further perversion of the genre they credit him with inaugurating. Another perversion of sorts is the decadent fairy tale's neglect of the many women writers who dominated the seventeenth-century vogue, but who were being steadily eclipsed by Perrault in spite of chapbook publications and stage productions of their tales throughout the nineteenth century.

Beyond Perrault, references to other traditions speak to decadent writers' acquaintance with contemporaneous scholarship and literature. Characters and settings from Arthurian legend (Morgane, Viviane, and the forest of Brocéliande), made prominent by nineteenth-century medievalists, appear in tales by Fersen, Mendès, and Ricard, among others. Also referenced is Melusina, who is featured in medieval French and German works and resurrected by nineteenth-century German writers and composers (Arnim, Goethe, La Roche, Mendelssohn, and Hoffmann). An important French influence was the vein of fantastic literature that appeared throughout the century, from Mérimée (*La Vénus d'Ille*, 1837) and Nerval (*Aurélia*, 1855) to Maupassant (*Le Horla*, 1886–87) and Villiers de l'Isle-Adam (*Contes cruels*, 1883). Following Tzvetan Todorov's well-known definition, the fantastic text, unlike the fairy tale, is predicated on a narrative hesitation about the reality of seemingly supernatural events. This hesitation is found in many of the decadent fairy tales, most notably those by Rachilde and Régnier. Decadent writers in France were also familiar with Victorian English fairy tales and incorporate into their stories the diminutive fairies and pixies of this tradition. Unlike the rewritings of Perrault's fairy tales, these borrowings aim less to rework plot than to put these characters into decidedly new and modern settings.

But decadent writers also invented their own characters, whose powers of enchantment they nonetheless place in question, frequently exploiting the genre to respond to present-day issues. Whether these writers situate their characters in settings that are magical or, on the contrary, realistic and contemporary, the trope of death and decline runs throughout their tales.[7] In many of them, fairies represent an endangered species; in others, their very existence is questioned. A common trope of decadent literature finds a maladapted but artistically refined protagonist, typically of noble birth, who represents the last descendent of a dying bloodline. The classic example, from Joris-Karl Huysmans's seminal decadent novel, *À rebours* (*Against the Grain*, 1884), is the androgynous character Des Esseintes, a physically and psychologically fragile young man whose family has fallen victim to hereditary degeneration. Among the tales that follow, Rachilde's "The Mortis" offers the example of the count Sébastiani Ceccaldo-Rossi who, like Des Esseintes, is identified as "the last of his clan." Similarly, the last remaining fairy is a recurring figure in these tales. In Daudet's "The Fairies of France," for instance, the last fairy appears in court as an angry incendiary who accuses modern rationality and the death of belief in the marvelous for the crime of killing off fairies. Both Pierre Veber and Catulle Mendès wrote tales entitled "The Last Fairy," and each attributes their demise to the contemporary moment: "there is no longer a place for fairies in the modern world" (Veber).

Mendès, by far the most prolific writer of fairy tales during this period, blames knowledge in particular: "men and women had become too wise to require the help of a little fairy." Erudition rendered obsolete the powers of fairies, previously sustained by folk wisdom. Not only does empiricism disprove magic; its gravitas threatens the lighthearted innocence associated with children and fairy tales. One nineteenth-century author described what he saw as a change in the way such tales were written, considered, and consumed:

> When we were children . . . we were given fairy tales at the new year for our amusement. . . . This no longer happens today. Fairy tales have acquired immense importance in literature. Now they have a genealogy or a history, like the great seigneurs. There is a geography, an astronomy, a zoology, and soon there will be a philosophy and a religion of fairy tales. *Analysis has arrived, goodbye jollity!* (Laboulaye 1–2, emphasis added)

According to Laboulaye, erudition and the marvelous are incompatible: "the wittier the man, the more artless and tedious his tales" (3).

Fairies are thus frequently seen to be the victims of modern cynicism and technological advancement. While plentiful in the French fairy-tale tradition of the seventeenth and eighteenth centuries, in this corpus they lose their homes owing to deforestation and industrialization: "there were no longer many fairies in the region since the ravages of the war, industry, and the attentive care of the government had cleared their forests" (Mockel). Simple country folk cease to believe in them. Fairies are sometimes obliged to move to Paris, center of manufacturing and science, which Walter Benjamin called the "capital of the nineteenth century." Urbanism incarnates everything that is antithetical to enchantment, including industry and cynicism. In the capital, fairies must beg to survive.

As a motif, the disappearance of the fairy echoes nineteenth-century folklorists' frequent laments about the rapid decline in oral storytelling, which was attributed to the modernization so forcefully derided by decadent writers. Although it is impossible to know for certain whether they were alluding to the contemporaneous work of those collecting and publishing oral folktales, this striking parallel points to a shared reverence for tradition in spite of very different, even antithetical means of expressing that reverence. Whereas folklorists employed the tools of modern erudition to preserve the record of endangered beliefs and stories— while distancing themselves from them—decadent writers used their fairy tales to counter positivistic rationalism. As does Catulle Mendès when he depicts young innocents who still believe in magic ("the illusions of a poor little girl") and the restoration of the powers of fairies ("The Lucky Find"). Still, typical of the cynicism of the decadents, Mendès undercuts this solution in his "Last Fairy," when another naive young girl chooses to follow a decrepit old man carrying a box of precious stones instead of saving the last fairy, thus assuring her death. The rejection of a happy ending, not unprecedented in folk- and fairy tales, here might be read as an indictment of an economy based on capital, but also as a jaundiced reflection on love. Whether it is celebrated or mourned, the marvelous becomes a means by which the decadent fairy tale casts a critical gaze on modern existence.

While fairies are frequently depicted as victims of the present day, tale writers just as often represent them as dangerous creatures corrupted by contemporary society, thus updating the traditional evil fairy character and using her to highlight modern perversity.[8] Willy's "Fairy Tales for the Disillusioned" informs its readers that "there are no good fairies: the bad ones killed them off long ago." They wreak havoc, from Mockel's spiteful fairies to vengeful ones in Lorrain, to the burning of Paris in Daudet. The depiction of bad fairies, or bad magic, also illuminates the sexual politics of the decadent moment, which was shaped by the postwar crisis of masculinity.[9] Just as the prominence of the femme fatale in decadent literature reflected this fin-de-siècle crisis, so did the fatal fairy reflect male anxiety about the dangers of female sexuality. Arène's "The Ogresses," a rewriting of Perrault's "Little Thumbling," presents a sensitive young painter "in love with the unreal" who falls in love with and falls victim to the Ogre's seven daughters, who are assimilated to contemporary Parisian women. As does Willy, France turns the tables to reveal Bluebeard to be the victim of his scheming wives. Other examples of the characteristically decadent trope of the femme fatale include Régnier's "The Living Door Knocker."

Nearly a century before postmodern fairy tales by Margaret Atwood, A. S. Byatt, Angela Carter, and others upend fairy-tale stereotypes about gender and sexuality, decadent writers created female characters unlike the virginal beauties of the classic tales and exposed the romantic myths associated with the genre. Mendès's Beauty refuses the prince's kiss, preferring her own dreams to the love and riches he offers. And in Willy's tale, the young couple Daphnis and Chloe are dissuaded from marrying each other after a troop of characters out of Perrault convince them not to believe in fairy tales: "People have filled your head with ridiculously optimistic notions and persuaded you to believe in good fairies. . . . All that, my children, is a farce, and you must believe the exact opposite of such nonsense." They are not, however, deterred from consummating their passion, and Chloe happily loses her virginity. Mendès also paints a cynical picture of love in "The Lucky Find," whose personified Love and Beauty lose "the respect and admiration of the human race" because they fail to conduct themselves "as honorable divinities."

Decadent writers frequently compared the decline of contemporary civilization to the fall of the Roman Empire, especially indicting what they saw as the perversity of modern gender roles and sexuality. Joséphin Péladan, a colorful, prolific, and extremely conservative monarchist and Catholic (who nonetheless was deeply interested in the occult) is a case in point. His fourteen-volume novel cycle, *La Décadence latine* (*The Latin Decadence*, 1884–1900), which he called an ethopœia (moral portraiture), presents Paris as a den of corruption, filled with depraved, sexually aberrant characters. Although Péladan did not write fairy tales per se, he showed interest in fairies and folklore in such works as his novel *Mélusine* (1895) and a treatise on femininity entitled *Comment on devient fée* (*How to Become a Fairy*, 1893). In the latter, Péladan condemns contemporary women for having usurped male prerogatives and suggests that gender confusion is a symptom of cultural decline: "Periods of decadence display an inversion in sex roles, and degenerate bloodlines are full of women doctors and women artists" (106). He posits the fairy as a sublime incarnation of nurturing femininity, a "queen of feelings" (167) who welcomes her ornamental role as counterpoint to the "master of ideas": "to be a fairy is to be beautiful in both heart and body" (166).

Characters manifesting nonnormative sexual and gender comportment are not infrequent in the sexually convoluted world of decadent fiction. Contemporary trends in such fields as anthropology, psychiatry, and criminology—which were keenly interested in what they viewed as sexual pathologies, chief among them homosexuality—contributed to the decadent fascination with perversion. Writers of the period regularly peopled their fiction with sexually deviant characters, thus mirroring the scientific work of men like British physician Havelock Ellis, German psychiatrist Richard von Krafft-Ebing, and Italian criminologist Cesare Lombroso, who categorized and documented erotic aberration. Androgynous, effeminate, and sapphic characters abound in decadent fiction, exemplified in this collection by Vivien's "Prince Charming" and Mendès's "An Unsuitable Guest." The former presents a charming prince who turns out to be a woman, the latter a less-than-manly prince who prefers collecting flowers to waging warfare. And in his tale "Isolina / Isolin," Mendès's title character is magically transformed into a man. Cahun's version of Cinderella paints her as a masochist, which, like the homosexual, was a category invented toward the end of the century. And Rachilde, whose prolific oeuvre is famous for its portrayal of nontraditional sexualities (one of her most notorious novels, *Monsieur Vénus*, 1884, features sadomasochism and gender role reversal), presents a prince who "loved in equal measure brunette ladies and blond pages, beautiful statues and heraldic dogs."

Decadents looked to Charles Baudelaire, author of *The Flowers of Evil* (1857), as an important influence. He described his aesthetic project as an alchemical process of extracting beauty from evil. We include his sole tale, "Fairies' Gifts," originally published in his collection of prose poems, *Le Spleen de Paris* (1869). In the sexualized landscape of the decadent fairy tale, flowers of evil abound. Jean Lorrain's "Princess of the Red Lilies" destroys the lilies of her garden; as she does so, soldiers fall on the fields of battle and princes die. Similarly, in Rachilde's "The Mortis," hoards of lovely flowers, "smoldering with forbidden fragrances," attack the city of Florence after cholera has wiped out its inhabitants, bathing it in a sea of color. To ease his hunger, the lone survivor eats rosebuds, likened to heads of women, which intoxicate and then kill him.

Such unnatural, deadly flowers incarnate both the decadent quest for beauty, aligned with the movement of art for art and its denaturalizing aesthetic, which privileged artifice and ornate refinement over crude realism. A sense of despair before the contemporary and contempt for the masses fed decadent preference for the uncommon, and even abnormal, excessive, and neurotic, over the commonplace. Arène's character Estevanet is an exemplary decadent hero: a painter of delicate sensibility, whose art "the public could not understand." Because he is out of synch with the vulgarity of the present, he is ill-equipped to withstand its barbarity and succumbs to the seven fatal ogresses.

Just as the decadent fairy tale repudiated positivism and naturalism by taking refuge in magic and the unreal, so did renewed fin de siècle interest in the occult, magnetism, and esotericism represent a reaction to scientism, the ideal of progress, and modern society. But even as decadents fled from the empirical world, in their fairy tales wonderment falls victim to the contemporary moment, and herein lies their cynicism. Palacio has suggested that the decadent tale is "devoid of naïveté." These tales both reject a conception of the genre dependent upon innocence and wonder, and renew it by infusing it with modern paradigms and opening up ways of critiquing them, albeit ambiguously.

Like the vast majority of seventeenth- and eighteenth-century *contes de fées*, decadent fairy tales were written for adult readers rather than children and so dispensed with naïveté and didacticism. Reveling in irony and dénouements that strayed from traditional morality, they often held ambiguous messages. The critique they perform of late nineteenth-century political, social, and intellectual worlds cannot always be reduced to the reactionary impulse at the heart of the decadent movement. And occasionally, some of these fairy tales swerved in a different direction to find inspiration, rather than annihilation, in modernity. At the turn of the twentieth century, one critic optimistically predicted that after their nineteenth-century decline, fairy tales would regain visibility, prompted by science itself. Were not electric lighting, horseless carriages, urban underground railways, and moving pictures all cause for marvel? Indeed, following the discovery of electricity and the 1881 Paris Exposition internationale d'électricité—which featured, among other things, Edison's incandescent light and Bell's telephone—electric current was frequently referred to as "la fée électricité." As the twentieth century dawned,

fairies and genies began once again to show themselves to people. The first automobiles they caught sight of con-

vinced them that the prophecy had been fulfilled. They believed that women traveling in automobiles were fairies
come to revisit the realms they once inhabited. (Goyau 18)

Technology might just have given new life to the "last fairy."

Notes

1. Illustrations with narrative captions on a single page that were ancestors of the comic book.

2. Including, most notably, Jean-François Bladé, François Cadic, Emmanuel Cosquin, François-Marie Luzel, Achille Millien, and Paul Sébillot. On folklorists in nineteenth-century France, see Hopkin, *Voices of the People in Nineteenth-Century France*, and Baycroft and Hopkin, *Folklore and Nationalism in the Long Nineteenth Century*.

3. For instance, the first vogue of fairy tales in France occurred during the waning years of Louis XIV's reign, a period Paul Hasard famously equated with a "crisis of European consciousness."

4. For example, in *L'Assommoir* (1877) Zola tackled the social plague of alcoholism among the working class, and in *Nana* (1880) he focused on the life of a courtesan. However, Zola himself published a rather conventional fairy tale, "La Fée amoureuse," in an early publication, *Contes à Ninon* (1864).

5. See Seifert, *Fairy Tales, Sexuality and Gender*.

6. Characters from fairy tales were also quite visible in such novels as these: Oscar Méténier, *Barbe-bleue* (1893); Gustave Claudin, *La Veuve au bois dormant* (1888); Emile Richebourg, *Cendrillon: la fée de l'atelier* (1892). And in plays: Maurice Maeterlinck, *Ariane et Barbe-Bleue* (1896); Jean Richepin and Henri Cain, *La Belle au bois dormant: féerie lyrique en vers* (1908).

7. See Chatelain, "Lorsque le titre se fait épitaphe," and Goyau, *La Vie et la mort des fées*.

8. See Viegnes, "La Force au féminin dans le conte merveilleux fin-de-siècle."

9. See Maugue, *L'Identité masculine en crise*.

TALES

CHARLES BAUDELAIRE

Fairies' Gifts

It was the grand assembly of the Fairies, who were tasked with distributing gifts among all the newborns who had come into the world in the preceding twenty-four hours.

They were a varied bunch, these ancient and capricious Sisters of Destiny, these strange Mothers of Joy and Sadness: some appeared gloomy and cranky, while others were playful and clever; the young ones looked as if they had always been young, the old ones as though they had always been old.

All fathers who believed in Fairies had come, each one carrying a newborn in his arms.

Gifts, Aptitudes, Good Luck, and Invincible Circumstances were piled high beside the tribunal like prizes on a stage during an awards ceremony. The peculiar thing here was that these Gifts were not granted for achievement, but rather accorded as a grace to one yet to live, a grace capable of determining a child's destiny, of becoming the source of unhappiness as well as of happiness.

The poor Fairies were very busy, since the crowd of applicants was large. And intermediary creatures who exist between humanity and God are, like us, subject to the laws of Time and its unceasing succession: Days, Hours, Minutes, and Seconds.

In truth, they were as harried as ministers of state before a hearing, as overwhelmed as government creditors when a national holiday authorized free paybacks.* I believe that they even watched the hands of the clock with as much impatience as human judges who, having presided since the morning, cannot upon occasion prevent themselves from daydreaming about dinner, their family, and their cozy slippers. Given that otherworldly justice involves a bit of hastiness and chance, it is not surprising to find that this is also sometimes true with human justice. We ourselves might be unfair judges in such cases.

So it was that upon that day the Fairies committed a few blunders that might strike one as bizarre—that is, if prudence rather than capriciousness were their distinct and eternal characteristic.

Thus was the power to magnetically attract fortune granted to the only heir of an extremely wealthy family. Having no sense of charity, nor being covetous of worldly goods, this child would later find himself prodigiously burdened by his millions.

Thus were Love of Beauty and Poetic Ability bestowed upon the son of a wretched pauper, a quarryman by trade, who could in no way nurture the potential or lessen the burden of his lamentable progeny.

I have forgotten to tell you that, on these solemn occasions, allocations cannot be appealed and no gift can be refused.

All the Fairies rose to leave, believing their task accomplished

---

* Mont-de-Piété: charitable public pawnbroker designed to assist the poor. Occasional free returns of pawned goods were authorized following the Revolution and over the course of the nineteenth century.

since no more gifts remained, no largesse left to toss to this human small-fry. But as they did, a good fellow, a humble shop-keeper I believe he was, stood up and seized hold of the nearest Fairy by the multicolored vapors of her gown and called out:

"Excuse me, Ma'am! You're forgetting my little one! I didn't come here to leave empty-handed!"

Given that nothing else remained, this might have been both-ersome for the Fairy. And yet she recalled a law that, while well known, was rarely applied in the preternatural world inhabited by those impalpable deities (Fairies, Gnomes, Salamanders, Sylphs and Sylphids, Nixes and Nixies, Mermen and Mermaids) who, as friends of humankind, were often obliged to adapt to its passions. I'm talking about the law that allows Fairies, in cases such as this in which prizes are out of stock, to bestow as an ex-ception one additional gift, provided that they are sufficiently imaginative to create one on the spot.

So the good Fairy replied, with composure worthy of her rank, "I give to your son . . . I give him . . . the Gift to please!"

"Please? To please how? And why?" the little shopkeeper asked obstinately, in the manner of one of those argumentative fellows unable to rise up to the logic of the Absurd.

"Because! because!" replied the angry Fairy as she turned her back to him. And as she caught up with the procession of her companions, she said to them, "How do you like this conceited little Frenchman who wants to understand everything? He re-ceived the best of all prizes for his son, and yet he dares to ques-tion me and dispute the indisputable!"

Le Spleen de Paris, 1869

ALPHONSE DAUDET

The Fairies of France

"Will the accused rise," said the presiding judge.

There was a stirring from the hideous dock of *pétroleuses*,* and something shapeless and shivering came to lean against the bar. It was a bundle of rags, holes, patches, strings, old flowers and plumes, and underneath it all, a poor, faded figure, leathery, wrinkled, chapped, whose malicious little black eyes quivered among its wrinkles like a lizard in the crevice of an old wall.

"What is your name!" she was asked.

"Melusina."

"What did you say?"

She repeated solemnly, "Melusina."

Under his mustache, as big as a dragoon colonel's, the judge smiled, but continued without raising an eyebrow: "Your age?"

"I've lost track."

"Your profession?"

"I'm a fairy!"

---

* Female arsonists who fought for the insurrectional government during the Paris Commune (1871) and used gasoline to set fires. Came to be used to as an epithet for radical women and feminists.

In response, everyone—the court, the counsel, even the prosecutor—burst out laughing. But that didn't bother her at all; in a small voice, clear and quavering, which climbed high in the courtroom and hovered like a voice from a dream, the old woman began again:

"Oh, the fairies of France! Where are they? All dead, my good men. I am the last, the only one remaining. In truth, it's a great shame, because France was much finer when there were still fairies. We were the country's poetry, its faith, its honesty, and its youth. We contributed something magical and grand to all our haunts: to the bottoms of overgrown parks, the fountain stones, the towers of old châteaux, pond mists, and great, swampy moors. In the fantastic light of legends, we could be seen going just about everywhere, dragging our skirts on a moon ray or running on blade tips in grassy meadows. Farmers loved us, they venerated us.

"For those with naive imaginations, our brows crowned with pearls, our wands, our enchanted distaffs lent a bit of fear to the adoration. As a result our springs remained ever clear. Plows halted at the pathways that we watched over; and as we are respectful of that which is old, we, the oldest in the world, people let the forests grow and rocks crumbled of their own accord, from one end of France to the other.

"But the century marched on. Railways arrived. Tunnels were dug, ponds filled in, and so many trees felled that before long we were lost as to where to put ourselves. Little by little the country folk stopped believing in us. When we used to rap on his shutters in the evening, Robin said 'It's the wind' and went back to sleep. Women came to do their washing in our ponds. From that point it was finished for us. Folk wisdom sustained us, and so when we lost it, we lost everything. The power of our wands disappeared and, from the potent queens we once were, we saw ourselves become old, wrinkled women, malicious like forgotten fairies who, with all that, still needed to earn our daily bread but had hands that were incapable of doing anything. For a while, people came across us in the forest dragging loads of dead wood or gleaning by the side of the road. But the woodsmen were harsh with us, and farmers threw stones at us. So like paupers who can no longer make a living in the country, we went to the big cities in search of work.

"Some of us worked in the mills. Others sold apples in winter next to bridges, or rosaries at church doors. We pushed orange carts before us; to passersby we offered cheap bouquets that nobody wanted. Children made fun of our quivering chins, policemen ran us around, and omnibuses ran us over. Then came illness, deprivation, a poorhouse sheet pulled over our heads . . . And this is how France let all its fairies die. The country has been well punished for it!

"Go ahead and laugh, my good people. In the meantime, we have just seen what it is to live in a country without fairies. We have witnessed as all those sated and snickering farmers share their provisions with the Prussians and give them directions.* There you have it! Robin no longer believed in magic spells, but he no longer believed in the country, either. Oh! if we had been there, we fairies, not one of those Germans who came into France would have left alive. Our dracos and our will-o'-the-wisps would have led them to the bogs. With the pure water from springs that bore our names we would have mixed magic potions that would

---

* The Franco-Prussian War (1870–71) was a devastating loss for the French.

have driven them mad. And with a magic word uttered during our moonlit assemblies, we would have mixed up the roads and the rivers so well, and with brambles and brushwood so well tangled the undergrowth, where they always huddled together, that Mr. Moltke's* little cat eyes would never have been able to find their bearings. With us there, the farmers would have marched! We would have made balms for the wounded with great flowers from our ponds, and bandages out of gossamer threads. And in the fields of battle, through half-closed eyes, a dying soldier would have seen his local fairy bending over to show him a bit of the woods or a bend in the road, something to remind him of home. That's how you go to war as a nation, how you make a holy war! But alas, in countries that no longer believe in fairies, that no longer have fairies, that kind of war is not possible."

Then the shrill little voice stopped for a moment, and the judge spoke:

"None of this explains what you were doing with the petrol found on you when the soldiers arrested you.

"I was burning Paris, my good man," the old woman replied tranquilly. "I was burning Paris because I hate it, because it scoffs at everything, because Paris is what killed us. It's Paris that sent scientists to analyze our beautiful, miraculous springs. On its stages, Paris laughed at us. Our enchantments have become tricks and our miracles dirty jokes. People have seen so many ugly faces go by in our pink dresses, and winged chariots under Bengal-lit moonlight, that they can no longer think of us without laughing. There were small children who knew us by name, who loved and

---

* Helmuth von Moltke the Elder (1800–1891), Prussian field marshal, architect of the Franco-Prussian War.

even feared us a little. But instead of giving them beautiful, gilt picture books where they learned our history, Paris now puts heavy tomes of science within their reach, books that exude boredom like gray dust, that wipe our enchanted palaces and magic mirrors from their eyes. Oh yes! I was happy to see your Paris in flames . . . It was I who filled the gas cans for the bomb-throwers, and I led them myself to the best places, saying, 'Go ahead, ladies, burn everything, burn, burn!'"

"This old woman is obviously mad," said the judge. "Take her away."

Contes du lundi, 1873

CATULLE MENDÈS

Dreaming Beauty

"Sleeping Beauty" is more than a tale put absentmindedly into writing: there is also a legend behind it. Let's bear in mind that the most conscientious and best informed of storytellers (even Madame d'Aulnoy or the good Perrault himself) sometimes fail to relate matters exactly as they occurred in fairyland.

Let me give you a few examples. Cinderella's oldest sister did not, as we have been led to believe, wear a red velvet outfit trimmed with English lace to the prince's ball: her dress was scarlet in color, embroidered in silver and embellished with orphrey. And I will grant you that, among the monarchs invited from all the countries of the world to attend Donkey Skin's wedding, some were borne in sedan chairs and others rode in horse-drawn carriages, with those traveling the farthest distances coming on elephants, tigers, and eagles. But it has never been told that the king of Mataquin* made his entrance into the palace courtyard sitting between the wings of a tarasquet† whose nostrils exhaled bejeweled flames.

---

* Fairy realm in Perrault's "Sleeping Beauty."
† Amphibious dragon-like animal from medieval Provençal legend. Described in Jacques

And don't hope to catch me off guard by asking from whom and in what manner I learned of these important matters. I once knew, a long time ago, an old woman who lived in a small thatched cottage on the edge of a field. She was very old, old enough to have been a fairy, which I always suspected her to be. As I sometimes stopped by to keep her company while she warmed herself under the sun in front of her little house, she took a liking to me. Just a few days before her death (or before returning to the mysterious land of Vivianes and Melusinas following her probationary period), she gave me as a going-away present a spinning wheel that was extremely old and quite extraordinary. Each time the wheel was spun, it would talk or sing in a quiet little voice that quavered a bit, just like a grandmother happily chattering away. It told many lovely tales, some entirely unknown and others it knew better than anyone. In the second instance it took a mischievous pleasure in pointing out and correcting errors introduced by those who have meddled in writing down such tales. You can imagine what I learned! And were I to recount all that the spinning wheel revealed to me, you would be astonished indeed.

For instance . . . you think you know down to the last detail the story of the princess who, after pricking her hand on a spindle, fell asleep and was laid on a bed embroidered with silver and gold in a castle in the middle of the wood? She slept so deeply that nothing could wake her, not even when the Queen of Hungary's Water was rubbed on her temples.* Well, it gives me no pleasure

---

de Voragine's *Légende dorée* (1261–66) as "a dragon that was half animal, and half fish, wider than a cow and longer than a horse, with teeth as sharp as swords and as thick as horns."

* Also called "Hungary Water," the earliest perfume made with alcohol, its formulation reputedly commanded by a Hungarian queen in the fourteenth century.

Figure 1

to inform you that you know nothing about how this adventure really ended, or that in the very least you are poorly apprised of its nuances. Were I not now to take it upon myself to enlighten you, you would forever remain in ignorance.

"Yes, yes," purred the Spinning Wheel, "the princess had been sleeping for a hundred years when a young prince, driven by love and glory, resolved to enter her resting place and wake her. Great trees, thorns, and brambles made way so that the prince might proceed. He walked toward the castle, visible at the end of a grand alleyway, and entered. He was a bit surprised that none of his entourage was able to follow him. After having traversed several marble-paved courtyards (red-nosed, pink-faced guards were sleeping, evidently from drink since in the goblets by their sides remained traces of wine), walked along spacious vestibules, and climbed staircases lined by snoring guards with shouldered rifles, he found himself in a gilded room where he saw, lying on a bed with curtains drawn open, the most beautiful sight he had ever seen: a princess fifteen or sixteen years old whose resplendent loveliness was luminescent and divine.

"I grant you that this all happened," continued the Spinning Wheel, "and that up to this point, Perrault was not brazenly misleading. But the remainder of his tale is entirely false. I cannot concede that, when awoken, Sleeping Beauty gazed lovingly upon the prince, nor that she said to him, 'Is it you, my lord? You certainly took your time.'"

Listen up if you want to know the truth.

The princess stretched out her arms, raised her head ever so slightly, and began to open her eyes. But she closed them just as quickly as if frightened by the light, sighing at length while her little dog Pouffe, who had also awoken, yapped angrily.

"Who is it," the fairies' goddaughter asked at length, "and what do you want of me?"

The prince, kneeling, exclaimed, "He who has come adores you and has risked great danger" (here he was boasting a bit) "to free you from the spell that held you. Leave this bed on which you have slept for a hundred years, give me your hand, and let us return together to the light of day and to wakeful life."

Astonished by these words, she contemplated him and could not suppress a smile, for he was a well-built young prince whose eyes were the loveliest in the world and who spoke with a most melodious voice.

"Is it true," she asked as she swept back her hair, "that the hour has come for me to be delivered from my lengthy sleep?"

"It is indeed."

"Ah!" said she. After reflection, she added, "What will happen if I leave the shadows to return among the living?"

"Do you not know? Have you forgotten that you are the daughter of a king? You will witness your delighted subjects rushing to greet you, crying out in pleasure, and waving multicolored banners. Women and children will kiss the hem of your gown. You will be the most powerful and celebrated queen on earth."

"I would like to be queen," said she. "What will happen next?"

"You will live in a palace as bright as gold, and you will walk upon diamond mosaics as you climb the steps to your throne. Courtiers will gather around you to sing your praise. The noblest of men will bow before the all-powerful grace of your smile."

"How delightful to be praised and obeyed," she replied. "Will I enjoy other pleasures?"

"Maids-in-waiting as skillful as your fairy godmothers will clothe you in gowns the colors of the sun and the moon, powder your hair, and apply beauty spots next to your eye or the corner of your mouth. You will wear a great cloak of golden cloth that will trail behind you."

"That suits me! I have always loved elegant clothing."

"Pages as fetching as birds will serve you the finest spices in silver dishes and fill your glass with sweet wines having the most delicate of bouquets."

"How excellent! I have always been fond of a well-provisioned table. Will there be other pleasures?"

"One more delight, the greatest of all, awaits you."

"Which one is that?"

"You will be loved!"

"By whom?"

"By me! That is, if you judge me not unworthy of aspiring to your affections."

"You are an attractive prince, and you are exceedingly well dressed."

"If you deign to accept my oath, I will give you all my heart over which to reign as sovereign, and I will never cease to greet even your cruelest whim with the most servile gratitude."

"Oh! What happiness you promise me!"

"Arise, then, dear heart, and follow me."

"Follow you? Already? Wait a minute. It's doubtless true that what you offer is quite tempting, and yet you realize, don't you, that I would have to give up better still to accept your proposal?"

"What do you mean, my princess?"

"I have not been merely sleeping for a century: I have also been dreaming during this time. And in my dreams, how divine the kingdom over which I reign! My palace has walls of light; my courtiers are angels who extol me in songs of infinite sweetness; the ground upon which I walk is strewn with stars. You cannot know how lovely are the dresses I wear, the incomparable fruits placed upon my table, the honeyed wines that wet my lips! And don't think that I am wanting for love, either! I am adored by a husband who is more handsome than all the world's princes and who has been faithful for a hundred years. All things considered, Your Highness, I don't think I would gain anything from having my spell broken. Please be so kind as to let me sleep."

She thereupon turned toward the wall, gathered her hair over her eyes, and returned to her long nap, while her little dog Pouffe ceased her yapping and happily settled her muzzle on her paws. The prince sheepishly withdrew. And since that time, thanks to the protection of good fairies, no one has come to trouble the sleep of "Dreaming Beauty of the Woods."

Isolina / Isolin

I

Once upon a time two fairies met at the edge of a forest near a big city. One of them, called Urganda,* was in a very bad temper because the pleasure of her company had not been requested at the festivities in honor of the baptism of the king's daughter. The other, named Urgèle,† was as happy as could be because she had been invited to partake in this joyous occasion. And it happens among fairies as it does among all humanity that contentment breeds kindness just as dejection begets wickedness.

"Hello, my sister," said Urgèle.

"Hello, sister," grumbled Urganda. "I suppose that you thoroughly enjoyed yourself with your friend, the king of Mataquin."

"More than I could express! The rooms were so brightly lit that

---

* Enchantress in *Amadis de Gaula*, Spanish chivalric romance of the fourteenth century.
† Good fairy appearing in Voltaire's *Ce qui plaît aux dames* (1764) and Egidio Duni's comic opera *La fée Urgèle, ou Ce qui plaît aux dames* (1765).

one would have thought we were in our underground palace, whose walls are made of gems and ceiling of sunlit crystal. The most delicate dishes were served in plates of gold on lace table-cloths. From lily-shaped goblets we drank wine so fragrant and so sweet that I thought I was drinking honey from flowers. After the meal, young men and lovely maidens, so svelte and well dressed in multicolored silks they looked like birds of paradise, danced the most charming dances in all the world."

"Yes, I know. I heard the violins from here. And I imagine that in recompense for such delightful hospitality you endowed your goddaughter the princess with very precious gifts indeed?"

"That goes without saying, dear sister! The princess will be as pretty as sunshine. When she speaks, her voice will sound like a warbler singing, and when she laughs, it will be like a rose blossoming. There is no perfection that I have failed to grant her, and when she reaches the age of marriage, she will marry a prince so handsome and so much in love with her, one more charming and more infatuated than any prince who has ever lived."

"How dreamy!" said Urganda as she ground her teeth. "I would also like to bestow my generosity upon your goddaughter."

"Oh, sister, please don't grant her a fatal gift! I beg you not to pronounce a terrible oath that cannot be retracted! If you had seen the little princess in her cradle, as sweet and as frail as a downy fledgling, if she had smiled at you with her eyes as bright blue as cornflowers and mouth the color of wild roses, you would be so moved that you wouldn't have the heart to harm her."

"Indeed, but I did not see her, did I! I grant you that she will be as lovely as sunshine, since no fairy can undo what another fairy has resolved; she will have a voice as sweet as a warbler's and lips

like a blooming rose; she will marry the most handsome and loving prince; however . . ."

"However *what?*" replied Urgèle, sick with worry.

"However, as soon as she marries, on her wedding night, she
will cease to be a girl and turn into a boy."

You can imagine how horrified the good fairy godmother was
by this prophecy! She begged and entreated, but Urganda
wouldn't listen to any of it. She sank snickering into the ground,
terrifying all the birds of the forest as she did so. Urgèle continued on her way with head hung low, wondering how to save her
goddaughter from so dreadful a fate.

II

At sixteen, the princess was so lovely that throughout the land all
anybody talked of was her beauty. Those who had seen her could
not help but adore her, and those who had not gazed upon her
were no less charmed, thanks to the renown of her loveliness.
Such was the case that ambassadors came from all around to the
court of Mataquin in order to ask for her hand in marriage on
behalf of the richest and most powerful monarchs. Alas! The
king and queen, who had been warned of the future awaiting
their daughter, did not know what to say to them. It would not
have been wise to give away in marriage a maiden who would be
so strangely metamorphosed on her wedding night. The king and
queen bade farewell to the ambassadors with great deference,
without consenting or refusing, both as upset as they could be.
As for Isolina, who was unaware of her cruel destiny, she cared
little whether she married or not. In her innocence she did not
bother about such things and was happy as long as she could play

with her doll and her little dog in the alleys of the royal garden. There the birds told her, "Your voice is sweeter than ours," and the roses said, "Your lips are rosier than we are." She was satisfied and wanted nothing more, just like a small flower unaware that it was destined to be picked.

But one day, as she was busy tying the stem of a morning glory to the collar of her happily barking dog, Isolina heard a great noise coming from the nearby road. She raised her eyes and saw a magnificent procession heading toward the palace. Leading the procession, astride a white horse shaking its mane, was a young prince so handsome, of such astonishing beauty, that it troubled her eyes and thrilled her heart. "Oh, how lovely he is!" she thought. And, contemplating such things for the first time, she avowed that if he deigned ask for her hand in marriage, it would not displease her in the least.

Meanwhile, the young lord had spied Isolina from the other side of the flowering hedge, and he stopped, equally charmed.

"If it please the good fairies," he cried, "may you be the daughter of the king of Mataquin! Because it is she I have come to marry, and there is no other on earth as charming as you."

"I am princess Isolina," she replied.

They spoke no more, but their eyes remained fixed upon each other. From this moment forward, they loved each other with ardor and tenderness greater than words can express.

III

You can imagine the king and queen's distress! This time it was their daughter, not a mere ambassador, to whom they had to answer. And Isolina was begging, crying, swearing that she would become ill and certainly die if she couldn't marry her beloved. What's more, Prince Diamond was not of the sort it was easy to dismiss: as the son of the emperor of Golconda,* he could summon four or five armies to wage war against his enemies, one alone of which would be capable of ravaging several kingdoms. There was everything to fear from his anger, and he would be greatly irritated indeed were the princess to be refused him. Nor would it have helped to tell him of the frightful destiny awaiting Isolina, since he would not have believed such an unlikely story, but would rather have thought that he was being mocked. Touched by their daughter and frightened by the prince, the king and queen therefore allowed the wedding to proceed as if no disaster would result from it. Besides, wasn't it possible that, after so many years, the fairy Urganda had lost her desire for vengeance? Thus, after much hesitation and many excuses and delays, did they consent to the marriage of the two young lovers. And truly never had there been a more beautiful bride nor a happier groom, even at a royal wedding.

IV

It is fair to say that the king and queen were far from feeling at ease. When they had retired to their rooms after the festivities, it was impossible for them to sleep. At every moment they expected to hear shouting and doors slamming and to see the prince arrive mad with despair and horror. Yet nothing troubled the calm of the night and, little by little, they took heart. They were undoubtedly right to think that the bad fairy had retracted her prophecy.

---

* Medieval sultanate known for its diamond mines.

The morning following the wedding, unconcerned, they entered the throne room, where the newlyweds would, as is customary, soon come to kneel before the royal and paternal benediction.

The door opened.

"My daughter!" cried the horrified king.

"Isolina!" wailed her mother.

"I am no longer your daughter, but your son, my father! Isolin rather than Isolina, dear mother!"

Thus speaking, the new prince, charming and proud with sword at side, twirled his mustache with a defiant look.

"All is lost!" said the king.

"Alas!" said the queen.

But Isolin's voice softened as he turned toward the door and said, "Come now, my lovely Diamond! Why do you tremble so? Your blushing would be annoying if it didn't make you lovelier still."

At the same moment that the princess became a boy, the prince had become a girl. And this is how the good Urgèle thwarted the vengeance of the evil fairy.

The Way to Heaven

Since the princess had refused to marry the emperor of Germania, her father ordered that she be put in the highest room of a very tall tower, a tower so tall it rose beyond the clouds, so tall the swifts did not nest in it because their wings tired before they could reach the top. Those who, from afar, saw the white dress of the captive princess blowing in the wind on the terrace halfway to the sky thought she was an angel who had fallen from heaven rather than a young girl who had ascended from the earth. And, all day long and all night, Guillelmine lamented her fate, not only because she had been separated from her companions, with whom she enjoyed playing card games or hunting for partridge or heron with a falcon, but also because she was separated from a good-looking page by the name of Aymeri, with blond curls and ever so rosy cheeks, to whom she had given her heart never to reclaim it.

For his part, Aymeri was no less distressed, and one day, leaning against the window of the jail cell where he had been locked up and lowering his head toward the rocky cliffs that surrounded the prison, he uttered these sad words: "What use is it for me to live since the one who is my sole happiness has been taken from me? When I was allowed to be with her, I rejoiced in the thought of many days full of noble combat and victorious adventure. I longed for every triumph, which I would have offered her just as a shepherd who returns from the plain gives his beloved a bouquet of flowers from the fields. I wanted to be illustrious so that she could reward me with a smile. But since she has been taken from me, I no longer care about victories or about my name, famous around the whole world. What is the use of picking flowers that those beloved lips will not kiss? I have not a single care for anything in this world. You can close your lids forever, miserable eyes that will no longer see Guillelmine!"

Once he had finished speaking, he climbed onto the windowsill and let himself fall toward the rocky cliffs.

But, a few instants before this, three swallows had perched themselves not far away on the branch of a flowering acacia. Flapping their wings and fluttering among the leaves, they had lost not one word of Aymeri's lament, even though they appeared not to be paying attention.

"Isn't it a pity . . ."
"There is so much pain . . ."
"In such a young heart . . ."
"So many tears . . ."
"So many bitter tears . . ."
"In such pretty eyes . . ."

There was nothing surprising about the fact that the birds were talking since they were not really swallows at all but angels who had taken that form, shrinking their wings. It often happens that celestial spirits transform themselves in such a way so as to listen, among the branches or through a chimney, to what is spoken here below. But they do not do this with bad intentions. They would be very happy to hear and repeat only honorable things. Sometimes, to spare our souls punishment, they even dare to lie to God, who does not hold it against them.

"Don't you think as I do . . ."
"That it would be just to save Aymeri . . ."
"From such a terrible death . . ."
"And that, without displeasing the Lord . . ."
"We could carry this child . . ."
"To our heaven?"

At that, they all three flew toward the despairing soul at the very moment that he fell from the window, and just before he hit the rocks of the cliffs, they lifted him toward the sky on their outstretched wings, which were now angel's wings.

Aymeri was astonished he had not died, and he was overjoyed when he realized where he was being taken. He was overcome with gratitude, which was not displeasing to his saviors. It is always satisfying not to encounter ungratefulness when obliging someone. Over houses and palaces, higher than the plane trees of the gardens and the pine trees on the hills, the airborne foursome traversed the azure sky, through the light and the clouds; they went so far that the wind, in spite of its desire to follow them, was obliged to give up and stopped behind them, out of breath.

But soon, when the city had disappeared below in the fog, Aymeri was gripped with worry.

"Beautiful angels," he asked, "you're not lost, are you?"

They could not keep themselves from laughing at these words.

"Child, do you believe . . ."

"That we do not know . . ."

"The way to heaven?"

A bit ashamed, Aymeri responded:

"Forgive me, beautiful angels. I asked you a silly question. I promise it won't happen again."

Their white wings continued to flap. Plains, forests, mountains disappeared in the gray depths. Above the clouds, Aymeri finally noticed the top of a tower.

"Ah!" he said in a cry of joy, "we've arrived!"

The angels were a bit surprised by these words.

"Not yet! Heaven . . ."

"Is not as close as you think . . ."

"To the dark dwellings of men."

"When we've passed . . ."

"To the right of the sun, up there . . ."

"Through flames the color of snow . . ."

"We'll still be far away . . ."

"From the resplendent threshold that protects . . ."

"The cherubs with golden armor."

Grabbing onto the feathers of the divine messengers, Aymeri cried out:

"We've arrived, I tell you! Heaven is in that tower where Guil-lelmine raises the sleeves of her dress toward me with arms more beautiful than your wings!"

The angels were more and more astonished.

"What! Crazy child, you do not want . . ."

"To follow us to the sojourn . . ."

"Of eternal delights?"

"You do not want, akin to the elect . . ."

"Who without end exult . . ."

"In the light and the music . . ."

"To see the miraculous gardens . . ."

"Where flowers, that are stars . . ."

"Overwhelm with luminous aromas . . ."

"And scented rays . . ."

"Those celestial bees, which are souls?"

"You do not want, from among Virgins . . ."

"Lilies more beautiful than lilies . . ."

"Whose nuptials make roses . . ."

"To choose for yourself a fiancée . . ."

"Who will scatter everlasting dreams . . ."

"Over your angelic wedding bed?"

But Aymeri, struggling, insisted:

"No! no! I will go no farther!"

So, the angels, justifiably irritated that he cared so little for heavenly pleasures, pulled away, and he fell through the air and slammed against the stone roof of the tower.

Poor Aymeri lay lifeless, with broken limbs and a smashed skull. Blood flowed from his mouth, his eyes, and his forehead. He knew all too well that he was going to die, and throughout his entire body he experienced suffering that he never believed one could ever endure. But Guillelmine, disheveled, took him in her arms, caressing his wounds and kissing his bloody lips. "I knew I was right," he said. "I knew the way to heaven better than they did!"

An Unsuitable Guest

Great alarm reigned at court and throughout the realm because the king's son had not eaten for four days. If he had had a fever or some illness, his prolonged fasting would not have been cause for such concern. But the prince's doctors agreed that, were it not for the weakness caused by his abstinence, he would be in fine form. Why then was he depriving himself of food? This was the only topic of conversation among courtiers and even the common people: instead of wishing each other good morning, people greeted each other by asking, "Has he eaten this morning?"

Nobody was as anxious as the king himself. Not that he bore a great affection for his son; the young man disappointed him in all sorts of ways. Although he was already sixteen years old, he showed the greatest aversion for politics and soldiering. While attending the Council of Ministers, he yawned in an unseemly fashion during the most eloquent speeches. And once, having been charged with leading a small army against a group of rebels, he returned before nightfall, his sword garlanded with morning glories and his hands full of violets and sweetbriar. The prince explained that he had come upon a ravishing vernal forest along the way, and that it was much more entertaining to gather flowers than to kill men.

He liked to walk alone under the trees of the Royal Park and enjoyed listening to the nightingales' song at the rise of the moon. The few people he allowed into his apartments spoke of books scattered across the rugs and musical instruments such as guzlas,* citharas, and mandolas.† Leaning against the balcony, he spent long evening hours contemplating stars so small for being so far away in the sky, his eyes wet with tears. Added to which, he was as pale and fragile as a young girl and preferred dressing in brightly colored silks that reflected the daylight to donning knightly armor.

All this will help you understand why the king was so shamefaced to have such a son. But since the young prince was sole heir to the crown, his safety was of great importance to the State. And so everything imaginable was done to prevent him from dying of hunger. His entourage begged and pleaded with him, but he shook his head in silent response. The best chefs prepared the most appetizing seafood, the most savory meats, the most delicate spring vegetables. His table was laden with salmon, trout, pike, haunch of venison, heads of newborn boars, bear paws, hare, pheasant, capercaillie, quail, woodcock, and water-rail, served at all hours, while from twenty platters arose the gentle aroma of freshly harvested greens.

When they suspected he was weary of ordinary game and native vegetables, the chefs prepared bison filets, saddle of Chinese dogs minced in tern nests, hummingbird skewers, barded marmoset grill, ragout of young monkey larded with Andean burnets, gundelia shoots cooked in antelope fat, *marolins* from Chandannagar,‡ and Brazilian *sacramarons* in a spicy turkey

---

* Balkan musical instrument having one string (also *gusla* or *gusle*).
† Larger, lower-pitched mandolin (also *mandora*).
‡ West Bengali city, formerly colonized as part of French India.

sauce. But the young prince let it be known that he wasn't hungry and, gesturing his boredom, fell to daydreaming once again.

This was the state of affairs, with the king becoming more and more distraught, when his haggard child, who was whiter than lilies and barely able to hold himself upright, said: "Father, if you want me to live, give me your blessing to leave your kingdom and go where I see fit, no questions asked."

"But my son, weak as you are, you would faint before taking three steps."

"I seek to go away only to regain my strength. Have you read what is written about the troubadour Thibaut, who was imprisoned by fairies?"

"It is not my habit to read," said the king.

"Know then that Thibaut led a very contented life among the fairies. He was above all happy at mealtime because small pages, who were gnomes, served him dewdrop soup on acacia leaves, roast butterfly wings glazed by the rays of the sun, and, for dessert, what remains on a rose petal that has been kissed by a bee."

"Such a meager meal!" said the king, who couldn't help but laugh in spite of his worries.

"And yet it is the only one that tempts me. I cannot nourish myself as do others on the flesh of dead animals and vegetables reaped from the earth by men. Allow me to go to the land of fairies and, if they welcome me to their table, I will eat my fill and return in full health."

What would you have done if you were king? Since the young prince was near death, it was wisdom of a sort to give into his madness. So his father gave him leave without hope of ever seeing him again.

Since the kingdom was near the forest of Brocéliande,* the child did not have far to go before reaching the land of the fairies. They welcomed him warmly, not because he was the son of a powerful monarch, but because he liked to listen to the song of the nightingale as the moon rose in the sky and to contemplate faraway stars as he leaned against his balcony. A party was given in his honor in a vast hall made of pink marble and illuminated by diamond chandeliers. For the pleasure of his eyes, the loveliest of the fairies danced in a circle as they held hands, their scarves trailing behind them. He felt such joy that, in spite of his agonizing stomach pangs, he wished the dance could last forever.

And yet he was growing weaker and weaker and understood that he would soon die without sustenance. He confessed the state he was in to one of the fairies and even dared ask her when dinner was served.

"Whenever you'd like!" she said and gave the order. A small page, a gnome, promptly brought the prince a drop of dew on an acacia leaf. Oh! What excellent soup! The fairies' guest declared that he couldn't imagine anything more delicious. Next he was offered a roast of butterfly wing glazed by the rays of the sun and cooked on a spit fashioned from a may thorn. He ate it in a single bite, with great pleasure.

"Have you dined well, my child?"

The enraptured prince nodded yes but, as he did so, dropped his head and died of starvation. Such is the fate of earthly poets, unfortunate beings too pure and not pure enough, too divine to share in the feasts of men and yet too human to dine among the fairies.

---

* The mythical forest of Arthurian legend that was the site of the adventures of Merlin, the fairies Morgane and Viviane, and the Knights of the Round Table.

The Three Good Fairies

In those days there were three fairies named Abonde, Myrtile, and Caricine who were good beyond what anyone could imagine. Their only pleasure came from helping the unfortunate, and that's what they did with all their powers. Nothing could persuade them to participate in the games that other fairies play on moonlit nights in the forest of Brocéliande, nor to wait in the festival hall where sylph cupbearers serve dewdrops in lily chalices—according to Thomas the Rhymer, there is not a more pleasant drink—unless they had first consoled much human suffering. And they had such a fine sense of hearing that they heard, even from afar, hearts breaking and tears flowing.

Abonde, who preferred to visit outlying districts of big cities, would appear all of a sudden in humble abodes either by breaking a galley window (which was quickly replaced by a diamond pane without call for a glazier) or by making herself into a body of smoke from the half-extinguished stove. Overcome with pity at the sight of these attic rooms where miserable families without work shivered, dying of hunger, she would quickly transform them into sumptuous dwellings having beautiful furniture, pantries full of victuals, and coffers full of gold coins.

No less charitable, Myrtile frequented country folk in their hovels, who lament their fate when hail bruises their orchards' blooming promise and who, between the empty bread bin and the armoire without linen, wonder if it would not be better to abandon their children in the woods since they cannot feed or clothe them.* She was able to restore their confidence easily by

---

* An allusion to the abandonment of the eponymous hero and his brothers in Perrault's "Le Petit Poucet" (Little Thumbling).

offering them talismans and advising them to make vows that never failed to come true. The man who, three moments earlier, had no alms to give to a robin pecking at his windowpane, became a rich bourgeois in a magnificently appointed house or a powerful monarch in a palace of porphyry and jewels.

As for Caricine, she was moved by lovers' sorrows more than any other sort of pain. She made coquettes and fickle men faithful, she moved to compassion miserly parents who refuse to consent to their children's happiness, and when she learned that an old beggar on the road was enamored of the daughter of a king, she would transform him into a prince as handsome as daylight so he could wed his beloved. And so it was that if things had continued in this manner, there would be no more misery or suffering in the world thanks to the three good fairies.

But this would not have been to the liking of a very cruel sorcerer who was filled with the worst of feelings toward men and women. The very idea that suffering and crying might cease on earth caused him intolerable torment. And so, he was filled with rage at these excellent fairies—unable to decide which one he hated the most—and he decided to render them incapable of making the misfortunate happy, as was their custom. Nothing was easier for him because of the great power he had.

He made them appear before him, then, frowning, announced that he would deprive them of their powers for many centuries. He added that he could easily transform them into vile beasts or senseless objects, such as blocks of marble, tree trunks, or woodland streams, but that, out of mercy, he consented to allow them to choose the form in which they would spend their time of penance.

One cannot imagine the sorrow of the good fairies! They were not really sad to lose their glory or their privileges. Giving up fairy dances in the forest of Brocéliande and parties in subterranean palaces lit by ruby suns meant little to them. What dismayed them was the thought that, stripped of their powers, they could no longer give aid to the unfortunate. "What!" thought Abonde, "men and women will die of cold and hunger in far-flung attics, and I will no longer console them!" Myrtile thought to herself: "What will become of peasant men and women in their hovels when hailstorms break the branches of flowering apple trees? How many little children will cry when abandoned in the bushes beyond the path, unable to see any light other than the distant lamp of the ogre's wife while the wolf lies in wait for them!" And Caricine, sobbing, wondered: "How many lovers are going to suffer! And just when I was informed that a poor little street singer, without home or family, is languishing for love of the princess Trébizonde. Alas! So he will not marry her?" And, together, the good fairies were thrown into the depths of despair for a long, long time, as if suffering all the sorrows they would not make into joys, as if shedding all the tears they would not be able to dry.

But if truth be told, they had one small consolation in their despair. They were allowed to choose the forms in which they would appear among humans. With the right choice, their goodness would perhaps still find a way to do its work. Although reduced to the impotence of mortal beings or perishable things, they would not be entirely of no use to poor folk. So they started to think, wondering what it was best to be so as not to cease being useful. Abonde, recalling the impoverished neighborhoods, at first wanted to be changed into a rich person who would give out innumerable alms. Then, remembering the stoves that went cold and the cots without blankets, she happily imagined becoming a warming flame or a good bed where exhausted workmen could rest. Myrtile dreamt of being a queen who would make richly clothed chamberlains of all the laborers dressed in rags, or the beam of sunshine that parts menacing clouds, or the wife of the woodsman who brings lost children back home. As for Caricine, with her intention to comfort hearts, she would have gladly consented to be changed into a beautiful wife, faithful and sincere, whose sole care was the happiness of her husband, or into a timid and loving fiancée. But then, other thoughts occurred to them, and they hesitated, comparing the advantages of different metamorphoses.

Then the Sorcerer cried out:

"Well! Have you decided? You've been mulling this over for far too long, and I don't have time to waste. What do you want to be? Hurry up and tell me."

There was a long silence, and then Abonde said:

"Let me be the wine that is drunk in the taverns of the slums! Drunkenness consoles tired bodies and hearts better than bread for the hungry, warm stoves, and bed rest."

"May I be strings on an old fiddler's violin!" said Myrtile. "More than gilded clothes that replace rags, the flight of menacing clouds, or the return of lost children, the song that makes people dance is good for the unfortunate."

"May I be the beautiful bohemian girl at the crossroads who offers laughter and kisses to passersby!" said Caricine. Free love— crazy, inconstant, risky, without disappointments or regrets—is what makes men forget the boredom and despair of life."

Since that time, Abonde laughs in the full glasses on tavern tables, and Myrtile makes people dance at peasant weddings under

Figure 2: The Forest of Brocéliande

the trees of a large clearing or in the courtyard of an inn. Stripped of their powers, these good fairies are happy with the joy they give, but they are also jealous of Caricine, because they know she is the one who gives out the best sort of charity.

The Last Fairy

One day the fairy Oriana, who was no bigger than your little finger, was heading back to Brocéliande forest where she lived with her kind. In a carriage made from a hazelnut and drawn by four ladybugs, she was returning from the baptism of three robins, which was feted in a hollow in a wall flowering with wisteria. It had been a very pleasant party in their nest under the leaves. The fledglings let out lovely cries as they shook their little pink wings barely covered in down, giving hope that the fairy's godchildren would one day be excellent singers. Oriana was thus in a very good mood, and, since joy breeds happiness, she granted favors along the way to everyone and everything she encountered. She placed mulberry bouquets in the baskets of little girls on their way to school; she blew upon sweetbriar buds to help them bloom; and she placed oat flakes on top of dewdrops to keep mites from drowning as they ran across them. Two young lovers, a peasant lad and lass, were kissing in a field where the green wheat barely reached their ankles: Oriana made the wheat grow and rise taller so no one would see their kisses from the road. And since doing good deeds inspired by joy makes one more joyful still, Oriana the fairy was so delighted that she would have danced in the nutshell were she not afraid of upsetting the carriage.

But soon the time for happiness had ended. Alas! What had happened? She was sure that she had taken the right road, and yet there where the gentle breezes of Brocéliande forest had so recently stirred the enchanted mysteries of its deep greenery, she saw nothing but a vast plain scattered with buildings under a sky dirty with black smoke. What had become of you, green and golden clearings where fairies danced by starlight? Where were the rose thickets and blooming thornbushes? What had happened to the aromatic and musical caves in which sleep smiled on golden moss, to the crystal-walled underground palaces, lit on feast days by a thousand chandeliers of living gemstones? Where had you gone, Urganda, Urgèle, Alcine, Viviane, pagan Holda and bewitching Melusina? And you, Mélandre, and you, Arie, and Mab and Titania?

"It's no use calling them, my poor Oriana," said a lizard who had stopped while scampering among the stones. "Men came running in throngs through your cherished solitude. They cut down trees, burned rose thickets and thornbushes, in order to open a passage for dreadful machines blowing steam and flames. They filled your mysterious crystal palaces with stones from your grottoes, upon which they built houses, and all the fairies succumbed during this disastrous upheaval. I saw Habonde,* who nearly escaped, die under the foot of a passerby with a tiny cry, crushed like a cicada." Upon hearing this, Oriana began to weep bitterly about the destiny of her dear companions and about her own fate as well, since it was a truly melancholic state of affairs to be the only fairy remaining in the world.

What would she do? Where would she hide? Who would protect her against the fury of malicious men? Her first thought was to run away, to escape from this sad place where her sisters had perished. But she could not travel by carriage as was her custom since her four ladybugs (to whom she had always shown such kindness) had taken flight (such was the ingratitude of all winged creatures) upon hearing the lizard's speech. This was a real blow

---

* Welsh goddess of abundance and joy.

for the unfortunate Oriana, all the more since there was nothing she hated as much as walking. And yet she resigned herself to doing so and set off upon her way with tiny strides among blades of grass taller than she. She had resolved to return to the robins' wisteria-covered wall. The parents of her godchildren would surely welcome her into their nest to take refuge until autumn. But such little legs fare poorly without a hazelnut shell borne by fluttering ladybugs, and three long days went by before she spied the flowering wall. You can imagine how weary she was. But she would finally be able to rest.

"It's me," she called as she drew near, "it's me, your fairy god-mother! Come collect me on your wings, my good birds, and carry me to your mossy dwelling." But there was no answer; not even the small head of a redbreast peeked out through the leaves to see who was there. And, as she opened her eyes very wide, she saw that there on the wall where their nest used to be, someone had affixed a piece of white porcelain that held the wire of a tele-graph line.

As she turned to leave, wondering what would become of her, she noticed a woman carrying a basket full of wheat in her arms pushing open a barn door. "Please, ma'am," she said. "If you keep me with you and protect me, you will never regret it. Fairies, like goblins, are better than anyone in separating wheat from chaff and in winnowing, even without a basket. I will be a very useful servant to you indeed and will spare you much labor." The woman didn't hear or pretended not to. She pushed open the door and threw the contents of her basket under the cylinders of a machine able to clean wheat without the aid of goblins or fairies.

A little farther along near the edge of a river, Oriana came upon some men standing idly beside enormous bundles; nearby there was a ship moored at the bank. She thought that these people didn't know how to go about loading their merchandise. "Sirs!" she said, "If you keep me and protect me, you won't regret it! I will call some gnomes to help you out, gnomes so robust they can jump with such burdens on their shoulders. They will make short business of transporting all these heavy things. I will be a very useful servant to you indeed and will spare you much labor." They didn't hear or pretended not to. An enormous iron hook held by no hand descended and dug into one of the parcels, which took a half turn in the air and landed gently on the ship's bridge without the help of any gnomes.

As the day advanced, the little fairy looked through the open door of a cabaret and saw two men leaning over a table playing cards. Because of the gathering shadows, it surely was becoming difficult for them to distinguish the suits and the colors. "Dear sirs!" she said. "If you keep me and protect me, you won't regret it! I will call into this room all the glowworms that light up at wood's edge; you will soon be able to see clearly enough to continue your game with great enjoyment. Truly, I will be a very useful servant to you and will spare you many difficulties." The cardplayers didn't hear or pretended not to. As one of them signaled, three great bursts of light shot up toward the ceiling from three iron lances, illuminating the entire cabaret much more brightly than three thousand glowworms could have done. With this, Oriana could not keep from crying, for she understood that men and women had become too wise to require the help of a little fairy.

And yet the next day her hopes returned to her, thanks to a young girl she spied daydreaming at her open window as she watched swallows take flight. "While it is true," thought Oriana, "that people of this world have invented many extraordinary things, even in the triumph of their knowledge and their power they surely can't have abandoned the eternal, sweet pleasure of love. I was foolish not to have thought of this earlier."

And the last fairy spoke to the young girl at her window, saying, "Miss, I know of a young man living in a faraway land who is more handsome than sunshine and who loves you tenderly, even though he has never laid eyes upon you. He is neither the son of a king nor the son of a rich man, but his blond hair sits upon his head like a crown of gold, and his heart holds infinite treasures of tenderness for you. With your consent, I will bid him come to you and, before long, thanks to him you will become the happiest person alive."

"What a wonderful promise you offer me!" said the astonished young woman.

"And I will honor it, I assure you."

"But what do you want of me in exchange for such a service?"

"Oh, hardly anything at all!" said the fairy. "I ask only that you allow me to tuck myself in the dimple that appears at the corner of your mouth when you smile. I can make myself even smaller than I am now, so as not to trouble you."

"As you wish! It's a deal."

The girl had barely stopped talking before Oriana, no bigger than a pearl and nearly invisible, was already nestled in the pretty pink nest. Oh, how good it felt there! She would forever be happy! Now she no longer cared that men had laid waste to Brocéliande forest. She was too happy to fail to keep her promise and immediately summoned from his faraway land the young man who was more handsome than the day. He appeared, crowned with golden curls and bearing infinite treasures of tenderness in his heart, and knelt before his beloved.

But at that very moment an extremely loathsome person showed up, an aging man with rheumy eyes and withered lips. He carried a million gems displayed in an open coffer. The girl ran toward him, embraced him, kissing him on the mouth with a kiss so passionate that poor little Oriana died smothered in the dimple of a smile.

Les Contes du rouet, 1885

The Lucky Find

The clerk in the Lost and Found office did not betray the least bit of astonishment when, upon opening his counter grille, he saw standing before him in the yellow and black corridor a young man as beautiful as daybreak in springtime, wearing only a crimson blindfold and a golden quiver slung over his shoulder. This young man was not alone. At his side was a lady, the loveliest in the world, completely naked save for the lilies and roses that bedecked her skin and the diamond star in her hair. The clerk, as I've said, showed no surprise. No old Parisian such as himself would have been worth his salt had he expressed amazement for such a trifle.

So he considered the pair with the greatest indifference and asked in a professional manner, "Have you lost something?"

"Yes," responded the young man wearing a quiver.

"Yes," responded the young lady dressed in the pinky whiteness of her skin.

"Your clothes, perhaps?"

"I have never worn any!"

"Wouldn't it be wrong of me to cover myself?"

The clerk grumbled, "Let's get to the point: I don't have time to waste in chitchat. What have you lost?"

"As I stand before you, I am Love."

"Come to the point!"

"As I stand before you, I am Beauty."

"To the point!"

"We have lost," they said, "the respect and adoration that the human race once vowed to us."

"Hmm . . . these are items that will no doubt be difficult to recover. But let's think logically. Have you any recollection of the time or place this misfortune befell you?"

The god and goddess tried in vain to conceal their discomfort.

"Many days have passed," said he, "and I have found myself in more than one place since leaving the land of Cythera for the city rising in the neighborhood of Bougival and Asnières."*

"It was longer ago than yesterday when I left the waves and the modesty my hair afforded me," said she. "I have long since dwelled in the capital called Paris."

"I have seen night fall in both the boudoirs of celebrated socialites and those of inconsequential tarts."

"I have not refused to show myself at balls and parties, nor behind the footlights in theaters and cabarets."

"I have sworn a thousand broken promises at the feet of as many lovers."

"I have offered and I have surrendered myself on many a capricious evening of tempestuous weariness."

---

* Parisian suburbs notably frequented by impressionist painters during the latter part of the nineteenth century.

"I have debased myself for pleasures of the flesh, overlooking wholesome jealousies and accepting sacrilegious infidelities."

"I have sold myself for necklaces made of pearls and amethysts, for banknotes and piles of gold."

"Good God!" exclaimed the clerk. "You've done some fine things! People as important as you should have exhibited more restraint and not led such foolish lives. Admit it, it's your fault if you've lost the respect and admiration of the human race; between us, I seriously doubt that you will get them back. Do you think that even the most altruistic coach driver would return this sort of thing? Oh, if you had lived in the provinces, in a small city or village where chaste engagements linger on, you would have had some chance of winning back what you lost. But in Paris, after so many intrigues . . . Well, we'll see what we can do. Please wait a moment while I do some checking."

They waited a long time, because this clerk was an infinitely conscientious man. He ferreted around all the boards, cubbyholes, and closets of his office. He found opera glasses that had coveted the layered garments beneath dancers' skirts and bosoms that throbbed in the cleavage of bodices; he uncovered mirrors having reflected the makeup of lying lips. In wallets lost by clubmen, he found checks that might have purchased smiles and, in the purses of prostitutes, gold coins solicited between gasps of ecstasy. In the jumble of so many assorted things, he found virtues and reserves left on carriage cushions, forgotten in the bedrooms of furnished flats, or fallen into the gutter of some alleyway to be snagged, along with other varieties of blemished innocence, by a ragpicker's hook. There were also the virginities of children, thrown to the shameful lust of old men and then, the following day, swept into the garbage by the procuress's maid! But the worthy clerk could not lay his hand on the respect and adoration that Love and Beauty had lost, and he returned to his counter window saying, "You know, it's time to grieve: we don't have what you're looking for."

Beauty and Love then displayed the utmost desolation. What good did it serve her to be the charm and amazement of eyes, what good to him the unique dispenser of singular raptures, if the esteem and fervor of living souls were henceforth unattainable? They were gods scorned by their priests! This situation was clearly rather troublesome.

"What do you want me to do?" said the clerk, with his pen behind his ear, "You should have conducted yourselves like decent divinities."

But then a loud voice, rough and true, exclaimed, "Come on now, don't despair! Hell, there's a solution for everything!"

It was a coachman for the Company who had just come into the yellow and black hallway. He looked like an affable drunk with his stalk-like nose and enormous mouth. Undoubtedly he was bringing in some object forgotten in his carriage.

"Yes," he began again, "I'd like to bail you out. Do you know what I just discovered on the cushions in my coach? Here, look at that! the illusions of a poor little girl, as fresh as flowers and pretty as birds. She was joyful when she got into my carriage yesterday with a handsome boy who held her by the waist, but was crying when she stepped out. Illusions make us believe all the lies, make us see stars when the sky is dark and roses in the middle of winter. They're yours, take them away, I'm giving them to you! Make a present of them to humankind, fill all eyes, hearts, and heads with them and, I promise you, the whole race of mortal imbeciles will encircle you with respect and adoration. You, Love, as if betrayal and debauchery had never muddied you. And you, Beauty, my unthinking angel of back rooms, as though you had never, with your leg showing and a bit of skin flaming above your garter in the gaslight, kicked the hat off the head of a bedazzled provincial with the tip of your boot!"

Les Oiseaux bleus, 1888

The Wish Granted, Alas!

Any delay now was impossible! With the most ardent prayers and unwavering gestures, I threw myself at the feet of that exquisite and cruel socialite. Was she finally going to set aside her barbarity, touched no doubt by my long suffering and convinced of the value of the knight's earnest feat? How wrong I was! With one glance she dashed all my hopes and said with a little laugh:

"Love a poet? That's a folly I'll surely never commit."

"For what crime have poets deserved to lose the respect of young women?" I asked. "Don't they know how to love just as well as other men, and, furthermore, don't they have the pleasing advantage of immortalizing the beauty of their beloved ones with enthusiastic praise?"

"Precisely, sir, their mania for praise, abundant in rhetorical figures, is what I fear. No, I would not want to have happen to me what happened to my friend Lise de Belvelize."

So, what happened to Lise de Belvelize? The cruel woman told me:

"Once, when my friend, in front of her full-length mirror, was getting ready for the ball, a china vase on the fireplace smashed into twenty pieces after the chambermaid left. And from the fragments sprang forth, hardly bigger than a bee, dressed in four or five pearls with a hat made of a sweetbriar petal in which diamonds portrayed the dew, a cute little figure immediately recognizable as a fairy.

"Lise," she said. "In the evening, my sisters take refuge in the calyxes of daisies and roses, where they are very comfortable. I too sleep in flowers, but in the flowers of bobble and embroidery that bloom on your bed curtains. As you'd expect, I hardly sleep at all, listening to the tender words and refined compliments with which you enchant your lover's fortuitous insomnia! And I felt much goodwill for you because of the pretty words you know how to say and the even prettier mannerisms at which you excel. Make a wish! On my honor as a fairy, it will come true."

What can a woman—even a very beautiful woman—desire? To be even more beautiful. Lise remembered—she loved an arranger of rhymes, the poor woman!—sonnets, rondels, ballades that celebrated, with so many metaphors and not without some exaggeration, the features with which she was blessed, and she asked to become as miraculously charming as she was in her lover's poems.

"Your wish is my command!" said the fairy, who burst out laughing. "Finish getting dressed. As soon as you are at the ball, your wish will come true."

Then she disappeared—the fragments of the china vase closed around her like a flower. Lise hurried to get to the party, where such astonishment and admiration would welcome her! But things were not to happen as she had hoped, not by a long shot. Hardly had she entered the hall lit up with candelabra than she was surrounded by mocking whispers and laughter, exclamations of "oh! oh!" and "ah! ah!" and fingers pointing at her. But what? What had happened? Worried, she ran to a mirror. The heart of a tiger would have been moved by the plaintive cry she let out. She saw herself just like the beauty created by the imagination of her lover. Her blond hair was no longer hair, but ears of gold tufts; instead of eyes, two sapphires glistened; her mouth, which was no longer a mouth, was a rose; she had, quite literally, the neck of swan; angel wings fluttered on her shoulders; and her bosom—once warm and quivering flesh—her bosom was marble! She shuddered at the thought of what so many other treasures, veiled by embroidery and silk, could have become, and she fled, pursued by the mockery of the women and the pity of the men. My poor friend! It took her no fewer than eight or ten flirtations with engineers, bankers, and captains of industry to get rid of all that poetry. And so you understand, sir, that I am wary of rhymers obsessed with images and little persons springing from china vases, and will refrain from exposing myself to the danger of being beautiful to the point of no longer being a woman at all."

And that's how the exquisite and barbaric socialite explained why she could not love me. But she didn't convince me, even if the appearance of the fairy made the story plausible. For I knew all too well that if she was rejecting my ardent prayers and the unwavering advances I made in vain, it was because, last Sunday, on the plaza, her heart had been struck by the banderilla of an agile and muscular torero, with a tanned face closely shaved like a provincial actor.

La Princesse nue, 1890

JULES LEMAÎTRE

The Suitors of Princess Mimi

. . . So Cinderella married the prince.

Several months later, the prince lost his father and became king in his own right.

Then Queen Cinderella gave birth to a little girl, named Princess Mimi.

Princess Mimi was as beautiful as daylight. Her pink face and her lightly golden hair, with hints of sunshine, made her resemble an effervescent rose. And she was very intelligent.

When she was fifteen years old, she had to get married, for such was the law of the kingdom.

But since she was a princess, she could only marry a prince.

However, in all the surrounding lands, there were only two princes: Prince Polyphemus,* who was seven times taller than Princess Mimi, and Prince Thumbling,† who was seven times smaller than she.

---

* In Greek mythology, the giant son of Poseidon and Thoosa, and one of the Cyclopes in the *Odyssey*.

† "Poucet" in French. This is a reference to Perrault's "Le Petit Poucet" (Little Thum-

Both of them loved Mimi, but Mimi loved neither of them: Polyphemus because he was too tall and Thumbling because he was too short.

Nonetheless, the King ordered the princess to choose one of them before the end of the month, and he allowed the two princes to court her.

And it was agreed that the one who was rejected would forgive the other one and not do him any harm.

Polyphemus arrived with presents—cattle, sheep, cheeses, and overflowing baskets of fruit. And he was followed by giants ready for battle, clad in animal skins.

Thumbling brought birds in a golden cage, flowers, and jewels, and he was followed by jesters and dancers dressed in silk and wearing caps with bells.

Polyphemus told the princess his story:

"Do not believe," he told her, "what a poet by the name of Homer has recounted about me. First of all, he said that I had only one eye, and you see I have two. Next, it's true that long ago I happened to eat the men who landed on my island. But if I did that, it's because they were very small and I didn't give any more thought to eating them than you do when, at the table of the King your father, you suck on the bones of a plover or a young rabbit. But one day a Greek man, named Ulysses, helped me understand that those little men were still men just like me, that they often had families, and that I was hurting them a lot by eating them. From that day on, I've eaten only the flesh and milk of my own

bling), a diminutive but crafty boy who saves his brothers from an ogre after being abandoned by their parents.

flock. For I am not evil. Even more, as you see, Princess Mimi, I who am so strong and tall, I am as tender with you as with a new-born lamb."

Out of vanity, Polyphemus did not say that Ulysses had triumphed over him in spite of his strength and had poked out his eyes while he was sleeping and that he had recovered his sight thanks to the remedies of a wise magician.

Mimi thought to herself: "He'd still be capable of eating me if he got hungry. But Thumbling is so small that I'm the one who could gobble him up if I felt like it."

Thumbling told his story next:

"Treacherous sorcerers," he said, "wanted to lead me astray in the forest with my six brothers. But I dropped white pebbles behind me so we could find our way. By misfortune, I met the Ogre. He took us to his palace and had us sleep in a large bed. I discovered he wanted to kill us the next morning. So, in our place, I put the Ogre's seven daughters in the big bed, and they were the ones who got their throats slit by the Ogre. Then I took his seven-league boots, which were a godsend during a war that I had to wage against a neighboring king. The boots allowed me to know all about the enemy's movements. And that's how I became a very powerful prince. But I stopped wearing those boots, and I put them in the museum of my palace because they are too rough on my feet and also because they're not well suited for taking walks, since they force whoever wears them to take strides of seven leagues. But I'll show them to you, Princess Mimi."

Out of vanity, Thumbling said nothing about being the son of poor lumberjacks. And just like Polyphemus, he mixed truth with lies; for love, self-interest, and sometimes imagination always make us lie a bit.

One day, lying with his legs stretched out in the princess's sitting room, which he completely filled, Polyphemus told her in his thunder-like voice whose rumbling made the stained-glass windows tremble and the fragile shelves shake: "I'm simpleminded, but I'm honest and I'm strong. I grab boulders and throw them into the sea, I kill cattle with the slightest punch, and lions are afraid of me. Come to my land. You will see mountains that are blue in the morning and pink at night, with huge lakes as smooth as mirrors and forests as ancient as the world. I will take you wherever you'd like. I will go to the highest summits to pick flowers no woman has ever adorned herself with. My companions and I will be your slaves. Isn't it rare luck to be like a tiny goddess served by giants? To be the only queen—as cute as you are—of the forests and mountains, the streams and big lakes, the eagles and lions?"

The princess was somewhat moved by these words. She shivered and yet was joyful, like a wren that, enclosed in the hollow of a big hand, could feel the love of that hand and know that it is he who holds the enormous bird-catcher captive.

But Thumbling, nestled in the fold of Mimi's dress, told her with his thin, clear voice: "Accept me! I take up very little space! As little as I am, you'll have the pleasure of knowing that you can do anything you wish with me. I'll have the intelligence to love you. I'll be able to tell you that in a hundred different ways, and depending on whether you're sad or happy, vivacious or languid, and whatever the hour of the day or the time of the year, I'll be able to adapt my words and my caresses to your heart's secret desires. And I'll have a thousand tricks to entertain you. I'll surround you with all that man's ingenuity has invented for the pleasure of life. You'll have only elegant objects before your eyes, and you'll enjoy beautiful fabrics, well-carved statues, jewels and perfumes. I'll tell you stories and will have ingenious minstrels perform plays for you. I know how to sing, to play the mandolin, and to compose verse. It is more beautiful to express things seen and felt harmoniously than to tame lions, more rare to beautify one's life with grace and intelligence than to exercise the muscles of one's body . . ."

And Princess Mimi lost herself in reverie, but with a smile, as if she found this speech to be deliciously soothing.

One morning she told her two suitors: "Compose some verse for me."

Prince Thumbling thought to himself for a moment, then recited these lines, as short as he:

> *A prince I am*
> *(They all acclaim),*
> *And thin I am,*
> *Thumbling, my name.*

> *Body like a blot,*
> *Smaller than a hair,*
> *Hercules I'm not.*
> *And I don't care!*

The tiniest droplet
Upon the bonsai,
Reflects, all wet,
The entire sky.

And a thousand roses
(What a task!)
Under our noses
In a flask.

But who cares what I am?
For within myself I hold,
Even if a frail and tiny man,
A love strong and bold!

"Charming! Exquisite!" said the princess.

And she felt proud to be loved by a little man who put words together with such facility.

"Bah!" said Polyphemus, "it can't be that difficult to come up with lines as short as those."

"Try for yourself!" said Thumbling.

The giant tried all day long, but came up with nothing. At times, with his closed fist he struck his forehead in anger. But that didn't make anything come out. He was astonished and irritated at being incapable of expressing what he felt so deeply. That seemed unfair to him. He held still, his mouth agape, and his eyes glazed over ... Finally, toward evening, he realized that *love* rhymed with *dove*. Several hours later, he came to tell Mimi: "I've got it!"

"Tell me!" said the princess.
"Here it is," said the giant.

> *You are as beautiful as a dove,*
> *And I assure that for you I have much love.*

The princess burst out laughing.
"Isn't that beautiful poetry?" asked Polyphemus.
Thumbling felt triumphant.
"It's not difficult at all!" he responded. "All you had to say was . . ."

> *You are so very small, my princess so blonde,*
> *But your small size makes me so very fond.*

"Or else . . ."

> *I am a good but very crazy giant*
> *Whose love makes me very defiant.*

"Or even . . ."

> *O little, little girl,*
> *Who a powerful arrow did furl,*
> *You no bigger than my thumb,*
> *How did my heart succumb?*

"Or, if you prefer . . ."

> *I'm going to tell you what everyone knows:*
> *There was once a big oak who loved a rose.*

"Amazing!" said the princess.

But, in the corner of the giant's eye, she saw a tear as big as an egg, and he seemed so unhappy that she felt sorry for him. At the same time she thought Thumbling was too proud of his skill and that was in bad taste, which made her all the more sensitive to the sweetness and the naïveté of Polyphemus.

"After all," she said to herself, "he could have crushed his rival with the flick of a finger, or simply put him in his pocket. And even though I'm taller than Thumbling, he could still throw me under his arm, carry me away, and do as he pleases with me. He must be very good since he's done nothing like that."

And so, she said to Polyphemus:

"Don't despair, my friend. Your poetry wasn't very good, but your heart was in it and, after all, it says what's most important."

"But," said Thumbling, "that wasn't poetry at all. The meter is all wrong."

"Well, then," said the princess, "it's the verse of a decadent poet. Be quiet, Prince Thumbling!"

Princess Mimi's palace was surrounded by a large park traversed by a blue river. In the middle of the river, on an islet resembling a bouquet, there was a pavilion of colored porcelain, with windows made of precious stones held together with silver. The clever architect had made the pavilion in the form of a huge tulip. The princess had the habit of spending long hours there to feel the joy of being suspended between the azure blue river and the azure blue sky.

One day when she was on the small island, daydreaming, eyes half closed and humming melancholy songs, she did not notice that the river was rising all around her. Finally, the lapping of the waves pulled her from her drowsy state, and opening the window, she saw that the bridge that led to the islet was submerged and that soon the pavilion would be flooded. She was struck with fear and screamed.

On the riverbank, her father the King, her mother Queen Cinderella, and Prince Thumbling all three raised their arms to the heavens in despair. All of a sudden Polyphemus appeared. He walked into the river, and the water barely came to his waist. In three strides he reached the pavilion, delicately seized the princess, and took her back to shore.

"Oh!" Mimi said to herself, "how wonderful it is to be big and strong! And how sweet it is to feel protected like that! With him, I could sleep soundly, and I would never have the slightest care or fear. I do think he's the one I'll choose."

She smiled at the giant, and the smile of that little mouth sent a shiver of pleasure down Polyphemus's spine.

The next day, she saw that Thumbling was so sad that, to console him, she proposed they go on a long walk together through the fields.

She held his hand, and she pretended to be languid so as not to walk too fast and wear out her companion.

They came across a flock of sheep. And, since Thumbling was wearing a cherry satin doublet, a ram, who didn't like that color, broke away from the flock and, horns lowered, headed right for the little prince.

Thumbling, who was quite proud, put up a brave face, even though he was very frightened. But at the moment the ram was about to reach him, Princess Mimi took Thumbling in her arms and, at the same time, adroitly threw her cape onto the ram's nose, which stopped him in his tracks and made him turn away.

"We should be leaving," said Thumbling. "I wasn't afraid of him, and you saw, princess, how ready I was to confront him."

"Yes, little prince, I know you are brave," said Mimi.

And she reflected to herself: "Oh! It's good to protect those who are weaker than oneself! One can certainly learn to love those for whom one is useful, especially when they are pretty and elegant like this little man."

The next day, Thumbling gave the princess a small rose freshly emerging from its bud, a rose like none other for its color and its aroma.

Mimi took the flower and said: "Thank you, my dear little prince."

All day she wore a dress of constantly changing hues that seemed as if it were made of dragonfly wings.

"Ah," said Thumbling, "what a beautiful dress you have!"

"Yes, indeed," said Mimi. "And look how well your rose goes with it."

"A rose!" Polyphemus thought to himself, "what's that? I'll show her what sorts of bouquets I have to give her!"

He went to the East Indies and discovered a tall tree with brilliantly colored flowers, as big as the bells of a cathedral. Uprooting it, he presented it to Mimi, triumphantly.

"It is very beautiful," said the princess, laughing. "But what do you expect me to do with it, my dear prince? I can't pin it on my dress or put it in my hair."

The good giant, very ashamed, didn't know what to say. While lowering his eyes, he noticed that Prince Thumbling was wearing clothes the same color as the princess's dress.

"Oh!" he said.

"Yes," she answered, "I had this handsome suit made for him with a remnant of the cloth for my dress. I couldn't give it to you because there wouldn't have been enough to make even a bowtie for you."

And turning to the King, she said, "Since the time has come for me to make my choice known, father, Prince Thumbling is the one I choose for my husband. Prince Polyphemus will forgive me. I have a lot of respect for him, and I regret his pain."

The giant let out a sigh that made the whole palace tremble. Then, since he was a good man, he gave Thumbling his enormous hand, in which the prince lost himself.

"Make her happy," he told him.

On her wedding day, Princess Mimi was neither sad nor happy. For she doubtless had friendly feelings for Thumbling, but she did not love him.

At the very moment the wedding party was about to leave for the church, it was announced that Prince Charming, who had been traveling for several years, had arrived and would attend the ceremony.

Prince Charming appeared. He was a bit taller than the princess, handsome, noble, and extremely witty. In sum, Prince Charming was charming.

The princess had never seen him and had never even heard of him. But as soon as he appeared, she became pale, then flushed, and she said in spite of herself: "Prince Charming, I was waiting

Figure 3

for you. I love you and I can tell that you love me. But I've given my hand to this poor little man, and I can't take it back."

As she said this she almost fell over in a faint.

Polyphemus leaned over to Thumbling: "Little Prince, do you have the courage to do what I did?"

"But I love her!" said Thumbling.

"That's all the more reason," said the good giant.

"Madame," Thumbling said to Princess Mimi, "this good giant is right. I love you too much to keep you against your will. We hadn't foreseen the arrival of Prince Charming. Since you love him, marry him."

Princess Mimi, transported by joy, lifted the little man from the ground and kissed him on both cheeks, telling him: "Ah, what you're doing is so nice!"

Crying, Thumbling said: "That's more cruel than everything else."

"Come with me, poor little prince," said Polyphemus. "You can tell me all your troubles. We'll talk about her every day, and we'll look after her from afar."

He placed Thumbling on his shoulder, and soon they both disappeared over the horizon.

Dix contes, 1890

Liette's Notions

My goddaughter Liette is ten years old. She's a very logical little girl. For her feast day, I'd given her a beautiful copy of Perrault's *Fairy Tales.* When I saw her again later, I asked her:

"Did you read my book?"

"Yes, Godfather," she replied.

"Did you like it?" I asked.

"Sure," she said with a frown. "But there's quite a selection."

"What do you mean by that, Liette?"

"Well, some of the stories are certainly very nice—the stories that end happily . . ."

"Which is to say?"

"Which is to say the stories where those who were bad are punished and where those who were good are rewarded. For example, *Sleeping Beauty, Cinderella, Riquet with the Tuft* all end happily. But the others . . ."

"What do you mean, Liette?"

"Come now, Godfather. Can you really accept the ending of *Little Red Riding Hood*? A little girl is eaten by the wolf, and why? Because she was polite to him and because, next, she had fun gathering nuts! And the grandmother, who is also eaten by the wolf, what did *she* do wrong?

"It's the same thing with the wife of the Ogre in *Little Thumbling*. She's very good. When she sees Little Thumbling and his brothers, she starts to cry and tells them: 'Alas, poor children, do you know where you are?' She has them warm themselves next to a fire and, when her husband returns, she hides them under the bed. She convinces the Ogre to wait a day before killing them, and she gives them something to eat. And how is she rewarded for her good heart? The next morning, she finds her seven daughters with their throats slit, 'swimming in their own blood.' Is that fair? I know that the little ogresses weren't pretty and were going to be very nasty. But still, she loved them as they were since she was their mother."

Liette said these last words with a lot of emphasis, as if she were onstage.

"Have you finished, Liette?"

"Oh!" she said, shaking her head and waving her curls, "I could go on forever if I said everything I have to say."

"We have plenty of time, Liette."

"Well," she said after a moment of reflection, "as I explained, in some of them, people are punished for doing nothing wrong. But some people are punished, not unjustly, if you will, but much more than they deserve to be."

"But that's life."

"What?"

"Nothing. Continue . . ."

"For example, what did the wife of Bluebeard do? She was curious, disobedient . . . And she was in her rights to go everywhere, since she was the mistress of the house . . . But isn't she punished enough by the fright she had in the dark room, and by seeing that the little key was splattered with blood, and the blood wouldn't go away? No, it seems that wasn't enough," continued Liette, sarcastically. "Her husband has to grab her hair with one hand while, with the other, he raises his saber to cut off her head. Fortunately, her two brothers finally arrive. But what the poor woman must have suffered! All that, for a trivial little act of disobedience!

"And in *The Fairies*! Of course Fanchon is stupid and boastful. But isn't it enough of a punishment for her to see her younger sister spew pearls and diamonds from her mouth with each word she speaks and then marry the prince? I repeat: I do not like Fanchon . . . But going to die in the corner of the woods and being unable to complain without vomiting toads and serpents—that's really too harsh."

"But, Liette, you'd at least approve of the success of the Marquis of Carabas and his faithful Puss 'n Boots, wouldn't you?"

"Oh! There are lots of things I could say about that story as well . . . Children are forbidden to lie, and your infamous Puss 'n Boots does nothing but lie from morning to night . . . And then, why does he eat the Ogre who'd welcomed him so civilly into his castle? The Ogre is stupid to change himself into a mouse out of vanity. But that still doesn't justify it. And that stupid idiot Marquis of Carabas, who becomes so rich without lifting a finger, is that fair? Don't you see, Godfather, your *Perrault's Fairy Tales* are very lovely, but they give children bad ideas."

*

A few days after this conversation, on Christmas day, in fact, Liette had assembled her little friends Zette, Toche, Dine, Pote, Niquette, and Yoyo and was telling them stories, which is one of her most favorite things to do.

Six pairs of bright eyes were riveted on Liette, and six rosy mouths drank in her every word.

Liette was telling them:

"In those times, Jesus was born in a stable, between the ox and the donkey. Mary and Joseph were near him, and the shepherds and Wise Men came to worship him.

"Around the same time, Little Red Riding Hood, who no longer recalled having met the wolf, was having fun picking nuts, running after butterflies, and making bouquets of flowers."

"Flowers at Christmastime?" Zette asked.

Liette ignored the objection, and continued:

"She hadn't noticed that night was falling. The woods were dark. The basket she was carrying on her arm, which held a cake and a little jar of butter, seemed very heavy to her. But she noticed a little light far off in the distance. She walked in that direction and arrived at the stable where Jesus was lying in a manger.

"She was surprised at first. But because baby Jesus was smiling at her, she kissed him and offered the Virgin her cake, her little jar of butter, and her bouquets. The Virgin thanked her and said: 'You were right to come here, my dear; otherwise, you'd have been eaten by the wolf. But the wolf was not even able to eat your grandmother because a man saw him as he was trying to enter her house and chased him away by throwing rocks at him.'

"So the Virgin asked one the shepherds to accompany the little girl home to her parents, who must have been worried. And one

Figure 4

of the Wise Men thought Little Red Riding Hood was so nice that he wanted to adopt her. 'Go ask my parents,' said Little Red Riding Hood. And the Wise Man adopted her and took her to his court with her father, mother, and grandmother.'"

*

"That's not all," Liette continued. "After Little Red Riding Hood left the stable, the wife of the Ogre arrived, in tears. She told the Virgin about her misfortune and that she had found her seven daughters with their throats slit. The Virgin answered, after whispering to baby Jesus:

"'Return home, poor woman. You'll find your seven daughters alive in their bed. They'll be even prettier than before and, instead of their long teeth and crooked noses, they'll have small teeth and little upturned noses. But warn your husband to stop killing little children.'

"'I will not fail to do so, Madame,' said the Ogre's wife. 'Besides, my husband is very upset that he inadvertently killed his daughters, and I believe his sorrow has made him a better person.'

"'If that's the case,' said one of the Wise Men, 'I'll hire him, and he'll be one of the Swiss guards who watch over my palace.'

"The Ogre's wife was very grateful and went away very happy.

"Then Mrs. Bluebeard entered the stable, her hair disheveled and a key in her hand. She told the Virgin her adventure and how much she feared her husband's return. The Virgin took the little key stained with blood and had baby Jesus touch it. The blood disappeared instantly.

"And the Virgin gave the key back to Mrs. Bluebeard, who thanked her profusely. Mrs. Bluebeard returned home, and her husband never knew that she had disobeyed him. So, he was very nice with her. But since he had been very evil for killing his first wives, he died a few days later in a hunting accident.

"And then it was the turn of Fanchon, the boastful girl who had been condemned to spew out toads and serpents with each word, to come to the stable at Bethlehem. She went toward Jesus, she knelt down, and trembling for what was doubtless going to happen, she said: 'Jesus, have pity on me.' But, instead of vipers and toads, Christmas roses came out of her mouth . . .

"As soon as Fanchon, with tearful gratitude, had left, a gentleman appeared, richly dressed with a large plumed hat on his head. He shouted at the shepherds: 'Make way, peasants, make way for the Marquis of Carabas!' And, approaching the manger, he finally took off his hat and said to baby Jesus: 'Cousin, I offer you my loyalty.'

" 'Marquis,' the Virgin told him, 'return home, please. First of all, you are not a marquis since you are the son of a miller. You are not one of my son's friends, for you do not have a humble heart. And you acquired your great fortune only through the trickery and lies of your cat. Aren't you ashamed to owe him everything you are? Return home, my boy. While you were on your way here, your beautiful castle evaporated, and you'll find only the foundation. But, if you start working and if you really want it, I promise, in the name of my son, that you will earn a very good living and will not be unhappy.'

"And the Marquis left amidst the laughter of the shepherds and the Wise Men.

"That's all," said Liette.

Zette, Toche, Dine, Pote, Niquette, and Yoyo appeared enchanted by these stories.

*

I had been listening from my corner, pretending to read my news-paper. When Liette had finished, I said: "You spoke eloquently. Through your childlike make-believe and with the refinement and the grace of a Frenchwoman, you've just shown that you've inherited the elegance of a conscience slowly purified by genera-tions of excellent Aryans."

"I don't understand what you're saying there, Godfather."

"Never mind, Liette. But you didn't speak of the fairies who are in Perrault's *Fairy Tales.* They also went to worship baby Jesus in the stable. And, since they were very beautiful and magnificently dressed, one in gold, another in silver, the third in crimson silk, the fourth in royal blue velour, and so on, and since they were sparkling with thousands of jewels, they were a truly beautiful sight: it would be less difficult for you to imagine this scene than for me to describe it . . . Baby Jesus received their homage, then he changed the fairies into saints, and he sent them off to the coun-tryside and the woods. They take care of the grasses and the flow-ers with which remedies are made, as well as the fountains that heal the sick. They protect travelers. They turn flocks of animals away from poisonous plants. They teach birds to sing . . .

"And it was one of these saints who was the first to speak to your good friend Joan of Arc, under the tree of the fairies . . ."

En marge des vieux livres, 1906

On the Margins of Perrault's Fairy Tales:
The White Rabbit and the Four-Leaf Clover

There was once a young peasant boy who went into the forest to gather kindling. He had a passion for flowers, trees, and animals. Following the path, he was very careful not to walk on insects and snails.

He gave birds most of the bread he'd brought from home for his afternoon snack.

Passing a fountain where only a trickle of water was flowing, he saw it was clogged with dead leaves and pieces of rotting wood. He cleaned it carefully because he knew that water likes very much to be clean.

At the foot of a tree, he saw a nest that had fallen from its branch. Several little gray eggs with blue spots had cracked open during the fall. He put the ones that were not broken back into the nest and put the nest back in the tree.

At that moment, he heard some moaning behind a bush. It was a deer that had hurt its leg and couldn't stand up. The young boy approached it and petted it. Then he cleaned the wound and dressed it with a piece of his shirt.

After all that, he gathered a bundle of wood and left the forest.

But the fairy of the forest had seen him. She had strong feelings of friendship for this young boy and decided to make his fortune . . . Here's how she did that.

*

One day when the little princess of the land was walking through the forest looking for mushrooms, a surprisingly beautiful white rabbit jumped on her dress. She leaned down, took it in her arms, and held it against her heart.

At that very instant, the fairy appeared and told her: "Princess, that white rabbit will bring you good fortune if you want. But for that to happen, you'll have to keep him with you and take good care of him, giving him only four-leaf clover. If he were to eat anything else, he would die and you with him. For your fate is tied to him, at least until you get married."

Having said this, the fairy disappeared into the hollow trunk of an old willow tree.

The princess took the rabbit to her palace and let him stay in her own bedroom. The next day, she made a proclamation asking all her subjects to bring her all the four-leaf clover they could find and promised good money for them.

The next day, all the children in the kingdom could be seen scouring the fields looking for four-leaf clover. In the evening, they went to the palace and paraded their harvest in front of a minister who had been named specifically to watch over feeding the white rabbit.

The first few days, supplies were quite abundant, and the white rabbit could eat to his heart's content. As he was vain, he was pleased to be given such refined food. But then the harvest became less and less plentiful each day. The rabbit began to get skinny, and the princess did as well.

She issued a second proclamation in which she offered an even higher price for four-leaf clover. Almost immediately, so many were brought that the white rabbit couldn't even eat them all. But they did him no good: he became very ill, and the princess had terrible stomach pains.

At this, the minister examined the clover the rabbit had left behind and discovered that they were three-leaf clover to which a fourth leaf had been glued. The princess was very irritated and made yet another proclamation in which she condemned all counterfeiters to be hanged, and she established an office for the inspection of clover.

*

From then on, people brought only clover that really had four leaves. But fewer and fewer were to be had. The white rabbit wasted away. His ribs looked as though they were collapsing, and he didn't even have the strength to wiggle his nose. The princess was so weak she took to her bed. She held the white rabbit in her poor little arms, and all they could do was wait to die.

In this dire situation, she let her people know that she would give her hand in marriage and her crown to the man who, by a miracle or some other means, could provide enough four-leaf clover to save her by saving her rabbit.

*

So the fairy went to find the little peasant boy she'd befriended. She led him through the forest to a hidden spot, protected by impenetrable bushes, where unbeknownst to others there was a field of nothing but four-leaf clover.

The fairy cleared a path through the bushes with her magic wand, and the young boy had simply to cut the clover with his scythe.

For several days, he brought cartloads full of clover. And in less than a week, the white rabbit regained its weight and the princess got her color back.

And, because the young boy was good-looking and the fairy

had groomed and dressed him herself, the princess married him, not only out of gratitude, but also with pleasure.

*

Since she was now out of danger, she let the rabbit eat whatever it wanted. But the rabbit was disgusted by four-leaf clover and ate so much lettuce, cabbage, and carrots that it died of indigestion.

La Vieillesse d'Hélène: nouveaux contes en marge, 1914

PAUL ARÈNE

The Ogresses

My boyhood friend Estevanet was a funny one. He had a bizarre mind, a truly original soul! Even as a young child, he had his own way of seeing things and viewing the world.

He was always wandering off, and when he returned to school after roaming thus he came bearing a bizarrely shaped stone, or the nest of a bird of prey acquired at great peril to himself, or strange mountain plants whose names were known only to shepherds. One morning he showed up with two frogs, a rare find, since in our rocky region ponds are not abundant. After a while the frogs started to waste away: they were motionless, with their white bellies stuck against the glass bowl, and they no longer had the heart even to swallow flies. This is when Estevanet imagined they were bored.

"Let them go in the Durance River," I said.

"No! They need their pond; anywhere else they'll feel exiled. And it's such a pretty pond! A water hole that's all blue and green with reflections from the sky and tall irises that look at themselves there. Over time, the water has dug away mossy hideaways under the river bank. That's where my frogs were happy, and that's where they'll be joyful again!"

During an entire afternoon we searched over hill and dale for the pond, whose location Estevanet couldn't remember. We finally came upon it at sunset, and I'll be if we weren't rewarded sweetly. Even with the pond far behind us as we doubled back to arrive on time, we could still hear the grateful frogs singing.

Estevanet was very reserved, even a bit of a loner, who rarely displayed the treasure of his delicate sensitivity, for fear of ridicule. During lost moments, he practiced his mouth harp, an instrument rarely played anymore, which is unfortunate, since it's a perfect instrument for timid souls such as he, guarded and withdrawn. Perhaps you're aware that the mouth harp is like a miniature steel lyre with a reed in the middle. It's easy to use: you place the lyre frame between your teeth and make the reed vibrate with your finger. In this way, anyone able to inhale the sound strongly enough can play the most enchanting music in the pit of his stomach. And the public doesn't hear anything, so only the virtuoso benefits from his genius. It's the height of Art for Art!

Estevanet always carried his mouth harp with him when we ran around the countryside. He would sit at the foot of a tree and begin playing. And in my role as trusted admirer, I imagined what interior melodies he was playing from the look on his face, by turns smiling and ecstatic.

We liked each other because we had a common bond: we were both in love!

First about me ... but then it surely is of little interest to you to know for whom I shed tears at the age of twelve.

He, ever in love with the unreal, ended up discovering an object worthy of his affections in a collection of fairy tales. You'll never guess who! It was neither the little girl with the red riding hood, who was too young when the wolf ate her; nor that sweet, innocent child who was rewarded so magnificently for having given begging fairies a drink by the side of the road, since pearls and diamonds came out of her mouth when she spoke; nor the melancholic chatelaine, Sister Anne's sister, whom it would have been nonetheless heroic and lovely to defend against her abominable husband; nor Sleeping Beauty, hidden away in her castle behind an impenetrable rampart formed by intertwined trees and brambles; nor the clever princess whom the Marquis of Carabas married thanks to the tricks of Master Cat; nor the one whom Riquet with the Tuft made intelligent. Nor was it Cinderella, who went to the ball in a carriage made out of a pumpkin, drawn by six mice who served as horses and six fat lizards as valets. Nor was it Donkey Skin, the radiant baby princess wearing gowns the color of the sun and the moon. As for Griselda, she couldn't have been involved since the adventures of the unfortunate Marquise de Saluces were missing from the cheap edition of Mother Goose we bought from a peddler.

No! He was in love with . . . (do you remember Little Thumbling?) . . . none other than the Ogre's seven daughters. All seven of them, you ask? Yes, all seven.

Boys that age don't do things by halves, and in explanation for such a choice, that sly Estevanet gave me the most convincing reasons. I reminded him in vain that good old Perrault's portrait of them was hardly flattering: "These young ogresses all had very fine complexions, because they ate fresh meat like their father; but they had little gray eyes, quite round, hooked noses, and very long sharp teeth, with big spaces between each one. They were not as yet overly mischievous, but they had great potential, for they had already bitten little children to suck their blood."

"That's nonsense," replied Estevanet. "Perrault was doubtless misinformed, either that or he knowingly falsified the facts in order to excuse the disgraceful conduct of his hero, who answered the good ogress's hospitality by getting her daughters' throats slit. 'They had very fine complexions . . .' Here their true portrait shines through, showing that they must have been adorable, in spite of what Perrault says about their round eyes and hooked noses! 'They were not as yet overly mischievous . . .' Why add this? And who says they wouldn't have grown up to be good and sweet like their mother?"

Thereupon Estevanet made up another ending to the story, which he claimed to have heard from his nanny, in which Little Thumbling and his brothers carried away the Ogre's daughters, married them, and became great lords.

He ended up by convincing me. We hoped mightily that one day we'd find the Ogre's castle deep in the woods. In which case, it was all settled! Estevanet claimed the eldest for himself, but deigned to let me choose from among the others. And at night, between two fanciful tunes from his mouth harp, we dreamt of the seven young ogresses in their big bed, rosy-cheeked, gorgeous, and wearing crowns of gold on their heads.

*

Later on, Estevanet and I lost track of each other. I knew that he had become a painter, making his Art pretty much for himself alone, just like the way he played his mouth harp! Nobody could capture the contemporary Parisienne as well as he: with her insolent bodice, cruel lips, and her doubly sensual charms, which combined a voluptuous body with pure artifice. But the public could not understand his paintings, so sophisticated were they in their *modernism*: light sketches that perpetually glorified womanhood, as subtle as flowers and as vague as symbols.

People said that Estevanet had come into an inheritance and that he had had love affairs.

I learned one day that he had died.

A common friend let me into his atelier. Seven portraits of women—of a questionable sort, to put it delicately!—adorned his walls. All seven shared a resemblance, having the same sort of indifferent and hard beauty. In the corner was a large canvas covered by a sheet.

"That's the one," the concierge told us, "that he was working on at the end . . . They say that the painting is quite beautiful, but nobody has been able yet to guess what it means."

It showed seven women, the same as those depicted in the portraits, sleeping in a sumptuous bed shrouded by rich fabrics. They were rosy red, full-bodied, and cheerful, all wearing crowns of gold upon their heads. And there beside the bed, standing on his tiptoes and holding his breath, a pale Little Thumbling watched over them with childish eyes full of desire and fright.

You must know, dear reader, that all intrepid boys who hide their naïveté behind skepticism are a bit like poor Estevanet who, in spite of betrayal and disappointment, persisted until his death in believing that ogresses could be good.

Les Ogresses, 1891

JULES RICARD

Fairy Morgane's Tales: Nocturne II

Morgane[*] entered my bedroom silently, through the closed windowpanes.

She gave me a slight nod and smiled at me, with her tender smile of the rosy hours. And, indeed, the star that shimmers on the sheen of her black hair was pink, an indescribable pink that in no way resembles the color of molten barley sugar that our real, terrestrial illuminations shine over things. The star reflected continuously but differently throughout the whole room, sometimes giving muted visions like those of beautiful Chinese porcelain or of the creamy hues of flowers. And then the faint glow blackened, became transparent, far off, whimsically tender, and a profound joy emanated from all of this shimmering, living, loving pink. A quiet stilled my heart. Life—hurried, abrupt, mean—had stopped for a moment to smile as a fairy smiles standing next to my bed, to smile the tender smile of the rosy hours.

"A story, dear friend!" I implored. "There has been nothing but bitterness and stupidity all day long. I saw people who wanted to

***

[*] Enchantress in Arthurian legend.

live to be very old, ugly women and intelligent men . . . Tell me a story! A story that consoles, a story as rosy as your smile."

Morgane thought for a moment.

"There's no such thing as a rosy story, you ought to know that," she said. "Would you like a mauve one?"

"No," I insisted grumpily. "Rosy! I want a rosy one!"

"And anyway, what is a rosy story?" continued the fairy, whose facemask of gentle white opal betrayed the suave ray of feminine indulgence.

"A rosy story," I asserted, "is a story that ends happily, of course."

"Ah!" said the fairy, in a way that seemed to be making fun of me a bit.

After a pause as noble as an actor's at the Comédie-Française, Morgane began:

Cinderella was sitting on a braided mat. She was thinking bitterly about how no one loved her or would ever love her, about how useless it would be for her to throw her heart in front of passersby. And Cinderella cried because she knew nothing of the science of life.

Then, as Cinderella's tears flowed and fell onto the light rug she was sitting on, one of these tears—like flat diamonds embedded on the golden hilt of curved sabers—gave off a bright flicker. Then, Cinderella saw in the room's blond shadows a strange being, diaphanous and smiling, who was standing before her and whose vague form seemed to be made of a bit of gray and blue smoke. As she was looking at the strange silhouette, it seemed to her that a voice was coming from it, a voice she heard not with her ears but with something vibrant and subtle, something like a new sense that had just appeared in her chest. The voice said:

"Do you want to be adored for all eternity, little Cinderella?"

"Yes!" answered the solitary girl, crying out from the depths of her soul.

Then, the frail, unreal form drew nearer to the young girl. She felt the grasp of a powerful arm around her waist, and the room disappeared. Cinderella was flying through the air, carried off by the genie.

Soon, they stopped at a place where countless roads met. The genie set Cinderella, shaking with anguish, on the burning ground.

"Listen," he began with that voice she heard with the new subtle and vibrant sense in her chest. "I didn't tell you everything. In order to be adored, little Cinderella, adored for eternity, you must give up the intoxicating feeling of loving."

"It doesn't matter!" she exclaimed. "I know what it's like to love, and it's too much suffering! What I want from now on is to be loved. Hurry, dream god, fulfill your promise!"

So, the genie put his finger on the sad child's head, and her forehead and cheeks, whose skin was like a delectably gilded sheen, turned into gold, as did her small body, elastic and supple. And her eyes, black as the dark enamel paint used to infill engravings, turned into enamel. Her lips, red like ivory stained with bold nopal purples, turned into ivory. Her hair, similar to black marble marvelously sculpted around her head, became marble. And her dress of light white cloth, which seemed to have silver reflections and whose intricate pink designs resembled coral, turned into a silver dress encrusted with coral.

Then, by the side of the road, the genie picked a broad blue flower that had instantly and radiantly grown. He put it in Cinderella's hand, and as soon as it touched her, the flower became a huge sapphire, hard and magnificent.

Next the genie, smiling sadly, said to Cinderella:

"You are no more charming than you were before. Your skin is no more finely gilded, your eyes no more purely enameled, your mouth of no fresher ivory, your black hair no more exquisitely marbled. But you have become impassive and impossible. You are the Idol. You shall be adored. Adieu, Cinderella. If ever you tire of your ferocious intoxication, throw the sapphire flower on the ground and I'll return to help you . . . if I can."

And placing Cinderella on the gold pedestal of a god that had once protected this crossroad and that an antiques dealer had carried off the week before, the genie disappeared into the morning air.

Shortly afterwards some men passed by who, struck with admiration and crazed at the sight of the Idol, bowed down before it, sobbing with love. All day long they came. Many stayed, their foreheads touching the mud of the path. Others left, their hearts poisoned by the irreducible memory. And Cinderella felt, under the gold of her pure breast, an ever-greater intoxication in this triumph that soothed the tortured pride of her soul. She exulted in her indifference as if it were a strong balm that, along with peace, delivers dreams of paradise.

At her feet, sons of kings stabbed each other, merchants fought with knives, men in rags with their fists. And with cries of deep sadness, they all repeated the same words. The same words, always the same:

"Ah! If the gold of your body could quiver and live, if the enamel of your eyes could see, if the marble of your hair were to soften, if the purple ivory of your lips could feel the warmth of kisses! If only, just as you are now, you were a woman!"

The Idol seemed to smile strangely, while her eyes looked off, far off, beyond the world. She remembered the time she was a woman with the same appearance whom no one loved. And, silently delirious, she exulted in her indifference.

Years passed. Bones piled up at the feet of the smiling Idol, cruelly impassive and drowning in her dream. Living men crawled upon these bones, some sobbing and crying, others dying in mournful silence with the bitter rictus of slow fevers on their lips.

But one day someone passed by without stopping. He was a simple boy who was whistling while walking to a neighboring city, doubtless to do something useful there. He looked at the Idol and continued on his way. So, suddenly, Cinderella was tired of her dream of being adored. And in the ardent and clear night, as sobs wafted toward her in an indistinct and distressing threnody, she felt the invincible disgust of life fall upon her and seize her, ferociously. She threw the big sapphire flower into the dust, and it cut through the air with a quick shimmer of light.

The genie appeared before her, diaphanous and smiling. Above the sobbing men kneeling under the polished pewter moonbeam, Cinderella said:

"I want the love of the one who passed by without stopping . . . And I also want to be able to love him. Give me my heart back, genie of dreams!"

And still smiling, he responded:

"He will love you, you will love him. But you must first comfort the men who are moaning, lovingly, at your feet."

"How can I do that?" asked the Idol.

The genie then picked up the big sapphire flower from the dust. He put his finger on the left breast of Cinderella, whose golden face seemed to pale and whose enamel eyes illuminated with ecstasy and sorrow. Like the blow of a knife, the touch of the diaphanous finger had made a hole in her breast. Blood flowed from her heart in large drops and fell into the sapphire flower chalice. When it was full, the genie continued:

"Give your heart's blood to these miserable souls. Then you will be loved by the one who passed by without stopping. You will love him. Adieu!"

And after touching the Idol's forehead with his unreal lips, the spirit vanished in the light air of the ardent and clear night.

Cinderella held the flower over the kneeling men who were sobbing and dying. A drop of her heart's blood fell onto the lips of the nearest one. He rose with a great cry of happiness:

"She lives!"

Indeed, she was alive. Her marble heart softened, the purple ivory of her mouth shivered, the dark enamel of her eyes filled with tears, the gold of her skin shimmered.

And the man repeated: "She lives!" Then, after he had swallowed the drop of blood, he continued:

"She's a woman, a woman like all the others . . ."

And with a sigh of relief, smiling at the thought of the folly that had filled his lost hours, he fled in haste. And all of them, likewise, were healed in a second of the love for the one who gave her heart's blood, because she gave them the blood of her heart.

At the end of the day, Cinderella was alone, down from her pedestal, and ineffably sad.

Suddenly, at the crossing of one of numerous roads appeared the man who had passed by that morning. Cinderella went toward him, holding out the big sapphire flower with only a single remaining drop of her heart's blood. The simple boy, who was returning quietly from the neighboring city, content to have carefully completed some humble task, took the shining lotus with a hesitant gesture. He looked at the flower, then looked at the woman whose gilded forehead paled.

"Drink," she said.

He obeyed, surprised. And when the drop of blood had reached his heart, the sapphire flower wilted, and Cinderella, upright and pale by the edge of the road, was nothing more than Cinderella. She clasped her hands on her chest and said:

"I love you."

"I love you too," answered the simple boy. "Come with me to my little house, you'll help me weave baskets, and we'll be very happy."

And Cinderella left with him.

"Do you think she was happy, dear fairy?" I asked, curious, perplexed especially.

"I never found out," responded Morgane. "I really don't know what to think about the happiness of that idol turned basket weaver."

"So, the rosy story?"

"Is a rosy story . . . Isn't that happiness? Giving the blood of your heart to an unknown passerby, and then following him . . . without knowing where you're going . . ."

Acheteuses de rêves, 1894

MARCEL SCHWOB

Bluebeard's Little Wife

"That's fantastic," said the little girl. "It's bleeding white blood!"*

Her playmate watched calmly as she scored the green poppy buds with her fingernails. They had played at bandits among the chestnut trees, pelting the rosebushes with fresh conkers, unhooding young acorns. They placed the meowing kitten atop the wooden fence. A forked tree grew at the bottom of the dark garden: this was Robinson's island. The rose of a watering can became their war horn during the attack of the savages. Tall, black-topped weeds were taken prisoner and decapitated. Some blue and green beetles, captured during the hunt and held in the well bucket, struggled to open their forewings. The sand of the pathways was furrowed by captains' maces during the armies' frequent passage. They had just mounted an attack on a grassy hillock in the meadow. The setting sun enveloped them in a glorious light.

Settling themselves into their captured positions, a bit weary, they admired the faraway crimson mists of autumn.

---

* The title above was the tale's first title, as it was published individually in a journal (1892). Retitled "La Voluptueuse" for inclusion in *Le Livre de Monelle*.

"If I were Robinson," he said, "and you Friday, and if there were a large sandy beach down there, we'd go looking for cannibal tracks."

She mulled this over and then asked, "Did Robinson beat Friday so he would obey him?"

"I don't remember," he replied, "but they beat the nasty old Spaniards and the savages from Friday's country."

"I don't like these stories," she said, "they're for boys. It's going to be night soon. Let's play fairy tales: then we'll really be afraid."

"Really?"

"Hey, don't you think that the Ogre, with his long teeth, comes every evening to the dark wood?"

He looked at her and, gnashing his jaws, said, "And when he ate the seven little princesses, he went *yum yum yum.*"

"No, not like that," she said. "You can only be the Ogre or Little Thumbling. Nobody knows the names of the little princesses. If you want, I'll be Sleeping Beauty, and you can come wake me in my castle. You'll have to kiss me really hard. Princes are tremendous kissers, you know."

Feeling timid, he answered, "I think it's too late to sleep in the grass. Sleeping Beauty was on her bed in a castle surrounded by thorns and flowers."

"Then let's play Bluebeard," she said. "I'll be your wife and you'll forbid me to go into the little room. Start with coming to marry me. 'I'm not sure, Sire, your six wives disappeared so mysteriously. It's true that you have a big, beautiful blue beard, and that you live in a splendid castle. You won't ever hurt me, will you?'"

She looked at him beseechingly.

"Okay, now you've asked me to marry you, and my parents have consented. We're married. Give me all the keys. 'And what is this

Figure 5

pretty little one here?' You do the mean voice forbidding me to open the door."

"Okay, now you're gone and I disobey right away. 'Oh! How horrible! Six murdered wives!' I faint, and you arrive in time to catch me. Like that. Go back to being Bluebeard. Do the mean voice. 'Sire, here are all the keys you entrusted to me.' You ask me where the little key is. 'Sire, I do not know. I didn't touch it.' Now shout. 'Pardon me, Sire, here it is; it was at the bottom of my pocket.'"

"Now you look at the key. Was there blood on the key?"

"Yes," he said, "a bloodstain."

"I remember," she said. "I rubbed and rubbed, but I couldn't get it off. Was it the blood of the six wives?"

"Of the six wives."

"He killed them all, didn't he, because they went into the little room? How did he kill them? Did he cut their throats and hang them in the dark room? And the blood ran down off their feet onto the floor? It was very red blood, nearly black, not like how poppies bleed when I scratch them. He makes them kneel before slitting their throats, right?"

"I think you have to kneel down," he said.

"This will be a lot of fun," she said. "But you'll cut my throat like for real, won't you?"

"Yes," he said, "but Bluebeard couldn't kill her."

"That doesn't matter," she said. "Why couldn't Bluebeard cut off his wife's head?"

"Because her brothers came."

"She was afraid, wasn't she?"

"Really afraid."

"Did she cry out?"

"She called for her sister, Anne."

"If it were me, I wouldn't have cried out."

"Maybe, but then Bluebeard would have had the time to kill you," he said. "Sister Anne was in the tower, looking at the green grass. Her brothers, who were very strong musketeers, arrived on their horses at full gallop."

"I don't want to play that way," said the little girl. "That's boring. Because I don't have any sister Anne."

She turned sweetly toward him: "Since my brothers won't

come, you have to kill me, my little Bluebeard, and kill me really, really hard!"

She knelt down. He took hold of her hair, brought it forward, and raised his hand.

Slowly, with her eyes closed and lashes fluttering, the corner of her mouth troubled by a nervous smile, she offered the down on her nape, her neck, and her voluptuously tucked shoulders to the cruel blade of Bluebeard's saber.

"Oh, ooh!" she cried. "This is going to hurt!"

The Green She-Devil

Buchette's father led her into the woods at the break of day, and she sat near him as he cut down trees.* Buchette watched his axe as it sank into the bark, at first letting fly only small wood chips. Often tree moss came crawling upon her face. "Timber!" Buchette's father would cry when the tree bent down with a crack that seemed to come from under the earth. She was a bit sad as she stood before the monster that lay stretched out in the clearing, with its broken boughs and wounded branches. In the evening, the reddish circle of charcoal kilns lit up the shadows. Buchette knew when it was time to open her wicker basket and pass her father the earthen jug and a piece of brown bread. He lay down among the small broken branches as he chewed slowly. Buchette ate her supper later at home. She ran around the marked trees, and if her father wasn't watching, she hid and said, "Boo!"

In the woods there was a dark cave called Saint Mary of the

---

* The title above was the tale's first title, as it was published individually in a journal (1893). Retitled "La Sauvage" for inclusion in *Le Livre de Monelle*.

Wolf's Maw, which was rife with brambles and ringing with echoes. Standing on the tips of her toes, Buchette contemplated it from afar.

One autumn morning in the forest, when the withering tree-tops were still burning with dawn, Buchette saw something green trembling in front of the Wolf's Maw. It had arms and legs, and its head looked like that of a young girl about the age of Buchette.

At first Buchette was afraid to go near. She didn't dare even call her father. She wondered if this were one of the people who called back from the Wolf's Maw when someone spoke loudly. She closed her eyes and was afraid to move for fear of being attacked. But as she craned her head to listen, she heard a sob coming from that direction: the strange green girl was crying. Buchette opened her eyes and felt bad. She saw that the green face, sad and sweet, was wet with tears, and that with two little green hands, the extraordinary young girl nervously clutched at her throat.

"Perhaps she fell in some rotten leaves that turned her green," thought Buchette.

Then, courageously, she walked through ferns that were prickly with hooks and tendrils, until she was so close she could almost touch the singular creature. Small, verdant arms reached for Buchette among the withered brambles.

"She's just like me," thought Buchette, "but she's a funny color."

The crying green creature was dressed in a makeshift tunic of leaves sewn together. It really was a girl, one who had the complexion of a wild plant. Buchette wondered if her feet were rooted in the ground, but saw that she moved them quite nimbly.

Buchette caressed her hair and took her hand. She let herself be led away, still crying. It appeared that she didn't know how to talk.

"My God, it's a green she-devil!" cried Buchette's father when he saw her coming. "Where do you come from, and why are you green? Can't you speak?"

It was impossible to know whether the green girl understood. "Maybe she's hungry," he said. And he offered her his bread and the jug. She turned the bread around in her hands and threw it to the ground. She shook the jug and listened to the sound of the wine.

Buchette begged her father not to leave this poor creature in the forest overnight. The charcoal kilns were shining brightly in the dusk, and the green girl trembled as she looked at their fires. When she entered the woodsman's small house, she fled from the light. She couldn't get used to the flames and let out a cry each time someone lit a candle.

Buchette's mother made the sign of the cross when she saw her. "God help me if it's a demon," she said, "but I know it's not Christian."

Because the green girl would touch neither bread nor salt nor wine, it was plainly clear that she couldn't have been baptized or taken communion. They sent for the parish priest, and he crossed the threshold just as Buchette was giving the creature some bean pods.

She appeared to be joyful and right away set about splitting the stem with her nails, thinking she'd find the beans inside. But she was disappointed and again began to cry, not stopping until Buchette opened a pod for her. Then she nibbled the beans as she considered the priest.

They called upon the schoolmaster, but he couldn't make her

understand a single human word or pronounce an articulate sound. Instead she wept, laughed, or cried out.

The priest examined her with great care, but could find no mark of the devil on her body. The following Sunday they brought her to church, where she showed no sign of alarm, although she whimpered when sprinkled with holy water. But she did not shrink before the image of the cross; indeed, she appeared distressed as she moved her hands over the Christ's holy wounds and lacerations left by the thorns.

People in the village were greatly curious, and some were afraid. Regardless of the priest's opinion, they referred to her as the "green she-devil."

She ate nothing but grains and fruit, and each time somebody handed her an ear of wheat or a branch, she slit open the stem or the wood and cried tears of disappointment. Buchette was unable to teach her where to look for the seeds or the fruit, and she was always disheartened.

But by imitating others, she soon learned to fetch wood and water, to sweep, to wash up, and to sew, although handling cloth seemed rather repugnant to her. And yet she never resigned herself to making a fire, or even to coming near the hearth.

Meanwhile, Buchette was growing up, and her parents wanted to place her in domestic service. She became sorrowful and sobbed quietly under her covers at night. The green girl looked upon her little friend with pity. In the morning she stared into Buchette's eyes, and her own eyes filled with tears. And when Buchette cried at night, the green girl's soft hands caressed her hair, her fresh lips brushed her cheek.

The moment was nearing when Buchette would have to enter domestic service. Now when she sobbed, she did so almost as lamentably as the green creature had the day she was found by the Wolf's Maw.

The evening before Buchette's departure, as her father and mother were sleeping, the green girl caressed her tearful friend's hair and took her by the hand. She opened the door and extended her arm into the night. And just as Buchette had once guided her toward the houses of men, the green girl led her by the hand toward an unknown freedom.

Cice

Cice curled up her legs in her little bed and placed her ear against the wall.* The window was pale. The wall was vibrating and seemed to sleep with struggled breath. Her small white slip was spread out over the chair, from which two stockings hung like black legs, limp and empty. A dress marked the wall mysteriously as if it had wanted to climb up to the ceiling. The floorboards called out feebly in the night. The pot of water was like a white toad, crouching in the basin and inhaling the shadow.

"I'm much too unhappy," said Cice. And she began to cry into her sheets. The wall sighed more loudly. But the two black legs remained inert, and the dress was no longer climbing, and the crouching white toad did not close its damp mouth.

Cice spoke again, saying, "Because everyone is mad at me, because people here only like my sisters, because they send me to bed during dinner, I'll leave. Yes, I'll go very far away. I'm a Cin-

---

* The title above was the tale's first title, as it was published individually in a journal (1893). Retitled "L'Exaucée" (The Fulfilled One) for inclusion in *Le Livre de Monelle*.

derella, that's what I am. I'll show them, I will. I'll have a prince, and my sisters won't have anyone, nobody at all. I'll come in my beautiful carriage with my prince, that's what I'll do. If they're good when this happens, then I'll pardon them. Poor Cinderella, you'll see that she's better than you, yes you will."

Her little heart grew heavier still as she put on her stockings and tied her petticoat. The chair stood empty and abandoned in the middle of the bedroom.

Cice went softly down to the kitchen, and she cried some more as she knelt in front of the hearth and plunged her hands into the ashes.

The regular sound of a spinning wheel made her turn around. A warm, furry body rubbed against her legs.

"I don't have a godmother," said Cice, "but I have my cat. Right?"

She offered her fingers, and he licked them slowly, as with a small, hot file.

"Come with me," said Cice.

She opened the door to the garden, and there was a great burst of fresh air. A darkly greenish color marked the lawn. The great sycamore tree trembled, and stars looked as though they were suspended between its branches. Beyond the trees, the vegetable garden was visible, and the cloches covering the melons were shining.

Cice tore out two clumps of long grass that were lightly tickling her. She ran among the cloches where short glimmers fluttered about.

"I don't have a godmother: can you make a carriage, cat?" she asked.

The small animal yawned toward the sky, where gray clouds blew.

"I don't have a prince yet," said Cice. "When will he come?"

Sitting near a big, purplish thistle, she looked at the garden hedge. Then she took off one of her slippers and threw it with all her might over the gooseberry bush. The slipper fell in the high road.

Cice caressed the cat and said, "Listen, cat. If the prince doesn't bring me back my slipper, I'll buy you some boots and we'll travel around to look for him. He's a very handsome young man. He's dressed in green, with diamonds. He loves me very much, but he has never seen me. You won't be jealous. We'll stay together, all three of us. I'll be happier than Cinderella, because I have been more unhappy. Cinderella went to the ball every evening, and she was given sumptuous gowns. But I only have you, my sweet little cat."

She kissed its wet, leathery nose. The cat meowed weakly and scratched its ear with its paw. Then it licked itself and purred.

Cice picked some green gooseberries.

"One for me, one for my prince, one for you. One for my prince, one for you, one for me. One for you, one for me, one for my prince. That's how we'll live. We'll share everything among the three of us, and we won't have mean sisters."

Gray clouds had gathered in the sky. A pale band was rising in the east. The trees were bathed in a pallid half-light. Then a sudden burst of frozen wind shook Cice's skirt, and everything trembled. The violet thistle bent over two or three times. The cat rounded its back and bristled from head to toe.

Cice heard the creaking sound of wheels coming from a distance down the road.

A dull light ran across the swaying crowns of the trees and along the roof of the little house.

Then the rumbling grew nearer. She heard the neighing of horses and the indistinct murmur of men's voices.

"Listen, cat," said Cice. "Listen. A big carriage is approaching. It's the carriage of my prince. Quickly! He's going to call me."

A leather slipper of golden brown flew over the gooseberry bushes and fell in the middle of the melon patch.

Cice ran toward the wicker gate and opened it.

A long, dark carriage lumbered forward. The coach driver's two-horned hat was lit up by a red ray of light. Two men dressed in black walked alongside the horses. The rear of the carriage was low and oblong, like a casket. A sickly odor wafted in the early morning breeze.

But Cice understood nothing. She saw only one thing: that her marvelous carriage had arrived. The prince's coachman was wearing a hat of gold. The heavy trunk was laden with wedding jewels. The terrible and majestic scent enveloped her in royalty.

And Cice reached out her arms, crying, "Prince! Take me away! Take me away!"

Mandosiane

Lilly and Nan worked as servants on a farm.* During the summer they carried water from the well by the narrow pathway that led through fields of tall wheat. And in winter, when it was so cold that icicles hung outside the windows, Lilly slept with Nan. They snuggled under the covers and listened to the wind complain. They always had a few pieces of silver in their pockets and

---

* The title above was the tale's first title, as it was published individually in a journal (1893). Retitled "La Sacrifiée" for inclusion in *Le Livre de Monelle*. Cf. Lorrain's "Mandosiane in Captivity" (1902), in this collection.

wore fine chemisettes with cherry-red ribbons. They were both blond, and they giggled in equal measure. Every evening they placed a bucket of fresh, clear water by the hearth. Each morning when they jumped from their bed, this is where they found the silver coins that they jingled between their fingers. People say that this is because pixies threw the coins in the bucket after bathing there. But neither Nan nor Lilly, nor anyone else, had seen a pixie, although in tales and ballads, they are nasty, dirty little things with spinning tails.

One night, Nan forgot to draw water; and because it was December, the rusty well chain was covered with ice. While she lay sleeping, with her hands on Lilly's shoulders, her arms and her calves were suddenly pinched, and the hair on her neck pulled cruelly. She awoke crying. "Tomorrow I will be black-and-blue!" she said to Lilly, "Hold me tight! I didn't fetch the bucket of clear, fresh water, but I won't leave my bed, in spite of all the pixies in Devonshire." So Lilly, good and sweet, kissed her, got up to fetch the water, and placed the bucket by the hearth. When she returned to bed, Nan was asleep.

While sleeping, little Lilly had a dream. She saw a queen, dressed in green leaves and with a golden crown on her head, who came to her bed and said to her, "I am Queen Mandosiane, Lilly. Come to me." And she said, "I am sitting in a prairie of emeralds, and the path that leads to me has three colors: yellow, blue, and green." And she said, "I am Queen Mandosiane, Lilly. Come to me."

Then Lilly buried her head in her pillow, dark with the night, and saw nothing more. In the morning as the cock crowed, Nan was unable to get up, and she gave forth sharp cries, because she couldn't feel her legs and could not move them. That day doctors examined her and, following their consultation, agreed that she would doubtless remain this way and never walk again. And poor Nan sobbed, for now she would never find a husband.

Lilly felt very sorry for her. As she peeled winter apples, put away the medlar fruit, whipped the butter, and wiped up the whey with her reddened hands, she imagined to herself that Nan could be cured. She had forgotten her dream, until one night when the snow was falling thickly, and everyone was drinking warm beer and eating toast, an old peddler of ballads knocked at the door. All the farm girls gathered around him, because he came bearing gloves, love songs, ribbons, Dutch linens, garters, pins, and golden head scarves.

"Here you have the sad story of the lender's wife," he said, "for twelve months pregnant with twenty sacks full of crowns, who was seized with the singular desire to eat fricasseed viper heads and grilled toads."

"And here the ballad of the big fish that came upon the coast the fourteenth day of April, left the water's edge by more than forty breaststrokes, and vomited five bushels of wedding bands, all greened by the sea."

"And here the song of the king's three evil daughters, and of the one who poured a glass of blood on her father's beard."

"And I also had the adventures of Queen Mandosiane. But a wicked gust of wind tore the last page from my hands at the crossroad."

With that Lilly remembered her dream, and she knew that Queen Mandosiane was ordering her to come.

That same evening, Lilly kissed Nan softly, put on her new shoes, and took to the road by herself. But the old ballad peddler had disappeared, and his ballad had flown off so far away that

Lilly couldn't find it. So she did not know who Queen Mandosiane was or how to look for her.

And nobody could tell her, although along the way she asked
some old laborers who, shielding their eyes with their hands, saw
her coming from afar. And she asked young pregnant women
who chatted indolently in front of their houses, and she asked
young children just learning to talk, as she lowered branches of
blueberry bushes so they could reach the fruit. Some said, "There
are no more queens," and others answered, "There aren't any of
those around here; that was in olden times." And others asked, "Is
that the name of a handsome lad?" And the bad ones led Lilly to
one of those houses in town that are closed during the daytime
but which open and light up at night, saying and affirming that
Queen Mandosiane dwelt there, wore a red nightdress, and was
served by naked women.

But Lilly was well aware that the real Queen Mandosiane
dressed in green, not red, and that she had to take a path in three
colors to find her. So she recognized that the bad men were lying.
She walked a long while indeed, and spent the summer of her life
trotting along dusty roads, trudging through thickly muddy ruts,
accompanied on her way by the carriages of wagoners. Sometimes in the evening, when the sky had a splendid red glow, great
wagons followed her, piled high with wheat sheaves atop which a
few shining scythes were balanced. But nobody could tell her
anything about Queen Mandosiane.

So as not to forget such a difficult name, she had tied three
knots on her garter. One day she had gone far in the direction of
the rising sun and came upon a sinuous yellow road that bor-
dered a blue canal. The canal wound along with the road, and

between the two there was a green embankment that followed their contours. Groups of bushes grew on both sides. And as far as the eye could reach, all there was to see were swamps and verdant shadows. Small, conical huts rose up from the marshy landscape, and the long road melded ahead into the bleeding clouds of the sky.

There she encountered a small boy with oddly cloven eyes, who was hauling a heavy rowboat along the canal. She wanted to ask him if he had seen the queen, but realized in terror that she had forgotten her name. She shouted and cried and felt her garter, all in vain. And then she cried out more loudly still, for she realized that she was walking on a road of three colors, made of yellow dirt, a blue canal, and a green embankment. She again touched the three knots she had tied on her garter, and she sobbed. And the small boy, seeing that she was suffering but not understanding her sorrow, gathered a simple herb from the side of the yellow road and placed it in her hand.

"The mandosiane is a healing herb," he said.

And this is how Lilly found her queen, dressed in green leaves.

She held it with care and returned to the long road right away. The trip back was slower than the first one because she was tired. It seemed to her as though she walked for years. But she was joyful, knowing that she would restore poor Nan to health.

She crossed the sea with its monstrous waves. Finally she arrived in Devonshire, clutching the herb between her shirt and tunic dress. At first she didn't recognize the trees, and it seemed to her that all the livestock had changed. In the great room of the farmhouse, she saw an old woman surrounded by children. As she ran to them, she asked for Nan. The old woman was surprised. She looked at Lilly and said, "But Nan left a long time ago. She is married now."

"And cured?" Lilly asked joyously.

"Yes, of course she's cured," said the old woman. "And you, poor thing, aren't you Lilly?"

"Yes," said Lilly. "But then how old can I be now?"

"Fifty years. Isn't that right, grandmother?" cried the children. "She isn't quite as old as you are."

And as Lilly smiled wearily, the strong scent of the mandosiane made her swoon, and she died under the sun. Thus Lilly went in search of Queen Mandosiane and was carried off by her.

Le Livre de Monelle, 1894

WILLY

Fairy Tales for the Disillusioned

Once upon a time there were two beautiful children who were named Daphnis and Chloé * and who knew nothing of life because they were convent schooled.

It happened that, on the eve of their wedding, they lost their way in the woods. They had lost their bearings, and they dared not continue on their way through the shadows for fear of becoming even more disoriented. And because the night is full of mystery, Daphnis and Chloé trembled like innocents before an examining magistrate.

The moon rose suddenly, revealing to them that they had come to a deserted clearing. But soon there arrived, in single file, a mangy wolf; a very ugly little weasel; a red-faced, mustached girl; a splendid, sleepy-looking creature; a large man; a slovenly woman; a woman dressed in a donkey skin; and many more besides.

The big man approached the couple, saying "There is nothing

* Early Greek romance (Longus, second century CE) about two foundlings raised by shepherds. They fall in love, but in their naïveté do not know how to act upon their feelings. The story tells of their adventures as they educate themselves about love, are recognized by their wealthy parents, and are finally married.

to fear, we mean well. Tomorrow you will be married, and yet you are ignorant of life's philosophy. We will teach you. Your lucky star led you astray to this glade. People have filled your head with ridiculously optimistic notions and persuaded you to believe in good fairies who guide the projects of poor mortals to fruition. All that, my children, is a farce, and you must believe the exact opposite of such nonsense.

"First be aware that there are no good fairies: the bad ones killed them off long ago. There are no more kings who wish to have children; on the contrary, the fewer they have, the happier they are. The only talisman that can help you open a door is a crowbar, and you would be wrong to count on magic wands capable of finding treasure—which in fact would surely be confiscated by the State. Princes can no longer be changed into animals; the closest thing to that is a beast transformed into a functionary. So here is my story, for your edification:

The Ogre's Story

"I didn't have a bicycle, much less seven-league boots, only big shoes. Far from eating young children, I took in orphans. I fed travelers without asking for payment. That little rascal Little Thumbling, along with his entire family, landed at my house, where he proceeded to make merry. With his brothers he fondled my daughters, not that I saw anything wrong with that (kids have to have fun!). Then one ugly morning I woke up, and there was nobody there! They had all left, carrying off everything down to my shoes. And on top of it all, that good-for-nothing Thumb said dreadful things about me so I could no longer do business with my merchants. Never give refuge to vagabonds!"

The Ogre fell silent, and the Wolf began to speak:

The Wolf's Story

"I was walking in the woods, starving, when I saw Little Red Riding Hood approaching. She said to me, 'My grandmother, a mean old woman who makes my life wretched, dwells five hundred meters from here. Dear wolf, would you be so kind, such a sweet little wolf, and go wring her neck? She is very fat.' Like an idiot I strangled the shrew. During this time, Little Red Riding Hood called the police and had them arrest me for being an anarchist. I did twenty years of hard labor, while the slut inherited her grandmother's savings, which she coveted so she could marry a hairdresser's assistant. Don't try to avenge other people's grudges."

The wolf stopped speaking, and the beautiful, yawning woman said as she stretched:

Sleeping Beauty's Story

"I was sleeping in the castle. The prince came looking for me, although I hadn't called him. I was waiting for Love, and I began loving the first one to come forward in its name. Alas! after only a few days, the prince was bored and began to yawn. He barely listened to me and gave me to understand that he was weary of me. When finally he fell asleep, even with my caresses I was unable to wake him. And in his insulting sleep, he dreamt of other women! Then I fled and now, even though I long to sleep, I cannot close my eyelids. My lovely dream is over, and I will never again escape Reality, which stares me in the face. I am punished for having believed in Love."

The slovenly woman stood up:

Cinderella's Story

"Like all unhappy people, I've had my troubles, but troubles of no interest to others. I sacrificed myself for my beastly sisters: I amassed dowries for them, and they beat me. Then I fell for a cobbler who stiffed me in turn. And my children imitated their father. Such is the destiny of women: to take knocks and keep house while dreaming of adventures that never come. No god-mother, fairy or otherwise, protected me; mice nibbled on my second-rate skirts and, as for glass slippers, all I ever had were worn-out shoes. Married life is a sham!"

A lord with a great beard cried out:

Bluebeard's Story

"What slander have I endured! I've had seven wives; the first six walked out on me to circle the globe with big shots. The seventh ran off with a contralto after having carefully packed up all the riches of my palace with the help of her two brothers and her sister: while those thieves were robbing me, Anne was keeping lookout. During the divorce proceedings, they accused me of all manner of crime, and the lies stuck. Young man, be wary of your wife! If I had killed mine, they wouldn't have ridiculed or robbed me, and I would still possess an excellent reputation."

A sly little man quickly entered the circle:

Riquet with the Tuft's Story

"Riquet with the Tuft at your service! Are you complaining about slander? And what about me? I had gold, hair, wit, and I fell for a

Figure 6: Riquet with the Tuft

little twit who was mean as a weasel. I imagined her to be sweet and good, and I thought she loved me when in fact she only coveted my dividends. As soon as she had become Mrs. Riquet, she ruined, deceived, and tortured me, and I had to kill her because I could no longer live with her. So don't think that love transforms everything that it touches."

A young woman began to speak:

The Story of the Girl with the Pearls
"I was so good and so beautiful that a fairy granted me the gift of spitting jewels. My mean, ugly sister received the more enviable ability to spit vipers and toads, with the result that everyone tried to stay on her good side. She was jealous; she belittled me fiercely and endlessly discredited my wares: 'Where did that jewelry come from? Stolen, no doubt; or else they were plated, made of glass, fake.' So my business failed, and I had to leave the area. My sister bought up the jewelry store for a song, married the clerk, and lived happily. To succeed in this vile and lowly world, you need to be mean."

Puss 'n Boots explained how he was taken in the matter of the Carabasville lands after having imprudently agreed to serve as front man for his boss. He was even obliged to bear all responsibility for murdering the Ogre. The forty thieves had duped Ali Baba so well that he was still in shock. Donkey Skin led a miserable life after being dumped by the king's son, who regretted having married beneath himself.

The Ogre summed up the situation, saying, "My children, don't believe in fairy tales; buy Roret's encyclopedia* instead. Cultivate your garden, and throw the stones in someone else's. Steal and slander, and you will be happy."

The next morning, having regained the path to the paternal

---

* Nicolas Roret (1797–1860), publisher of "L'Encyclopédie Roret," a large series of practical manuals on a wide variety of topics, also know as the "Manuels Roret."

foyer, Daphnis and Chloé resolved not to get married. In fact, they had lost no time during the small hours that night, and Chloé was no longer what one could call a virgin.

This tale has no moral.

Une Passade, 1894

HENRI DE RÉGNIER

The Living Door Knocker

I was born and grew up in this house. Nothing has changed about it since as long as I can remember. Vast bedrooms and spacious drawing rooms, the same bizarre nooks, that complicated succession of vestibules, corridors, and labyrinthine landings in a solid architecture, behind a long façade of gray stone that looks out on the square with the sparkling indifference of its windows and the precise blinking of its dormers. On top of the vaulted and tiled ground floor are two unequal floors, the first with curved ceilings, the second with its attic rooms.

That is where I was born and where I have lived. The curiosity of my childhood and the desires of my youth wandered all around it. I went up the stairs thousands of times. I opened all the doors. Actually, no! For two remained closed, one at each end of the house: the rooms where my father and my mother died before I knew them. She, put to sleep by the surprise of Death in the flower of her youth; he, not before slowly suffering its meticulous torture.

I possessed no portrait of either of them, nothing except, from my father, a study full of books, mirrors, and swords and, from my mother, a gallery filled with shells in glass cases and tables with mosaic tops. The keys to the mortuary apartments had long ago been thrown into a deep pond in the middle of the garden.

That garden, by the way, is unique. You will see it presently and almost exactly as it has always been. High walls surround it on three sides and connect it to the house. It is not vast, but square. Along the walls are arcades of old bushes that form, on the end, two niches where there are two statues, one of a Faun crushing a cluster of grapes under its sabot, the other of a Centaur rolling out a wineskin. In the center is a pond, also square, with edges of greenish stone, in the middle of which stands a statue in green bronze of a nude man who seemed to listen attentively to the surroundings.

Since there are neither trees nor flowers in this garden, neither leaves nor petals fall into the water. It shimmers, clear, deep, and black. When you walk by the statue, its reflection seems to follow you as if looking at you, for it presents four identical faces atop four bodies that, by an optical illusion, appear to be a single one as you circle around it.

I often wandered in that garden. The sun hardly ever reaches it; the rain keeps the bushes green and makes snails crawl all over. The place was always sonorous and extraordinarily quiet; the water grew stagnant without the noise of a fountain. I spent many hours walking by the high walls along the pathway. Leaving it to return to the house, I found the same solitude from one room to the next.

During the winter months, I sat next to the fire. The heat of the flames crinkled the bindings of old books or melted the sealing wax at the bottom of parchments. Sometimes, I would leave my isolation to look at the swords and the shells in the rooms they filled. I would take a sword from its display or remove a shell from its case.

Whether the sword was heavy or light, straight or curved, with the unsheathed weapon in my hand I stood immobile, lost in long and violent reverie in contemplation of its sharp, shining blade.

The shells interested me; I weighed their fragility cautiously. Some were clever and confidential; some still held grains of sand. They were bizarre and eloquent. I would put them against my ear, listening to the sound of the sea for a long time, indefinitely, until the evening. The murmur seemed to come closer, grow, and end up stunning me, permeating my whole being to the point that, once, I felt as if a wave was enveloping and submerging me. I dropped the conch and it broke.

I did not return to the gallery with the shells, and I abandoned the study with the swords because of a mirror in which, looking straight at myself, I had instinctively crossed swords with myself.

From that time on, I went less into the garden and spent my days at the windows of the façade watching the square.

Townspeople walked through it without even looking up at the house. No one knocked at the door since they knew it would inevitably be closed. Only wandering beggars or traveling salesmen would sometimes raise the door knocker. Those salesmen sold chapbooks crudely colored, romantic and brutal, famous adventures, melodramas, all of life . . . * They would let the wrought iron knocker hit the door with all its force, and the blow would resound throughout the house. My entire solitude would jump,

---

* This is a reference to the *images d'Épinal*, inexpensive chapbooks that were an important means by which fairy tales (and other stories) were circulated in print throughout the nineteenth century.

and in that muffled rumble I heard the provocative sound of a horseshoe, the departure, the gallop, the saliva in the bit, the wind in the mane . . .

That door knocker was quite remarkable, more so for its form and singularity than for its blow's rumbling summons of some withheld Destiny. It took the shape of a woman's bust, in iron, with a scroll edge. She had a face of furious sadness, with disheveled hair, heaving breasts, an astounding neck, twisted lips. She let out her mute anger through the jolt of the metal and stiffened her obstinate and captive appearance.

Days followed upon days. My solitude, prisoner of itself, stuck its face against the windows, forehead to glass, whose immobile transparency separated me from the outside. Sometimes, I thought I could feel the glass melt like water on my cheeks, and sometimes it also seemed as if the crystal cracked and split as if struck by a rock from a slingshot.

One evening at dusk, after a day when neither beggars nor salesmen had walked through the square, when the knocker had not sounded once, just as I was leaving the window where I followed the meandering of a bat flying in the still, clear sky or drifting along the pavement like a dead leaf, this evening at dusk I saw a woman pass by. She looked at me.

I followed her, and followed her, and followed her! Oh, sir, I can still hear in my mind the sound of the door which, like a madman, I slammed shut once I had run down the stairs. It seemed as if the house was collapsing forever from the sound, as if nothing existed any more but that passing woman who, walking in the deserted street, turned around, and smiled.

Her gaze was like the blade of the swords, her voice like the deep sound of the seashells. Sometimes she laughed, with a little laugh. Her naked beauty was the statue of love; her flesh seemed to be above an eternal dawn. We went from city to city. I walked with her through wheat fields. I bathed in glacial lakes and cool rivers. There were great storms that tore up the sky with lightning as if her hair, feverous and inflamed, hastened the gathering clouds and provoked their clash.

Her smile created the beauty of spring. She set me alight with summer embraces and corroded me with the rust of autumn.

Through her I knew all contentment and all suffering. She was the song on my lips, the wrinkle on my brow, the wound on my breast—she was my life.

We sat in taverns where the red of the wine we drank foreshadowed the spilling of blood. Desire rumbled around us. One night, by torchlight, in front of people drinking at tables, I kissed her on the mouth. Swords were drawn; people killed. Murder riddled her face with beauty spots, and she laughed out loud in the bloody coquetry of her ferocious adornment.

All kinds of rage entered my soul. Devious or violent, they made my hypocrisy pale and my brutality redden.

I dragged her by her hair! How hard it was raining that night! It was along a green marsh, near yellow bulrushes, under a gray sky. We were up to our waists in the mud we had fallen into. It smelled of rotten bulrushes, moss, water . . . Rain washed from our faces the filth of our embrace; but, when we returned to the palace, the muddy traces of our feet on the paving stones followed us like frogs that had walked in our footsteps.

There was a celebration of gold and joy! She danced until dawn; a thin fabric stuck to the sweat of her breasts. Her entire body collapsed, panting and heated; she hit the pavement with her drunkenness and, since I loved her, I struck her on the face.

Then we lived on the banks of a river. She cultivated a little garden where roses and gladiolus grew; she was contented like happiness itself.

I followed her—I also followed her through the tiny streets of a foreign city that night she hugged the walls furtively. I had caught a glimpse of her treason. Her hand already on the secret key and her foot on the adulterous threshold, noticing me, she turned around so quickly that her coat came unbuttoned and exposed her breast. She leaned her back against the door, arrogant and vicious, her hands like claws. I grabbed her by her throat, warm with lust. We were silent; her body tensed; she couldn't breathe; her eyes widened; her mouth twisted and was moistened by pinkish saliva. Occasionally a jump. The toenail of her bare foot scraped the stone. When I felt she was dead, without loosening my stranglehold, I kissed her bloody lips.

I let her go; she stayed upright for an instant, then slumped to the ground. The folds of her coat covered her, and she was little more than a gray mass with a pale hand sticking out, her opened fingers in a little puddle of blood.

I walked for a long time through the countryside until I arrived at the seashore. I had never seen it before, but I didn't even look at it. It seemed to me as if I had already borne it all within myself, with its roaring, its sighing, its bitterness, and its changing colors. I had borne the sea from its waves' softly furrowed lips licking cheeks of sand, to its frothy maw biting the contracted face of rocks. The closer I walked toward its murmur, the more it seemed to retreat from me. Peace entered me.

Each dawn this feeling of peace grew. I wandered for a long time; the wheat fields yellowed, trees lost their leaves, winter came. I cried when I saw that snow had fallen, and I returned to the house of my birth. I saw once again the square, the gray façade, the door.

The door knocker contorted its female torso. I recognized her. That face appeared to me to be an image from my past, hardened, shrunken in its metallic effigy. It was the exact same face that, warm and living—on a tragic evening long ago—died in my grasp. Her bare breast expanded with the same sigh, and her sorrowful and frenetic face suffered there too, but its mouth and eyes closed definitively in minuscule repose. With an indifferent hand I lifted the cold metal torso. The hammer resounded and I entered my dwelling once and for all.

That, sir, is why I will die in the house I was born in. I live here at peace with my thoughts. I have exorcised myself from myself; what I killed came from me and called me from outside. I had to kiss life on the lips and to grab it by the neck to be free of its ghosts.

I answered the call of my Destiny. It has ceased to call me. Now I no longer look out the windows; I no longer handle the swords; I no longer listen to the conches. I wouldn't hear anything in them any more. My deafness is full of the intimate voices of my silence. At dusk, I walk in my garden, along the pruned bushes. The green stone Faun that was crushing a porphyry cluster seems to have fallen asleep from drunkenness; he has fallen down. The Centaur that was trampling a wineskin has crumbled as well. Its croup is destroyed, but the smiling man remains. And the four-sided bronze statue that stood on a pedestal in the middle of the pond now pays attention only to himself.

La Canne de jaspe, 1897

RACHILDE

The Mortis
to Alfred Jarry

Under the amorous conflagration of a June sky, by the ever-white stair steps that crumbled toward the blackened Arno River, the wildest flowers, like warriors accustomed to surmounting obstacles, launched an attack on the city and overran it utterly.* Meanwhile garden flowers, less free, suddenly became libertines, climbing iron gates, overflowing their bronze urns, trailing down over golden balconies. They broke their noble ties to unite with the vagabonds in a monstrous celebration. Smoldering with forbidden fragrances, seasoned with human sewage, they were seen throwing the regal locks of their foliage onto the aggressive tips of the blackberry bushes that climbed from the river's somber embankment. The winds of rebellion entwined branches to branches, braided garlands, hung wreaths, erected triumphal arches, and sang an epithalamium amidst the great silence of death.

With mouths of ember and flesh-like flames, roses licked in-

---

* The tale's title derives from *mors, mortis*: Latin, he who belongs to death. Alfred Jarry, the dedicatee, was a French symbolist writer (1873–1907).

corruptible marble and splattered long pure columns up to their summits with stains as red as wine, crimson as blood, which at night formed round signs extravasated to brown, marking the skin of pale monuments with violet shadows that looked like traces of deeply dug fingers. Roses of all colors, from saffron to every shade of wine, from furious scarlet to the tender tones of newborns' limbs, shouted out their liberation. Their gaping maws clamored tirelessly, unseen and yet somehow divined. Above the carnage, they shook their plump buds, feverish with the desire to bloom, boils bursting with sap, ready to erupt in spurts of pus. This horrible menace culminated in torrents of intoxicating odors, as violent as infuriated screams.

There roamed in Florence only a few rare phantoms, larval men wrapped in filthy rags, creatures struck with vertigo who spun faintly before dropping to the ground. Roses repopulated the deserted city. They came to life tumultuously, rushing forward with heads knocking together like troops of children in love with ruins for the disorder they provide. These were no longer bouquets, but rather gangs. The capricious horde broke into palaces, entering through cellars and attics. They besieged fortresses, scoured inns, climbed churches, and settled into places for which they were not intended. They were truly leading the battle; their boldness resembled a military strategy.

A climbing plant had crept into a bell tower and launched its forest of ferocious thorns through a pointed arch. It grasped onto a rope, which swayed under the weight of its young buds, and when the hundredth dewy bud blossomed, its calyx heavy with tears, the rope strained and vibrated: the sound of a bell rang out. The roses were sounding the alarm! The inferno of their impassioned fragrances joined the conflagration of the amorous sky.

Praise be! Life was beginning anew in war. Seeing that walls were all that remained standing, the flowers sought to bring them down in order to affirm their independence from humanity.

The entire army responded to the call of its queen, and innumerable regiments of flowers rushed forth unchained, tumbling over one another in multiple avalanches. They climbed from the naked ground to the sculpted pediments of museums and temples. They bedecked watchtowers, upholstered the ramparts, and jostled each other through windows and crenels. Choking colonnettes and latticework, breaking apart balusters, wearing away stucco and paint, they rebounded in cascades from all the bright angles of cornices and poured forth from all the dark corners at crossroads to swing their censers in victory.

Finger-pistilled honeysuckles moved along as if on clawed hands. In their voiceless fury to arrive, their native virginal blush darkened quickly to the sulfurous yellow of desire. Through air perpetually dirtied by road dust, couch grass, lycopods, and mignonette flowers (oxidizing plebeians dressed in green and gray) multiplied into immense carpets, overrun by crazy morning glories on the front line. From the cups they bore flowed a blue intoxication, one drawn from the sky itself. Their tendrils widened cracks and enlarged fissures, showing the way to the more tightly formed squadrons of chiseling ivy, boring lichen, and moldering damp moss. Intersexed vines—bearing neither flower nor fruit and producing who knows what kind of poisoned clusters, hops, and clematis with crests like spiderwebs—wove shrouds over doors. Like green curtains flapping from dormer windows, this fine and shining liana appeared as smooth as silk from a distance and, from close by, looked like a lacework of snakes.

Grass, simple turf, ploddingly did the work of a gravedigger and unearthed enormous slabs for the sooty cadavers still piled high in the middle of streets and squares.

A swarm of emerald flies rose in the air, buzzing on all sides. Living seeds broke away from their plants, going to others to spread news of the battle that surged on, irrespective of victory.

No stone would be left standing!

A less bellicose but more plainly carnivorous activity followed the triumphant fanfare of the roses and the exquisite violence of their invasion. Flights of white butterflies, emblematic of innocence, forsook the flowers' blandness and fiercely attacked the liquefied eyes of cadavers, drinking molten souls, sugary in taste, from the tips of their small, voluptuous proboscises. Bees, hornets, wasps, dragonflies, misshapen and swollen like whipped horses, giant mosquitoes with venomous stingers, stag beetles with horns of steel, dung beetles, and, much lower down, snails, dragged behind them the final breaths of the dying.

All day long the vile *ichneumon* fly sang. In the evening the moon, that eternal widow of the sun, cried amidst these ruins, which were pompously adorned in honor of the eternal ceremony of death.

Nothing more than an Italian springtime was needed for Florence's desolation to be covered by flowers and to transform the abominable pestilence into the sweet contagion of fragrance.

Flowers, flowers, more flowers, and still more flowers! An astonishing blossoming that threatened to suffocate the few people remaining, barely alive and stunned to be able to breathe such air. Encroaching ever more, the rose queens blanketed all avenues, as if lying in wait for a hero or a god to pass by.

The churches had been closed for a year.

Priests who were able to flee had gone underground in faraway convents.

No women walked the streets of the city, and among the rotting corpses heaped in public squares there was nary a trace of a skirt. Women had disappeared, leaving no reminder of their grace. Had they fled at the start of the plague? Were they the first to die—of fear—before the scourge?

Ah! now the viols of love, which once had rasped under the fingernails of nervous pages, were utterly mute! And behind the shadowy velvet of masks that once peered through windows, gone were the gazes glaring with ardent light. Truly there was no one left since the ladies had gone.

Only flowers remained, sovereign mistresses of the ancient city of war and pleasure.

Only flowers rained from all the empty glasshouses where kisses once rained, as frequently did streams of boiling oil.

It was at the decline of this springtime that Count Sébastiani Ceccaldo-Rossi left his palace, chased by hunger. He was the last survivor of the powerful Ceccaldo-Rossi family, which was both Guelph and Ghibelline,* thanks to its numerous and precious alliances that reached across the entire Tuscan Republic.

Giovani-Sébastiani Ceccaldo, his father, was dead.

Lucrecia-Bella-Ginevra, his mother, was dead.

He had lost his fiancée, Violante Arnoldo, duchess of Fiesole.

His three mistresses, Ilda, Léone, et la Grippé, were dead.

His favorite, Angelo, the page who never left his side, was dead.

---

* Twelfth–fifteenth centuries, opposing factions supporting the pope on one side and the Holy Roman emperor on the other.

Even his dog, Lazar, a pearl-gray greyhound adorned with soft ears, had dried up from starvation.

All that remained were two lowly black servants who, naturally, could not be numbered among the ranks of men.

Sébastiani Ceccaldo left his palace wearing a bizarre ensemble, a vision that must have horrified nature. He pushed open the colossal bronze door leading to the terrace, already gripped by the destructive claws of a treacherous vine. He battled with his sword to free his home from these unforeseen chains and emerged, armed from head to toe against the somber *Enemy*.*

There had been a plague. Miracle! He alone in Florence had had the plague and had not died. But hunger was beginning to drive him mad.

He left the palace as if leaving a tomb, wearing a costume so farcical it would have made passersby laugh.

(But alas! In Florence there was no one left to pass by!)

Count Sébastiani Ceccaldo was dressed in a long and ample gown of Moroccan leather that swept the ground, whose stiff folds made it difficult for him to walk. He wore a form-fitting hood adorned with an enormous beak, which imprisoned his nose just as the brodequin compresses the legs of a condemned man during the administration of his torture. Two sinister glass eyes, hardened to the poor world, magnified whatever they fell upon and allowed him to make his way. His right hand was solidly gloved in buffalo hide and brandished a sword capable of scaring off anyone not of a mind to take him seriously.†

* Feminine in the French (*Ennemie*), so applicable grammatically to the plague ("la peste"), but also to the flowers.
† In the seventeenth and eighteenth centuries, some physicians known as plague doctors wore such outfits: "The hat, mask suggestive of a bird beak, goggles or glasses, and long

Figure 7: Plague Doctor

The noble Count Sébastiani had dreamt up this farcical disguise because he was young and whimsical, as well as quite shrewd. His getup was outrageous, but it isolated him from the rest of humanity and protected him from any hazards of contagion. Part necromancer, part buffoon, he lived according to secret manuscripts that he owed to an Eastern inheritance. Moreover, he had a skeptical disposition and made fun of doctors by imitating their chief idiocies. He claimed that the mere sight of his masquerade could frighten off death.

In truth, he had immured his father and mother behind the palace chapel wearing this profane outfit and had buried his favorite, the lovely Angelo, at the bottom of the gardens in front of a statue of Diana, whose amber-colored buttocks brightened stormy nights, this without the accursed plague bringing him down.

All his people, with the exception of those servants too black to blacken further, had fallen. The skeleton of his greyhound Lazar, lying curled up on the step of the staircase that descended toward the Arno, waited in vain for the return of his caresses. As for his mistresses and fiancées, they were carbonizing somewhere in town, buried hastily under the flagstones of their oratories or thrown pell-mell into public fires.

This now mattered little to Sébastiani Ceccaldo, because he was dying of hunger. The two slaves had stopped supplying him with bread made of crushed bones and spoiled meat. And, for

---

gown identify the person as a 'plague doctor' and are intended as protection. Descriptions indicate that the gown was made from heavy fabric or leather and was usually waxed. The beak contained pungent herbs or perfumes, thought to purify the air and relieve the stench. The pointer or rod was intended to keep patients at a distance" (Byrne, *Encyclopedia of Pestilence*, 505).

some time, the water in the oubliettes gave off a putrid smell that was absolutely intolerable.

He had eaten candied fruit discovered in the palace attic, where gluttonous servant girls had once secreted them, now reduced to something resembling splintered wood; figs that had been gnawed on by vermin; bitter orange peels; and flattened watermelons with seeds as hard as rosary beads. He did not dare roast rats, which were few in number and quite sick, since all other animals perished before they would consume such dubious prey. The birds were occupied in town: funereal crows and solemn magpies rarely alighted on rooftops and, seen from afar, looked like a confraternal procession of theologians wearing black doublets with white arm slits.

Sébastiani Ceccaldo made his way, pruning ivy and cutting back liana with his sword as he went, to the amber-bottomed nymph that reputedly shone on stormy nights, and knelt piously by the tomb of his favorite, the page Angelo. As he arose he noticed that the marvelous statue's two arms had been broken by two branches of an acacia tree. So distressed was he upon seeing the mutilation of this chef d'oeuvre that he forgot to visit his parents' tomb.

So he wandered aimlessly, in search of scraps to eat.

From high balconies the view of the city was panoramic, the beautiful city abandoned under thick veils of flowers. It was the picture of a great banner, embroidered with dazzling jewels, of an enchantress's dalmatic robe, laméd with every metal and encrusted with all kinds of gems. The contemplation of this paradise produced a mysterious drunkenness that stirred one's imagination. And in deserted streets it had to smell so sweet, so good, and so strong, that the mere idea of breathing freely made the grotesque pilgrim stagger with emotion. With his nose in his cormorant beak, Count Sébastiani could only inhale the odor of herbal remedies, and he had had enough. The musk, benzoin, sandalwood, clove, aloe, and chives all turned his stomach.

He passed beyond his garden gates, ever fighting against the tide of wild plants. He walked across thick grass that wrapped around his ankles like monkey tails and battled hand-to-hand with unidentified bushes that had sprung up spontaneously. He encountered a celery plant as high as a man and stumbled into a cabbage that could have sheltered a dozen children in a rainstorm.

It seemed as though the noxious air, deadly to Christian men, made vegetables flourish in abundance, distilling a benign dew that was capable of enhancing the cucumber race to the point of producing one that reached the size of an entire monk.

He encountered curtains of gentian and *Aristolochia* that became heavier as he progressed, and branches of thorny bushes lashed his mask. Meanwhile, high above all this diabolical growth gleaming with the human putrescence in which it grew, monstrous corollas, unimagined flowers, of snow or of blood, diadems of a thousand golden insects blossomed.

It was quite lovely.

But along the deserted streets, it was lovelier still.

Rosebushes, joyously thriving in the wind, spread atop spent pyres where those stricken by the plague had been piled, since fire purifies all. A shoot from a wild rose freed itself from the baluster upon which a Lord had crucified it with care, and rushed toward the ground where it found nourishment amidst the ashes. It grew to be tall and vigorous, offering the bountiful treasures of its smoldering fragrances to the sun. Garlands entwined from one balcony to the next shed petals that fell softly like an ambrosial shower, and here and there a bare lemon or orange tree—alas! denuded of its fruit—contributed, from the shadow of a portico, reflections of nuptial satin.

Not seeing another living soul, Count Sébastiani took off his Moroccan leather robe, because he was dying of heat. He went to the nearest church in hopes of finding a priest. No priest would refuse him a pitcher of water, even if he had to draw it from the font of holy water, or, for want of bread, a few rancid holy wafers.

It became hotter as he made his way, and with his desire to breathe fresh air growing, Count Sébastiani lost all sense of decorum. He tore off his leather hood, his glass-eyed mask, and his horn beak, and took off his buffalo gloves and shoes, leaving him as naked as the divine bambino when he issued forth from the Virgin Mary's womb. He kept his sword to cover his front.

Then all the roses of Florence, adorning the city's balconies as women's heads once did, seemed to shiver in modesty and lean over curiously.

Who was this man cavorting across their city dressed like an angel of death?

The winds of love shook the roses, making many of them fall upon the head of the archangel.

Ceccaldo gathered others with the tip of his sword and, when no priest appeared at the church door and as the font was decidedly dry, for lack of better fare he drank and ate of the flowers.

His thin serpentine body, still youthful and ivory white despite all the suffering it had endured, slid into snow-white thickets. The only mark remaining of the dreadful malady was the crown of brown roses that the plague places on the brow of its rare victors. And there, joyful with the joy of wild plants, supple with the suppleness of liberated branches, the first Florentine of Florence grazed to the point of drunkenness like a crazy goat.

Gone the danger! Gone the hood! Gone the herbal remedies!

Flowers, flowers, and more flowers! Although there were no lemons or oranges, there were yellow roses! Although pomegranates, melons, and watermelons failed to ripen, there were purple roses, red roses, and pink roses! And although the wine of Asti was not flowing in abundance this tragic year, its sweet, sparkling foam could be inhaled in the delicate aroma of miniature white roses, whose buds split open in one's mouth like simple hazelnuts!

He inhaled roses of all colors, ate them of all flavors until weariness. He smelled far too many and ate more than his fill.

Stumbling, his chest heavy and his head aching strangely, the poor young man was obliged to return home.

He didn't have the plague. No, it couldn't be the plague, because he had already had it. But he was very drunk!

He was seized with dizziness as he climbed laboriously up the palace steps, past the sleeping skeleton of his dog, Lazar, which still awaited the resurrection of his caresses. He uttered a cry and gripped his sword, forcing his head to remain raised. Treacherous plants grasped him by the ankles like monkey tails, and he dropped with his arms crossed and his mouth open. His proud, slightly cruel eyes became fixed, his black hair stuck to his head with the sweat of his last agony, and, from the crown of mourning that the plague leaves upon the brow of its rare victors, blood dripped: the blood of all the roses!

And thus, for having smelled the flowers, strangely perished Sébastiani Ceccaldo-Rossi, the last of his clan, a prince and count of the Tuscan Republic, an heir to several centuries of glory and crime, aligned with the Guelphs for the assassination of the Boldi d'a Ponte knights, allied with the Ghibellines for the dam erected against the Arno during the great flood, an accomplished gentleman and the pride of Florence who loved in equal measure brunette ladies and blond pages, beautiful statues and heraldic dogs. He was, finally, a *mortis*, whom the plague had spared, but the roses had poisoned without mercy.

Contes et nouvelles, 1900

JACQUES D'ADELSWÄRD-FERSEN

Sleeping Beauty Didn't Wake Up

Young Prince Charming, a pilgrim eager to worship beauty, a poet transported ecstatically in search of Eden—point of departure for Cythera—opened the château gate with great difficulty. It is old and heavy for his thirteen years. And the lover is obliged to take off his pretty ribbons before entering the garden, whose branches tear at his lace finery.

He is wearing pink silks under gray brocade. The undergrowth is dense, and his blond hair, lighter than a ray of sunshine, catches on flowering thornbushes. But this does not concern him because the image of a beautiful little princess, dancing in the corner of his eyes, moves him. Clear-eyed and fresh-faced, this is his first desire . . .

A dark and formidable fir tree, an evil sorcerer like those found in Norway, spreads its arms and stops him. With girlish fingers, the young prince grips the sword given to him by Merlin and the Mouse Fairy, and he slashes and cuts . . . Oh! if you had seen him thus, Mr. Perrault, perhaps you would have spoken more of him in your tales.

After a quarter hour, the young prince was quite heated and covered with twigs and drops of blood from the bleeding fir tree. He progressed a few steps. He had his viol with him and, to work up his nerve and faith in his Beloved (for this is the aim of all chivalry), he sang a virelay that he had written for her.

The birds of the woods and those of the thick forest heard his voice and were so enchanted that they forgot their pact (having agreed to pierce his heart with their yellow beaks) and came trembling with pleasure and beating their wings.

A swallow, who had been moved by his tale of woe, alighted on the young viol player's shoulder and said to him in his swallow tongue, "If I were stronger or if I were a fairy, I would bear you quickly to the palace, which is masked by climbing vines, and your heart would be renewed. But I am weak, and we would perish before arriving. And yet I feel sorry for you and would like to help. Tell me what I can do."

Prince Charming bowed most graciously toward Madam Swallow and answered, "Carry a bit of my soul to her, which will transform her dream with kisses."

Saying this, he unfastened his ruff, placed his hand against his heart, and brought forth three pearls. The first was mauve, the color of violets in autumn: Tenderness. The second was pink, Joyfulness. And the last one was sky blue and of such perfect harmony that it resembled a teardrop fallen from an angelic eyelid: this was Grace.

The bird then flew away chirping joyously.

The valiant little prince continued his journey, discouraged neither by the giants encountered along the way, nor by tangled thickets, nor the snakes secreted in tussocks. From time to time he climbed atop a leaf to see whether he could discern in the faraway blue distance some shadow of his sweetheart's château. But he could see nothing yet . . .

He was now as hungry for food as he was for caresses; a purplish sage plant, like a bunch of young strawberries, offered its seeds to him. He ate them and drank a drop of dew more pure than a diamond, which the sun had forgotten. I swear to you that no one had never before dined so royally in a fairy tale. As he gathered the sage and dewdrop, he thought melancholically, "My princess's lips are redder than this flower, her eyes sparkle more than this diamond, and her skin must have the delicate scent of roses in the rain.

"My princess is tender, and her fingers are like pearls; the enchanter or knight who returns her to life will find in his beloved a treasure. My princess is happy and her songs are gay. Some troubadour bearing an ornate lute could implore her for a song to ease his soul.

"My princess is prettier than sweetbriar in springtime, because her body is as pure as that of a newborn. The pagan Venus would have envied its splendor. Alas! My princess is asleep and her eyelids are shut, her gaze turned toward an interior sky. Oh! when will I again see her softness?"

His enchanted axe was in a pitiful condition. Never had it worked so hard, for since entering through the old gate, the prince had chopped down no fewer than two thousand trees. But rather than tiring him, this gave him strength. His blood was boiling with joy and hope, and the vines above his head were flying like woodchips.

Finally, after immeasurable effort, including the slaying of many enemies come to assail him, the Baby Prince glimpsed an ancient, timeworn arbor at the end of a thicket. And his small squire's heart beat very fast, faster than it had ever beaten before. When he reached the thicket and the bower, he bent to the ground and, although he could not yet see the château, so fine was his hearing and so immense his love, he could hear the breath of the slumbering Child.

This made him mad with joy, so much so that he danced a minuet, without music and off beat. If only you had seen him, Mr. Perrault . . . , but then, why did you not speak of it in your tales?

Because he was in a hurry and slender enough, he tried slipping under the lowest branches. A terrifying voice made him start . . . What a coward! He pulled himself together and prepared to move forward, placing his hand on the hilt of his sword. But an unknown force made him drop it and, full of emotion and terror, the poor little prince heard the big voice say, "I am the enchanted bower, and you will not pass. You're nothing more than a naughty little boy. Let the princess sleep; besides, she needs it. As for her waking up (and here the branches snickered), that depends on a certain red bird that will come from Utopia. Get back, or I'll eat you with gravy, your Lordship!"

His Lordship, with beating heart and dry throat, was not much worried about being eaten, even with gravy. He begged the bower to calm down and assured it that he would return when the red bird showed up, then drew back far from the reach of this dreadful creature.

When he was alone, all alone but for the little insects and florets and grass, he cried bitterly with all the force of his thirteen years.

Now the sun was shining and quickly discovered the sorrowful prince. The sun is a good sorcerer, since it gives life to both people and plants. So it understood, better than the sparrow whose wings had offered to carry a bit of soul and longing, and it felt compassionate. And quickly, more quickly since the prince's tears flowed abundantly, the sun became hotter so as to change them into a frail vapor, like a pink pearly cloud, on which Charming lay down. And gently they rose like a butterfly into the air, Prince and Cloud, Love and Smoke, like a butterfly toward the Ether.

Meanwhile the old bower screamed from down below as it shook its branches, "You troublemaker! You'll never get her!"

But he did, and after an aerial voyage upon a cloud that traveled like the wind, a journey of a hundred days and a hundred nights, he landed with his pockets stuffed with stars that he had gathered along the way. Viviane had banded his eyes so that he could not see the fairies' realm, and Eliacinde had tied his wrists and ankles so he wouldn't fall from his mist.

As a result, he neither saw nor felt a thing at first. But when the enchanters had sent Irish elves to free him, he opened his eyes and was dazzled!

He was in the courtyard of a splendid castle, with ivory towers and golden doors, but it was so old that it shook with each step the prince took. Vines had eaten away at even the smallest stones, and leaves that reached to the tower's pinnacle obscured the reflection of its stained-glass windows. An enormous spiderweb, shimmering with gnats and dragonflies, stretched across the drawbridge, which was watched over by sleeping guards.

Then the prince's heart was transported by the memory of Merlin's promise. He had said that each word spoken by the elected one would awaken somebody. Thus as he went in search of the princess, Charming looked around himself to see which person it would be fitting to speak with first.

Figure 8

A majestic Swiss guard, more majestic than the ones you see at the theater (isn't this so, Mr. Perrault?), stood tall with a silver staff petrified in his hand.

"Swiss guard, sir," said the small prince as he touched his tricorn hat, "I would greatly appreciate it if you would wake up."

"Oomph!"

Charming was answered by a gigantic snore, and he was so startled that his collar fell off into the dust. He picked it up with a distraught gesture, because this inamorato was very stylish. He straightened the fold that had come undone and even took the time to adjust his aiguillettes. And, confident in the strength of his philter, he called again, "Mr. Swiss Guard!" The guard yawned

a formidable yawn and stretched himself so mightily that the
prince nearly got one of the giant man's fists in his socket. Then
he answered with a Teutonic accent, "You should know, guv, that
I wasn't sleeping!"

"In a rush, old man, and I don't care." And the prince, reas-
sured, took off with a condescending nod. He had had a moment
of fright, thinking that he wouldn't be able to wake anyone. He
then returned a whole host of people to life, taking the same care
but with more patience: courtiers, sommeliers, guards, valets,
who had all until this point been snoring in unison with Beauty.
Everyone was loud and joyous, feeling the need to move around
after so much rest.

Think of it, good reader, scores of myriads of centuries!

Some went to eat and found, despite the passage of time, all
their food where it had always been in their kitchens. The wine
had aged to perfection. It is not known what had happened to the
cheeses. Others whose digestion was slower recalled the lunch
they ate before their famous sleep and straightaway organized a
great game of blindman's bluff in the courtyard.

Meanwhile young Prince Charming crossed many apartments
all covered in dust and cobwebs and arrived at the gold and blue
door behind which reposed the princess. An old duenna whom
he had encountered along the way, tucked in the crook of a deep
wing chair, made an effort to find the key. But her memory was
faulty, and it was no use. So they were obliged to break down the
lovely blue door inlaid with gold, which they did, taking all possible precautions.

Charming entered on the tips of his darling toes, shod in pearl-
colored stockings. And he saw, oh! he saw, in a bed nearly as small
as a cradle, a sleeping baby, a little princess like those painted by

Carpaccio,* who held a lily upright in her minuscule hand, clothed in heavy brocade. Her hair, the color of summer nights, was parted on one side with velvet bows. And beneath this hair, which could have damned an angel, was a face with great big eyes, lowered under golden lashes, a mischievous nose, and lips like gladiolus in April.

Charming felt somewhat vexed. "The fairy made a mistake," he said. "She gave me a little sister!"

And leaning toward the cradle, which was whiter than milk, he said with a kiss, "Wake up, my darling baby!" But there was only silence from the cradle, neither the sound of opening eyelids nor the sound of a jingling rattle.

"Wake up, my darling baby!" repeated the prince with a kiss. The courtiers and the duennas, valets and sommeliers, all gazed upon the child, who in her sleep maintained a lovely smile. Then someone said, "Your Majesty, Crown Prince, give her her doll. Before, ten thousand years ago or more, she always asked for it upon awaking."

But they looked for the doll in vain. The frightened prince said for the third time, "Wake up, my darling baby!" Oh joy! The princess moved, and he took up his viol and sang of his jubilation. But he was so moved that he lost his head, and what he sang was folly:

"Lullaby and goodnight, Lay thee down now and rest, may thy slumber be blessed . . ."

When he realized what he had done, it was too late to start over with a gavotte. Raising his head, he saw to his horror that everyone had fallen back asleep, magically soothed by his lullaby. The same doll-like gestures and inattentive poses, according to

---

* Vittore Carpaccio (1465–1525), Italian painter.

the person's rank and function, the same castle in the Sleeping Wood. He ran to the window and rubbed the glass, opaque from so many centuries, to discover that the games in the courtyard had stopped.

Then he cried with trembling voice, "Noble Sires, awake!" But none responded, because the enchanter had predicted a single awakening. And the little prince sobbed, understanding that he too had to fall asleep and wait for the time when they both would be old enough and have permission to marry. With the lightness of a feather, he returned to the cradle and gazed at length upon the five-year-old girl whose breath was calm, so calm (did you mention this, Mr. Perrault?). Taking up his viol of love, he played a tune by Gluck, modulated in a minor key, lento.

And thus, next to Beauty, next to Sleeping Beauty of the Woods, did the child close his eyes for more than a thousand centuries, as he kissed her delicate hand.

Ébauches et débauches, 1901

JEAN LORRAIN

Princess of the Red Lilies

Haughty brows crowned the eagle-gray eyes of this austere and cold descendant of monarchs, so white that her hands looked like wax and her temples pearls. She was called Audovère.

The daughter of an old warrior king who was forever busy with faraway conquests when not doing battle at the border, she grew up in a cloister among the tombs of her royal forebears. Her mother had died in childbirth, and so from infancy Princess Audovère had been raised by nuns.

The cloister in which she had spent the sixteen years of her life was situated in the shadows and the silence of an ancient forest. Because the king alone knew which pathways led there, the princess had never seen the face of a man other than the one belonging to her father.

This was a harsh place far from roadways and safe from wandering gypsies. Nothing but the sun could reach it, and even then with rays weakened by their passage through oak trees' thick vault of leaves.

Sometimes at the fall of day Princess Audovère went walking beyond the cloister's walls, accompanied by two rows of processing nuns. She was serious and thoughtful as she ambled, as if burdened by the weight of a proud secret, and so pale that she looked as though she would soon die.

A long gown of white wool with large golden clovers embroidered at its hem trailed at her feet, and a light veil of blue gauze, held in place by a band of chiseled silver, softened the coloring of her hair. Audovère was as blond as lily pollen and the slightly faded gilded silver of ancient altar vases.

Such was her life. Calm and with a heart full of hopeful joy, she awaited the return of her father as another would have awaited the return of a betrothed. In the convent she passed her time and her most loving thoughts dreaming of battles, of armies in peril, and of massacred princes defeated by the king.

In early spring, high embankments flowered about her with primrose; in autumn they were bloodied with the red clay of the earth and dead leaves. Whether in April or in October, ardent June or November, Princess Audovère walked ever silently among the oak trees, be they russet or green, forever cold and pale in her white woolen gown hemmed with golden clovers.

Sometimes in summer she would gather the great white lilies that grew in the convent garden, and since she herself was so white and so frail, she seemed to be their sister as she held them in her hand. In autumn she gathered purplish foxgloves at the edge of clearings and worried them with her fingers. The sickly pink of her lips resembled the flowers' winey purple. Oddly, although her fingers seemed to take pleasure in tearing apart the lilies, they never stripped the petals from the foxglove, but often kissed them absentmindedly. At such times, a cruel smile parted her lips, as if she were carrying out some obscure ritual. As people would later learn, this shadowy and bloody ceremony corresponded to some faraway preoccupation that transcended physical distance.

Each gesture of the virgin princess was linked to the suffering and death of a man. The old king was well aware of this and as a result kept her macabre virginity hidden in the unknown cloister. The cunning princess knew this too, hence her smile as she kissed the foxglove or tore apart lilies with her deliberate and lovely fingers.

Each lily she plucked was the body of a prince or young warrior fallen in battle, each foxglove kissed an open wound, an injury enlarged to make way for the free flow of blood from the heart. Princess Audovère had lost track of her far-off victories. In the four years since learning of her bewitchment, she had gone dispensing kisses to the poisonous red flowers, mercilessly butchering the lovely innocence of white lilies, giving death with a kiss, taking life in an embrace, acting as a funereal aide-de-camp and mysterious executioner of her father, the king. Every night she confessed her sins to the convent chaplain. This blind old Barnabite absolved her, since the sins of queens damn only their people, and the smell of cadavers is like incense at the foot of God's throne.

Princess Audovère was neither remorseful nor sad, since she knew herself to be pure by absolution. Besides, battlefields in defeat at day's end, where agonizing princes, highwaymen, and beggars raise their maimed arms toward the red sky, flatter the pride of virgins who do not share the anguished horror that mothers have for blood, mothers ever quaking for beloved sons. But then Audovère was above all her father's daughter.

One evening, a wretched fugitive, who had somehow found his way to this unmapped cloister, collapsed before the door of the sacred refuge crying like a child. His poor body, darkened with sweat and dirt, was lacerated and bleeding from seven wounds. The sisters collected him with more terror than pity and placed him in the coolness of the funerary crypt.

They left a jug of cold water by his side that he might drink his fill, and a cross and aspergilla full of holy water to accompany him as he passed from the living to the dead. Indeed, he was already in the throes of death, his chest seized with the first signs of agony. At nine o'clock, the mother superior had the anxious nuns recite a prayer for the dead in the refectory, after which they returned to their cells and the convent fell to slumbering.

Audovère alone did not sleep, but mused about the escapee. She had barely glimpsed him as he crossed the garden aided by two elderly sisters. One thought obsessed her: this dying man was certainly an enemy of her father, a deserter who had escaped the massacre, a last human wreckage stranded at this convent by some horrifying panic. The battle must have been waged nearby, closer than the nuns had guessed, and at that moment the forest had to be full of other bleeding and moaning wretches. Before dawn the cloister would be surrounded by a miserable throng of suffering men, hideous for their rotting flesh and mangled limbs, whom the nuns would welcome in their indolent charity.

It was July, and long flowerbeds of lilies perfumed the garden. Princess Audovère went there.

She moved through tall stems, bathed in moonlight and standing high like wetted lance blades, and began slowly to pluck the petals from the flowers.

But what happened next was strange! They emitted sighs and gasps, and cried out lamentations. The flowers met her touch with flesh-like caresses. At one moment something warm fell on her hand, which she took for tears. Now the lilies' smell sickened her, for they had singularly changed; heavy and dull, their blossoms emitted a noxious incense.

Although failing, Audovère relentlessly carried on her murderous labor, decapitating pitilessly, tirelessly plucking calyx and bud. But the more she smote, the more they repopulated. They were innumerable, now appearing as a field of tall, rigid flowers rising up in hostility before her, a veritable army of pikes and halberds blossoming fourfold under the moon. Painfully weary and yet overcome by a giddy fury of destruction, the princess went on tearing asunder, mutilating, and crushing everything before her until a strange sight stopped her.

From one of the tallest sprays of flowers, of a bluish transparency, emerged the cadaver of a man. Its arms were spread out in the form of a cross and its feet drawn one atop the other. The wounds on its left side and its bloodied hands were visible in the night, and the crown of thorns encircling its head was splattered with mud and rotting flesh. The frightened princess recognized the wretched deserter welcomed that very evening, the wounded man who lay dying in the convent crypt. He painfully raised a tumid eyelid and asked reproachfully, "Why did you strike me? What did I do to you?"

Princess Audovère was found dead the next morning, clutching lilies to her breast with her eyes rolled back into her head. Although her body lay across an alley at the entrance to the garden, she was surrounded by lilies, and all the lilies were red. They never again flowered white.

Thus died Princess Audovère, for having smelled the nocturnal lilies of a cloister garden in July.

Princess Snowflower

When Queen Imogene discovered that Princess Snowflower had not died, that the silk band she herself had tied around her neck had only partially strangled her, and that the dwarves of the forest had placed that gently lethargic body in a glass coffin—and, even worse, that they were keeping it out of sight in a magic cave—she went into a rage. She sat up straight in the cedar seat she would reflect in, in the highest room in her tower, and she ripped apart, lengthwise, her heavy dalmatic robe with yellow brocade overlaid with lilies and pearl leaves; she smashed against the ground the steel mirror that had just informed her of the unbearable news; and grabbing with a manly rage the hind leg of the enchanted frog she used for her curses, she threw it with all her force into the fireplace where it sizzled and popped until it disappeared like a dry leaf.

Once she calmed down, she opened the tall casement window, whose stained glass depicted horn-blowing dwarves, and looked out on the countryside. It was completely white with snow and, in the cold night air, slowly drifting flakes, like wisps of cotton, made the horizon look like heraldic ermine, but strangely in reverse, with white spots on a black background. A large red patch illuminated the snow at the base of the tower, and the queen knew it was the fire from the royal kitchens, where kitchen boys were preparing the evening feast, since it was Epiphany Sunday and there was a great party at the castle. And from the depths of her evil soul, a smile appeared on the face of maleficent Queen Imogene, for she knew that at that very moment a magnificent peacock was being roasted for the king. She had treacherously switched the liver of this peacock with a stew of lizard eggs and henbane, a horrible concoction that would alter the mind of the old monarch and forever banish from his flagging memory the sweet thought of Princess Snowflower.

Who did Snowflower think she was, that frail and sickeningly sweet little twit, with her porcelain blue eyes and insipid doll face, to surpass the beauty of the marvelous Queen Imogene of the Isles of Gold? Had Imogene come to this pitiful little kingdom in Aquitaine so she could hear it exclaimed loudly all day long, hither and yon by the wind over the hedges and the roses of the flowerbeds, and even by her mirror, a truth-speaking mirror given life by the fairies: "Your beauty is divine and enchants both birds and men, great Queen Imogene, but Princess Snowflower is more beautiful than you!" That little nuisance! So, she had never had a respite from it all. And there were no vile thoughts that she, as a true evil stepmother, had not conceived to destroy the king's love for her. But the old imbecile was blinded by tender feelings and only half listened to her, smitten as he was with sensual passion for her magical queenly beauty. Even poisons had no effect on that frail little childlike body. Her innocence or the fairies protected her. Imogene was still enraged remembering the day when she could stand it no longer and commanded her ladies-in-waiting to undress the frightened little princess and whip her trembling shoulders until they bled. She had wanted to see that spectacular nudity wounded and disfigured by their switches, but the switches in the hands of the crones had changed into peacock feathers that only just barely grazed the skin of the shivering virgin.

Then and there, exasperated by her spite, she resolved to kill her. She had strangled her with her royal hands and had had her body carried to the edge of the park, ready to blame the murder on a troop of bohemians. Unexpected fortune! She had not had to use this excuse on the king since the wolves had taken charge of things. Princess Snowflower had simply disappeared, and the conceited stepmother had triumphed when, all of a sudden, her magic mirror disappointed her. She had gotten her revenge, to be sure, by smashing it at that very instant; but that hardly did her much good seeing that her rival was still alive sleeping under the watchful guard of the dwarves!

And so, very perplexed, she went to an armoire and from the very back took out the dried-up head of a hanged man that she consulted on grave occasions, and, placing it on a large open book in the middle of a desk, she lit three green wax candles and fell into sinister thoughts.

II

Imogene wandered far, far, far from the sleeping palace, in the utter silence of the frozen forest, which resembled an immense coral reef. She had thrown a brown wool shepherd's cloak over her white silk dress, which made her look like some old sorceress. And with her noble profile hidden under the dark hood, she hurried beneath the enormous oak trees whose trunks, white with snow, resembled tall penitents. Some of them, with their branches reaching up into the shadows, seemed to curse her with all the strength of their long bony arms. Others, weighed down into strange postures, appeared to be kneeling by the side of the road. Hooded in frost, they looked like monks in prayer. They were all processing in a bizarre fashion, their hands oddly folded and stiff above the snow, which muffled their steps. It was almost mild in the forest, as if the frost had taken the edge off the cold. And the queen, absorbed by her plans, quickened her silent pace, the flanks of her coat hermetically wrapped around some object that vaguely shook and cried out.

She was carrying a six-month-old child she'd stolen away while passing by a maid's bedroom, whose throat she planned to slit at the stroke of midnight at the crossing, just as it is prescribed, on that calm and mild winter night. The elves, enemies of the gnomes, would run forward to drink the tepid blood, and she would enchant them with her crystal flute, with three holes for unfailing magical incantations. Once enchanted, the obedient elves would lead her through the maze of the immobile forest to the dwarves' cave. The night of Epiphany, the entrance was visible and wide open, as it was on Christmas Eve. Those two nights, enchantments are suspended by the omnipotent grace of Our Lord, and every cavern and hiding place of the gnomes, guardians of buried treasures, become accessible to humans. She would enter the lair, making the troop of kobolds scatter, and would approach the glass coffin, force the lock, smashing open the sides if necessary, and stab the heart of her sleeping enemy. She would not escape from her this time.

And as she hurried, ruminating on her vengeance, under the delicate white coral and the branched vault of the frozen forest, hymns and voices suddenly sounded out, a crystal vibration rang out through the numb branches, the whole forest shivered like a harp. And the queen, immobilized in her amazement, saw an odd cortege advancing toward her.

Under the cloudy winter sky, in the sparkling decor of a snowy clearing, she saw elegant and svelte camels and horses, palanquins covered with shiny striped silk, standards topped with crescents, golden globes strung on long spearheads, litters and turbans. Thoroughly diabolical little black men in green silken gandouras timidly trampled the snow, amulets glistening with jewels jingled on their ankles, and, save for their ear-shattering laughter, one would have thought they were little black marble statues. They followed in the footsteps of majestic patriarchs bejeweled with soft cloth streaked with gold. The gravity of their haughty profiles blended into the silky froth of their long white beards, and enormous silken burnooses, from the silvery white of their beards, opened onto heavy robes of night blue or dawn pink, decorated with jewels and golden arabesques. And the palanquins, in which veiled women could be glimpsed as in a dream, oscillated on the backs of the camels. The moon, which had just risen, shimmered on the silken lining of the standards. Aromas, heavy and scented with myrrh, frankincense, and muskroot, wafted through the air in thin bluish swirls. In the guise of incense burners, ciboria ornamented with enamel shone between ebony black fingers, and, under the rising moon, psalms broke out, murmured more than sung in a sweet Oriental language, as if rolled up in the gauze of veils and the smoke of the censer.

The queen, hiding behind a tree trunk, recognized the wise men, the black king Gaspar, the young sheik Melchior, and the old Balthazar. As they had done two thousand years ago, they were going to pay homage to the Holy Child.

Then they passed by.

And the queen, livid under her shepherd's coat, realized too late that on the night of Epiphany the presence of the wise men on their way to Bethlehem breaks the power of evil spells, and that no curse is possible in the night air pregnant with the myrrh of the censers.

She had set out on a vain journey. All for naught were the leagues she had traveled through the ghostly forest, and she had to set out once again on the perilous path through the cold and the snow. She intended to turn around and walk back, but the child she held under her coat was weighing strangely on her arm. It had become a leaden weight, and it froze her in the snow, which mounded around her strangely so that her stiff feet could not move forward.

A horrible spell held her prisoner in the spectral forest. She was sure to die if she could not break free from it. But who would come to her rescue? All the evil spirits remain safe in their hideouts on the luminous night of Epiphany. Only good spirits, friends of humble and long-suffering souls, risk wandering about. It occurred to the insidious Queen Imogene to seek the help of the good gnomes, clothed completely in green with primrose in their hair, the same gnomes who had taken care of Snowflower. Knowing their childlike passion for music, she pulled the crystal flute from her coat and brought it to her lips.

She stumbled under the weight of the child, now like a block of ice. Her feet, tense in the snow, were turning blue, but her violet lips still found the melancholy and sweet sounds, poignantly sad and tenderly voluptuous, painful and captivating farewells from a dying soul. Resigned but with vague hope, she tried one final time to summon help.

And, as the deceit of her entire life whined on her lips, her eyes searched the semidarkness of the clearing, the shadow of the trees, the twisted folds of the roots, and even the stumps left by the lumberjacks—evocative profiles of plants where gnomes appear.

All of a sudden, the queen was startled. From the edges of the clearing, a multitude of shining eyes were watching her, like a circle of yellow stars all around her. They were in between the trees and in the roots of the oaks. Some were far away, others were close by, and, in the night, each pair of eyes gave off a phosphorescent light, at half the height of a full-grown man.

They were the gnomes . . . finally! And the queen repressed a cry of joy that almost immediately was stifled by horror when she saw two pointy ears above each pair of eyes and below them a hairy muzzle, lips drawn back, with white teeth.

Her magic flute had called nothing other than the wolves.

The next day, they found her body, dismembered by the beasts. And thus by a clear winter night perished the evil Queen Imogene.

Mandosiane in Captivity

Princess Mandosiane was six hundred years old: for six centuries she had existed, embroidered on velvet with face and hands of painted silk.* The arabesques of her gown were of the finest gold, covered with pearls, and her collar was so heavy with embroidery that it weighed her down.

An ultramarine mantle, flowered with anemones, was caught at her breast with real jewels, and uncut sapphires trimmed the hem of her gown.

She had figured in many processions and royal fetes, where

___

* What appears here is an unattributed translation first published in *The Parisian* as "The Princess Mandosiane." Slightly modified. Cf. Marcel Schwob's "Mandosiane" (1893), in this collection.

she was carried aloft on a standard to be viewed with joy and acclamation by the people. This was in the happy time when, through the flag-bedecked streets, under the fluttering, flamboyant streamers, they cheered Princess Mandosiane. Then she was ceremoniously returned to the Treasury of the Cathedral, and shown to strangers in exchange for small sums of gold.

This marvelous and miraculous princess was born in the dreams of twenty nuns, who for fifty years had worked with skeins of silk and gold upon the delicate and hieratic figure.

Her hair was of yellow silk, her eyes two tourmalines of the most beautiful blue, and she held a sheaf of white velvet lilies clasped to her heart.

Then the era of processions passed, thrones were abolished, kings disappeared, civilization marched on, and the princess of pearls and painted silk remained thenceforth confined in the shadow and silence of the Cathedral.

She passed her days in the chiaroscuro of a crypt with a lot of queer things grimacing in the corners; there were old statues, goblets side by side with ciboria, and old church ornaments; and now as the door of the subterranean chapel was never opened, these old things slept, forgotten; and great despair filled Princess Mandosiane's heart.

And she gave an ear to the counsel of a red mouse, an insidious little mouse, lively as light and tenacious of will, who had beset her for many years.

"Why do you obstinately remain here a captive, cuirassed in pearls and beautiful embroideries? This is not the life for you; you belong to the time when, resplendent under the blue skies of high festivals, the people received you with acclamation. I will gnaw away, one by one, with my sharp teeth the silken points and the golden cords that have held you for six hundred years immovable to this glittering velvet, which is now of no use. It will probably hurt you a little, especially when I am gnawing near your heart; but I will begin along your gown, and then when your hands and face are loose you will see how good it is to be free. You are so fair, with the face of the princess in the story, and rich with the fabulous treasures that make your gown so resplendent, that you will be taken for the daughter of a banker, and you can marry a prince.

"Then you will have thousands of jewels: come! let me deliver you; you will cause a sensation in the world.

"If you knew how good it is to breathe the fresh air and follow your own fancies! You are cumbered with opals and sapphires, as a warrior in his armor, but you have never fought. I know the road that leads to the country of Happiness. Let me release you from your silken chains; we will make a tour of the world together, and I will find for you a throne and the love of a hero."

And Princess Mandosiane consented, and the little red mouse commenced his deadly work. His teeth cut, gnawed, and filed in the velvet, already eaten by the moths; the pearls loosened and fell, one by one, and at night by the light of the moon, as well as by day in the light of the sun, in the crypt where all light was dim, the little red mouse cut and gnawed and worked always.

When he began on the famous collar of pearls, Princess Mandosiane felt a cold, sharp pain at her heart. For many days she had had a feeling of lightness, and, singularly supple, she swayed in the breeze, and waited impatiently until the mouse could accomplish his work.

As the teeth of the rodent entered her breast, the poor princess of spangles and silk began to fail altogether. There was a crumbling of dust in the dusky chapel, a falling of flakes of silk, and shreds of braid, and luminous pieces; uncut gems rolled down like grains of corn, and the old moth-eaten velvet of the banner fell to pieces from top to bottom.

Thus died Princess Mandosiane for listening to the insidious counsel of a little mouse.

Princesses d'ivoire et d'ivresse, 1902

RENÉE VIVIEN

Prince Charming

Told by Gesa Karoly

My curious little girl, I promised to tell you the true story of Saroltâ Andrassy. You knew her, didn't you? You remember her
black hair, with a reddish-bluish sheen, and her amorous eyes,
imploring and melancholy.

Saroltâ Andrassy lived in the country with her elderly mother.
Their neighbors were the Széchenys, who had recently left Buda-
pest once and for all. A bizarre family, if truth be told! Béla
Szécheny could have been mistaken for a little girl, and his sister
Terka for a young boy. The strange thing is that Béla possessed all
the feminine virtues and Terka all the masculine vices. Béla's hair
was a greenish blond and Terka's, more lively, a pinkish blond.
The brother and sister resembled one another in a strange way—
and that's quite rare among members of the same family, no matter what they say.

Béla's mother had not yet resigned herself to the need to cut
the little boy's beautiful long curls and to trade his graceful mus-
lin or velvet skirts for ordinary knickers. She coddled him like a
little girl. As for Terka, she grew in her own way, like a weed. She

lived outdoors, climbing trees, marauding, pillaging vegetable gardens, insufferable and a pest with everyone. She was a child without tenderness and sentimentality. Béla, on the other hand, was the very definition of sweetness. His devotion to his mother took the form of incessant hugs and caresses. Terka loved no one and no one loved her.

One day, Saroltâ visited the Széchenys. Her amorous eyes called out from her thin, pale face. She liked Béla a lot, and they played together for a long time. Terka watched them warily from afar. When Saroltâ spoke to her, she ran away.

Mysterious Terka could have been pretty, but she was too lanky for her age, too skinny, too gauche, too gangling. Béla, on the other hand, was so cute and so sweet . . .

The Széchenys left Hungary a few months later. Saroltâ cried bitterly for her playmate. On the doctor's advice, Béla's mother took him to Nice along with his reluctant younger sister. Béla had an excessively sensitive stomach. In any event, he wasn't very robust.

In her dreams, Saroltâ always conjured up the overly frail, rather too pretty little boy whose memory lingered within her. She would say to herself, smiling at the blond image: "If I must get married later, I would like to marry Béla."

Several years passed—oh, how slowly for the impatient Saroltâ! Béla must have been twenty, and Terka seventeen. They were still on the Riviera. And Saroltâ was inconsolable during those joyless years brightened only by the illusion of a dream.

She was dreaming at her window one violet evening when her mother came to tell her that Béla had returned.

Saroltâ's heart burst out in song. And, the next day, Béla came to her.

He was the same, and yet far more charming than before. Sa-roltâ was happy he had kept that soft and effeminate look she had liked so much. He was still the fragile little boy, but now this boy possessed an indescribable grace. Saroltâ searched in vain for the cause of the transformation that made him so attractive to her. His voice was musical and remote, like an echo from the moun-tains. She admired everything about him, down to his stone gray English suit and mauve tie.

With his changed eyes, his strangely beautiful eyes, his eyes that were not like the eyes of other men, Béla gazed at the young girl.

"How skinny he is!" observed Saroltâ's mother, after he left. "Poor boy, he must still be quite sickly."

Saroltâ did not answer. She closed her eyes to see Béla's image on the back of her eyelids . . . How very pretty he was!

He returned the next day, and every day. He was the Prince Charming who exists only in the childish pages of fairy tales. She couldn't look at him face-to-face without swooning ardently, lan-guidly . . . Her face changed with each expression of her beloved's face. Her heart beat in cadence with that other heart. Oblivious and puerile tenderness had become love.

And Béla turned pale as soon as she entered, glowing in her white summer dress. He sometimes looked at her without speak-ing, like someone meditating before a flawless Statue. Sometimes he would take her by the hand. She had the feeling she was touch-ing the hand of someone sick because his palm burned hot and dry. Béla's cheekbones grew flushed with fever.

One day, she asked him for news about the undisciplined Terka.

"She's still in Nice," he answered nonchalantly. And they spoke of other things. Saroltâ understood that Béla did not like his sister. That was hardly surprising, of course, since she was such a taciturn and timid little girl!

What was destined to happen happened. Béla asked her to marry him a few months later. He reached his twenty-first birthday. Saroltâ's mother was not opposed to the union.

Their engagement was unreal, as refined as the white roses that Béla brought each day. Their declarations, uttered with heartfelt excitement on their lips, were more fervent than poems. Their nuptial dream passed into the depths of silence.

"Why," Saroltâ asked her fiancé, "are you more worthy of being loved than other young men? Why do you have a softness they know nothing of? Where did you learn the divine words they never utter?"

The ceremony was private. Candles enlivened the pinkish luster of Béla's blond locks. Incense drifted toward him, and the thunderous organ exalted and glorified him. For the first time since the beginning of the world, the Bridegroom was as beautiful as the Bride.

They left for the blue shores that provoke the desire of lovers. They were seen, the Divine Couple, eyelashes to eyelashes and eyelids to eyelids. They were seen, amorously and chastely interlocked, the black hair of the Beloved spread out on the blond hair of the Lover.

But here, my curious little girl, is where the story becomes a bit difficult to tell. A few months later, the real Béla Szécheny appeared, but he was not Prince Charming. Alas! He was only a pretty boy, nothing more.

He searched desperately for the identity of the young usurper.

And he discovered that the usurper in question was his sister Terka.

Saroltâ and Prince Charming did not return to Hungary. They hid themselves away in a Venetian palace or a Florentine house. And sometimes they are encountered, akin to a vision of ideal tenderness, amorously and chastely intertwined.

La Dame à la louve, 1904

ALBERT MOCKEL

The Story of the Prince of Valandeuse
For Charles Tardieu

The fairies had assembled in the clearing: Lazuli, Novéliane, Mélivaine, and the dwarf Lull, their brother, who was prime minister of the country of Golgoride.

Princes and princesses had come from all around to watch the fairies, who took no notice of them. Fairy Novéliane, suspended from a garland of honeysuckle, put a stop to the whims of a dragonfly by flapping her wings. Fairy Mélivaine was just as busy teaching daisies to lie when interrogated about love. And little Lazuli, obstinately coquettish, was powdering herself with pollen under a flowering broom bush.

The entertainment consisted of stories and tall tales, and soon it was the turn of the heir to the throne of Valandeuse to tell one. He was a bit dull, but as pretty as could be. The princes and princesses made a circle around him, and he began:

"One day it was very sunny in the garden where I was wandering, feeling melancholy, angry at life because my beloved had not smiled at me. Trying to cheer myself up, I thought of ancient legends about love, and I think I added new verses to my memories. When one is in love, one becomes a poet.

"The garden was full of the most beautiful flowers, so I picked two for every stanza: a big one to celebrate a sonorous rhyme, a fragrant one for a lighter rhyme, and so on, one after the other, following the music. In time I had an entire bouquet, and I playfully raised it far above my eyes to salute my lessened pain and my finished poem. But as I was admiring my double harvest, I was very surprised to see a sort of strange flower, shiny and mobile, suspended in the wind in the air.

"'Oh!' I asked myself, 'is that yet another verse that I neglected to compose and that is flying around to attract my attention?'

"But that moving flower was a living being—a bird or a butterfly, yes, a bird, very pale gold with vibrant blue wings and crimson spots. Lively and alert as if it had bounced off its wings, it climbed to the highest clouds and descended back toward me. And all of a sudden, with outstretched feathers, it landed on my bouquet."

"Prince of Valandeuse, hello!" (The little fairy Lazuli spoke from beneath her tuft of hollyhock.) "Your story delights me, and I'll like it even better if you keep it short. I once saw a very beautiful princess who was smitten with a prince as handsome as you. And without knowing it, the prince had a passionate heart. But all he cared about was smiling and arranging his outfit to please her. They say that when he was in her presence he couldn't even think straight."

"The strangest thing is that he didn't even know what she looked like," added Mélivaine. "When they were apart, he wove dream upon dream for her, and they all blew away in the wind.

Fée Novéliane.

Figure 9: The fairy Novéliane

Yes indeed, enough to make twenty dresses that fit her perfectly! Let me tell you all: those dresses were the closest he ever got to her!"

"He was an idiot," said the prince. "But let me continue my story."

"As for me," interrupted Fairy Novéliane, "I was really angry at that princess. 'Don't you know how to love,' I told her, 'or what is it exactly that you think you love about your suitor? He stutters at your feet . . . Well, what is he supposed to say to you! Poor birdbrain, you adore his graceful face, his doublet, his lace. And since he doesn't understand himself, he likes them because you like them. But is that really what your lover is? Do those things come from his heart, his soul, and his flesh? And can't you guess the dream with which he'd fill the earth if his lips touched heroic lips?'"

The prince shuddered.

"I don't dare try to understand your words," he said. "But listen. The bird was flying toward me, and it seemed as though it loved me, the way those frivolous souls love. I held it among my flowers, I caressed its belly, I was amazed to see its wings straighten out like hair and the pinkish gold of his belly shiver like a woman's flesh. 'Charming little thing,' I said to it, 'I love you because you are soft and pretty like my beloved.' And, by instinct or fancy, I gave it a kiss—a voluptuously strange kiss, as I felt the feathers melt away on my lips, the body grow, the wings enfold me, and suddenly I was holding my beloved, alive and completely naked!

"Oh! the divine instant of that union! Our lips locked together searched for each other through the desire that animated them. I felt hers come to life and die in my kiss. She lived through me, I breathed my soul into her, I thought I felt her soul brushing against mine. And when we finally had to unlock our bodies, I noticed on her mouth the first word, that first word whose meaning must have been eternal . . ."

The dwarf Lull let out a laugh so shrill it stopped the prince right then and there. The royal assembly laughed as well, but without knowing why. Then Lazuli drew near, mischievous and curious.

"And what did the princess say after such a kiss?"

The prince sighed.

"She said: 'kiii, cuic, kiii' and then 'Tiii, ti, pitiki! Ritipitiki, kiiiiiii . . .' Ah Novéliane, what have you done?

"She was speaking in bird language, and the worst part about it was that she was delighted by it. It was as if her soul had finally found the language that suited it. She was chattering like mad, *tikii!* Joyful, coquettish, enchanted with herself. But I was devastated, and recognized in her face the confused features I'd noticed in the bird. Like the bird, she bounced about. Her eyes were clear and animated, like a hummingbird's. Oh yes, it was indeed my beloved, her svelte and adorable body, every bit hers! There was her little head with its quivering, lively and impish as it pecked. There was her mouth—alas! my mortal delight—and I even recognized the inflections of her voice in it.

"'Ti, ti, tikiti!' she spoke at a breathtaking clip. 'Kiiiiii!' she kept going. And I quickly embraced her so she would be quiet."

"So!" Mélivaine said, "that's how one puts a stop to chattering?"

At these words, the elegant group listening to the story became agitated.

"Oh!" murmured several princes whose age had taught them wisdom.

"Ah!" a young princess much too free with her appearance exclaimed impetuously.

The other princesses thought it indecent to shout out in such a manner, although in the end they too drew attention to themselves, since they were all jabbering at once. This went on for a long time. Two or three of the most mature ones even seemed incorrigible.

Fortunately, valiant Prince of Féragator and the formidable King of Aktschwz-Kwkwkw were there. They were insistent that everyone quiet down so the Prince of Valandeuse could finish his story, which he continued thus:

"That kiss, I must confess, was not as intoxicating as the first. However, I again felt her coming to life and dying with my breath. Her breast rose as my desire increased. Alas! alas! my lips were still touching her lips when she began to speak again. 'Pihii-ki!' She just had to speak.

"I waited, hoping she would stop on her own. But she continued, smiling; she still had things to say. She told me things, explained things, laughed, was indignant, scolded me, praised me: she was unstoppable.

"I cried at her feet, I held on to her knees, I beseeched her elegantly. But she responded: 'Ripitiki!' with lighthearted grace. I gently put my hand over her mouth, but tiny bird noises still came through my fingers!

"So I became furious. I grabbed her wrists and, wanting at all costs to speak louder than her warbling, with my eyes gazing into hers I sang—no! I *screamed* into her face the poem in which I had celebrated her. But just as I was finishing the lines that called her so beautiful, I saw her suddenly stumble, fall, and faint... Ah! Novéliane, it was horrible because I no longer knew what I was holding in my hands: a woman's body, a bird's body perhaps, or a sort of soft rag emptied of life that was changing form under my fingers and that still resembled her!"

The prince stopped, reflecting on what he had said. Half-mocking and half-compassionate, the little fairy Lazuli came to take his hand.

"Prince of Valandeuse," she said, "what sorry fortune you've had! To have seen your love in all its simplicity! But one can't show oneself to everyone without finery. Nakedness is so difficult to wear, in both the moral and the physical sense ..."

The prince wasn't very sure whether he was being made fun of. He arranged the ribbons around his collar. From a small pocket he took a silver mirror so he could check the curves of his moustache. Then he pursed his lips, for he had chosen the path of recrimination.

"I thought you wanted to heal me, Novéliane. I'm healed, but am I happy? The same peeping of birds follows me on all lips, and

I no longer believe in words. No, I no longer believe, I no longer believe! And I have to believe in order to sing."

"Liar!" said Mélivaine. "You still sing, I know it."

"Yes," he said sadly. And all of a sudden, he threw down his mirror. "There are times when I try to sing rhymes, but I'm ashamed of them. They're words like yours, words like those of birds and women. I arrange them as they come to me, and with them I satisfy my fantasy, but their music doesn't move me. For I needed to shudder at your beauty, to let myself be enchanted and dazzled by you all, poor soulless shapes. Yes, all you in whom I blow life as I please!"

The prince fell silent. Among the group there was a long murmur of reprobation, then a silence pregnant with fright.

"Handsome prince, sir, you are insolent," said Novéliane. "We too will breathe into you, if you please! Oh, and we're only forms without life? But perhaps, without us, you would be nothing but a beautiful soul without substance, you who speak only because you've seen us, and spend your life expressing nothing more than what we are."

She approached him, beautiful and smiling, as supple as the garland of flowers she was hanging from.

"Beware of my kiss!" she said, warning him with her finger.

The prince gave a sign he was not afraid at all. He felt the touch of her supernatural lips . . .

But the fairy had taken his head in her two hands, and suddenly, maliciously, she blew so hard into his mouth that he inflated like a wineskin and was wider than he was tall.

And it was a good thing too because truth does not suit women, and it's irreverent to pronounce it—even to fairies.

*

And so, the heir apparent to the throne of Valandeuse was freed from his finery. Much too ugly to think of embroidery, lace, or hats with feathers, he might have died of despair. Indeed, at first he concluded it was rather unpleasant to be wider than he was tall. Such proportions are awkward. To accustom oneself to them, one has to be philosophical.

However, he kept on his lips a smooth quiet, like an unspeakable caress of light that continued to intoxicate him. Cured of a strange care, his soul lived on magically. In it, he heard the climbing, growing, and unfurling of a sea of returning waves where a thousand wild voices mixed with very soft ones. Since he had stopped contemplating his face, he decided one day to contemplate the world. So, the universe was born for his eyes, offering an immense mirror in which the images of stars move among the images of men.

The prince learned to discover things and to discover himself in them. The wind, the sea, and the sky spoke to him. The earth revealed to him the heroic work of love, and the eternal effort of the Being that desires, and the new harvests in fields plowed by Death.

Two years passed thus. And here is the astounding conclusion to this double story. The prince lost his puerile foolishness more and more, and his belly shrank as his intelligence expanded. At first, he felt great joy. Indeed! But when he found himself to be sufficiently slender, he neglected to take note of his progress, since his face was still deformed. So, he was very surprised one day when, walking on the banks of the Argilée River, he looked down at his feet, in the crystal waters, and saw a marvelous face . . . What? Was he really that person, such as he had been before?

It truly was he, most assuredly, but no longer as he had been before. Henceforth, he was more handsome, more noble, stronger. Now his reflection was visible on his forehead, and his heart sang in his eyes. His whole being was harmony. When he wanted to recount his joy to the earth, his voice let out vibrant and prodigious melodies to the heavens . . .

The fairies had arranged things thus, and we know that his mouth was forever dedicated to the expression of Music because he had inhaled a divine breath.

The Pleasant Surprise

for Rachilde

The time was approaching when the Queen of Gerdriance's loyal efforts (not to mention those of the King) would finally culminate in the continuation of the dynasty.* Thus began the search for a kindly fairy to be the godmother of the successor to the throne.

There were no longer many fairies in the region since the ravages of war, industry, and the attentive care of the government had cleared their forests. Even so, one was discovered in a clearing as she was weaving gossamer threads to make herself a pretty dress. She was as welcoming as could be, small and pretty, and reassuring in appearance, although a tad mischievous. Because she had been a friend to the Wise Men, she could predict the future as well as any woman under the influence of hypnosis.

She was invited by special envoy, and for a long time she hesitated. But then one day, just when they were beginning to lose

---

* The dedicatee of this tale, Rachilde, is the author of "The Mortis," in this collection.

hope, she arrived by air, swift and joyful, wearing a dress brighter than the moon. Lazuli, the tiny Fairy of surprises, alighted from her chariot.

The Queen was already in the throes of labor, and it was heart-rending to hear her cries. Even as her pain was subsiding, she continued to whimper, alas, nearly as much as she did when her husband the King ventured to scold her about household expenses or the cost of her wardrobe. But suddenly she moaned a great moan, and a little prince was born.

The Fairy took him in her arms, and she sang to him in a low and mysteriously sweet voice:

> *Alas, alas! What can my enchantment bring you?*
> *Tears that these eyes will cry,*
> *joy that fades before it blooms,*
> *such is life . . .*
> *Soul at dawn, seized from the shadows,*
> *what gift shall I bestow upon you?*

"We don't expect the impossible," allowed the King. "Give him the gift of happiness, and that will content us."

"Sire," responded Lazuli, "Your Majesty is demanding in his humility. But I'll do all I can with my magical science."

She smiled as she touched the newborn child's brow with her finger, kissed his eyes, which were still closed to all that light can teach, and calmly tossed off these frighteningly flat and heavy lines:

> *From disappointment, let your soul remain free!*
> *So that you may cultivate a cautious wisdom,*

To protect from evil your innocent weakness,
The gift I grant you is Low Expectations.

The King of Gerdriance wasn't very adept at poetry, and yet he did not applaud these lines. On the contrary, he found them detestable, as was evident from the dismayed look on his face. He was searching painfully within himself for words with which to answer the Fairy when from her bed the Queen, who was a bit deaf, asked, "What did she say?"

The King was diplomatic and, afraid of the consequences, would have preferred not to answer. From the other end of the room, all the way to the grand entry hall, courtiers were lined up symmetrically with their backs to the wall, according to rank. And they maintained a respectful silence, the better to hear what was being said. Because happy princes make for loyal subjects, the news of such a dire augury risked discouraging loyalty toward the dynasty . . .

The Queen, losing patience for waiting so long, cried out again, this time with all her might, "What present did she grant?"

The King leaned over and said in her ear, "The gift of Low Expectations."

After raising his arms up to the sky as witness, he then lowered his right hand to his lips to counsel prudence.

"What! Low Expectations?" said the Queen.

She had spoken softly, or at least so she thought. But the High Custodian of Secrets, who was closest to her, had overheard, almost unintentionally.

He whispered to the Great Eunuch: "The Fairy granted *Low Expectations.* This is awful."

And the Great Eunuch murmured to the High Chamberlain, "She granted *Low Expectations*. Shh! It's dreadful."

"Which gift?" asked the High Carafe Bearer.

And when he had heard the answer, he confided to the High Marshal of Mouths: "Between us, this isn't good." And with a bitter laugh he added, "Alas! What good can we expect from a prince of *Low Expectations?*"

Then the High Marshal told the Squire of Pleasures, who told the Tutor of Morals, who told the Grand Pontiff of the Useful Hypothesis, who told the Wielder of the Halberd. And when the Wielder of the Halberd had told the duenna, his cousin, the entire capital knew that it was possessed of a prince who had received the gift of *Low Expectations*.

This caused much gossip. In the street the townspeople greeted each other by saying,

"Alas!"

"Oh, alas!"

"*Low Expectations!*"

"*Low Expectations*, alas!"

"Oh, alas!"

Men and women arriving from the town's poor neighborhoods questioned each other and lamented in unison. A huge, tumultuous crowd eventually gathered before the royal residence, and it began to shout so loudly that in all the corners of the palace could be heard the thundering cry, "Down with the King!"

Then did the King come out of his torpor and find the response he was seeking for the Fairy.

"Ah! madam," he moaned, "what does this mean? You announce that this child will receive a gift comparable to happiness, but then, either I'm nothing but a jackass or, by God, yes, you cast a bad spell upon him! I don't know what prevents me from telling you . . . Oh, madam, in truth I do not know what is stopping me."

(Now we know very well, and perhaps the King knew it too, that it was the fear of evil charms that stopped him. Nevertheless, there are things that people think that are best kept to oneself.)

The clamor of the crowd was not subsiding, but rather it grew louder by the minute, filling the entire palace like a resounding and furious wave. With the force of its indignation, it chanted in cadence:

"Down with the Fairy, down with the Fairy!"

"What's this?" she said. "All this noise is on my account?"

She gave a little laugh, so flippant and improper that it chilled the court. But she had once more taken up the little prince and, as she rocked him in her arms, kissed him, coddling him with a thousand little favors, she murmured with a smile:

> Receive, since I have not been understood,
> The lovely gift of Pleasant Surprises.

With this it became clear that it was not bad poetry that had saddened the King, since he found this delightful.

"He's been given the gift of *Pleasant Surprises!*" he cried to the Queen.

The High Custodian of Secrets repeated this immediately to the Great Eunuch, and thus the good news began to spread just as the bad had spread. But not quite as quickly, because nothing flies so rapidly as wickedness, and happiness has always been heavy in flight.

The Great Eunuch then repeated to the High Chamberlain, "He has received the gift of *Pleasant Surprises!*"

And the High Chamberlain told the High Carafe Bearer, who told the High Marshal of Mouths, who told the Squire of Pleasures. But since the Tutor of Morals was attending to the duties of his office with a lady-in-waiting, the Squire told it to the Great Mender of Traditions, with the result that the Wielder of the Halberd didn't hear a thing. The Mender of Traditions told his neighbor, the Suppressor of Revolts, who told the Exterminator of the Wretched, and when this one had told the Great Keeper of Beliefs, there was a long delay, because this lofty personage, a man of scruples, hesitated feverously between the desire to speak and the desire to accomplish the duties with which he was charged.

But the Keeper of Beliefs ended up asking the advice of a lady-in-waiting who was well disposed toward him; and as soon as he did, the assembled crowd learned that the successor to the throne had received the gift of *Pleasant Surprises*, and that the Wielder's cousin had lied through her teeth.

"Long live the Fairy! Long live the King!" cried the people in a great frenzy of jubilation.

His Majesty appeared on the balcony with the little prince and his godmother. The enthused populace yelled twice as loudly, making so much noise that the palace windows broke into a thousand pieces. Little by little the rabble grew calmer, since cheering quickly becomes boring. But suddenly it began to yell even louder and went running off to raise hell with the Wielder of the Halberd's cousin. After this it fanned out through the streets to smash lanterns and to better propagate the news. People came out of their houses with hands in the air from despair, only to go back inside waving their hands in jubilation. Others barricaded themselves for fear of the uproar, taking up position on their roofs with hands cupped to ears.

La vieille loyaliste.

Figure 10: The old loyalist

People yelled to them, "The gift of *Pleasant Surprises!*"

And right away they began to dance for joy among the chimney stacks.

There was one old woman to whom the Pleasant Surprise brought bad luck. She had never seen the King nor the Queen, but she revered them because it is so ordered by police regulations. The excellent news took such hold of her that she went out of her mind with joy.

As prescribed by law for crazy people, lest they have the misfortune of offending His Royal Majesty with rash words, her tongue was cut out. And this unexpected turn was the only recognition she ever received from the Crown.

Meanwhile, in the middle of the palace court, the King thanked the Fairy as best he could, placing the treasures of the monarchy at her feet.

"Oh, madam!" he said, "I don't know what prevents me from expressing my complete joy to you. Oh! I really don't know . . ."

And this time, the King truly had no idea what held back his words, apart perhaps from his lack of eloquence.

"Sire," responded the smiling Fairy, "You have had time to appreciate the gift I have granted, and I have thus learned to know you. I want no other recompense than the entertainment it has given me."

She bade farewell to the court with a nimble curtsy and climbed into her chariot made of tulips and irises. But the King detained her still.

"Oh!" he said, "Pardon my disconsolate words regarding your first gift. I'm embarrassed, I assure you. But the other, the second one ..."

"The second?" asked the Fairy.

It then became quite evident that these kinds of winged maidens are not of our world. This one was in fact quite ill-mannered, and she began to laugh wildly without concern for etiquette. And at the height of her laughter she picked a tulip from her chariot and threw it in the face of the dumbfounded King.

"What a simpleton!" she exclaimed. "But I granted only one!"

With this her chariot bore her away amidst a great flowery scent, and she disappeared in midair.

The King remained speechless, not so much for having had a flower thrown in his face by the Fairy Lazuli as out of perplexity.

"A single gift," he murmured, "Only one! But then which one is it?"

And he was greatly aggrieved for having, just the preceding day, handed over a philosopher to the Suppressor of Revolts for execution, a philosopher who might have been able to explain to him ...

Contes pour les enfants d'hier, 1908

PIERRE VEBER

The Last Fairy

She was, irrevocably, the last Fairy. All the others had died off, one by one, just like Marshals of France, who aren't replaced when they die.* The old ones had gradually been carried off, one in some battle with a rival, another dragged away out of love for a mortal, still others killed off by progress. And as they disappeared, those who survived them divvied up their belongings among themselves.

The last Fairy lived deep in a Thuringian forest (the most impenetrable forests are typically found in Thuringia). Once in a while a dwarf visited with news of the demise of yet another of her sisters, bringing as he did her share of the dead fairy's inheritance. Talismans, magic wands, enchanted chests, and other professional accessories at length piled up in the Fairy's burrow. And when the last of her kind but she had passed on, a deputation of

---

* Maréchal de France was the title of highest distinction in the French army, granted for life. Because the title ceased to be conferred at the beginning of the Third Republic (1870), during the end of the century the number of those previously named thus grew smaller by attrition, with the last one dying in 1895 (the honor was subsequently reestablished during the First World War).

elves arrived to inform her that she was, henceforth, the only remaining Fairy. Since she had never left her forest, she felt neither
pride nor sorrow for being named the Queen of Fairies. When all
was said and done, she had only herself to govern and, if it's difficult to obey oneself, it's even harder to command oneself (the
significance of this philosophical observation will not be lost on
the wise). This Fairy's power, which had grown commensurately
as she collected her comrades' inheritance, thus went largely un-
used, although she occasionally distracted herself by changing
deer into swallows, or swallows into deer. As one might imagine,
the novelty of this pastime quickly wore off, and the Fairy succumbed to an ennui particular to fairies, whereby they begin to
envy the lot of ordinary women. For that matter, the forest demanded a lot of attention, if you really want to think about it!
Granted, there is a certain mystical poetry to moonlight in a forest glade, to the opalescent mist that gathers over ponds at nightfall, to the sounds of the wood at dusk. But all that had been well
worked over in romantic verse, with which the Fairy was only too
familiar.

Sometimes she went in search of her only friend, the old Genie
of quarries, keeper of the secrets of the earth. They chatted about
common interests, first and foremost about supernatural beings
practicing crafts destined for obsolescence. But they also ex-
changed stories about famous enchanters and discussed the best
way to distill potions. The Genie had composed an authoritative
Perfect Genie Manual. As the day broke, the Fairy returned home
to sleep. Sometimes the old Genie would go to her house and
examine her collection of talismans, rather judgmentally, and
make swaps. This peaceful exchange had gone on for centuries.

Then one day, the Queen who had no realm went in search of her old friend and told him, "I've had enough. I want to travel."

"Is that so?!" he responded in surprise. "Where will you go?"

"Straight in front of me," she answered, "and in this way I'll surely stumble across an objective. You can see that it's just idiotic to have absolute power and not take advantage of it! I have piles of talismans that I don't employ, and nothing breaks down faster than a talisman that isn't used. It's all well and good for me to practice on harmless animals, but I feel the need to move on to other exercises. I'm heading for bigger fish."

"I get it. You're a flirt: you're eternally young, and you want to see what effect you have on men."

"And what if I do?! I'm tired of changing animals into animals. I want to transform men into animals!"

"You don't need to be a fairy to change men into animals," the Genie sighed. "You just need to be a pretty woman."

"I want to make use of my riches. I have the purse of Fortunatus, which is constantly replenished; the carpet of the four Facardins, which flies in the air; the magic lamp; the wand that turns people to stone; the ring that makes its wearer invisible; the enchanted root, which can penetrate fortifications, among other things. You have to admit that it's hard to keep all that to oneself."

"So you've decided to go?"

"Absolutely."

"Then when are we leaving? Because I hope you didn't think for a minute that I'd let you leave alone."

"I'm so glad! You're the dearest old Genie who ever walked the earth. We'll leave in the morning."

They spent the night talking and fixed upon a plan of action. The Fairy wanted to travel like the simplest of mortals. They agreed on a leisurely itinerary to give themselves the time to take in the sights and people. This is in keeping with what is written in fairy tales, where it is demonstrated that these all-powerful creatures employ the most rudimentary means of transportation and, whether by modesty or by curiosity, travel by foot in the manner of honest women.

As soon as Dawn had tickled the mountain passages with its rosy fingers, the Fairy set out in the company of her old friend. Their luggage followed slowly in the distance, carried by impalpable servants. The first stop led the tourists outside of their cordial forest, in the direction of the closest town.

"What if we went by rail," suggested the Genie, who had no appreciation for hoofing it.

"As you please, although I don't know what that means," responded the Fairy.

They reached the nearest station, and the approach of a train was announced. But when the locomotive appeared as it emerged from a tunnel, roaring and blowing fire and smoke from its long neck, the Fairy took fright, thinking it was the legendary dragon-serpent bursting forth from the entrails of the earth. And before the Genie could stop her, she raised her wand and uttered the spell that immobilizes people and things. The locomotive stopped instantly, so brusquely that its wagons crashed into one another, and there followed a horrendous catastrophe, whose true cause was never known. Stationmasters and signalmen went before tribunals and finished their poor lives in comfortable prisons for unintentional homicide.

The two divine persons ran away from the clamor of this prodigious event and abstained from traveling by railway. Taking the main roads in the west, they made their way southward. They begged for shelter, as if they were poor homeless people, and, in accordance with their moralizing mission, they meted out rewards or punishment depending on whether the welcome they received was good or bad.

However, the justice they distributed did not achieve the intended results. At the very first farm, the voyagers were welcomed with such goodness that they resolved to honor their hosts by showing their gratitude. In the morning, while the farmers were still sleeping, they departed, leaving a sack of gold on the table. But when the farmers found the sack upon awakening, they believed they had lodged robbers who had off-loaded a part of their loot. "This is what happens when you take in vagabonds!" said the farmer's wife. "We'll make sure that never happens again. In any event, we'll have to bring this money to the authorities: a whole day of work lost!"

When they were poorly welcomed on another farm, the Fairy and the Genie avenged themselves by condemning the mean rich man's barn to be burned. But the next day this man had drifters, harmless all of them, arrested within a ten-league diameter. Punishment reaches only the truly guilty parties in fairy tales: in real life it usually falls upon the innocent, and in so doing makes life in this lowly world that much more unpredictable.

The enchanted wanderers took to the road once again. When a peasant showed disrespect to the Fairy, who was quite lovely, she punished him on the spot by changing him into a pig. "You're making progress there, aren't you?" scolded the Genie. "Do you really think you've punished him? You've hardly succeeded in increasing the number of pigs in the world! Besides, it's your fault: you should have made yourself ugly."

They went through market towns and then cities. Everywhere they traveled, they accomplished miracles that surprised no one, since we now have explanations for everything that once appeared extraordinary. The Fairy was annoyed by such human indifference; she wanted to astound people. "Wait until we get to Paris," said her companion. "You're sure to make a big impression there."

At last they arrived at the gates of Paris, the end of their journey. The Fairy couldn't hide her delight, declaring, "They're going to see some incredible things!" As she reached the exterior boulevard, she saw passing suddenly before her eyes a car that was drawn by no horse, and it was going so fast that it was hard to make out. "Look!" cried the Fairy. "A horseless car! It must be enchanted: a hellish smell is trailing that magic carriage!"

At that moment she raised her eyes and perceived a long object in the air that was maneuvering in all directions: it was the Santos-Dumont dirigible number 125, which was winning the Deutsch de la Meurthe prize once again.* "Look at that!" said the Fairy. "Now there's a talisman just like my carpet! Are we in a city of sorcerers?"

The travelers went to their hotel, where a handsome young man dressed in a tasseled uniform, following the customary negotiations, bade them enter a small room. He touched the wall, and suddenly the room rose up by itself, traversing floors with

---

* Alberto Santos-Dumont (1873–1932) was a pioneer in aviation who invented the first dirigible airship. He became famous when in 1901 he was the first to fly round-trip between the Parc Saint-Cloud and the Eiffel Tower in thirty minutes, thus winning the Deutsch prize. He accomplished this in his dirigible number 6.

phenomenal ease. "What's this?!" cried the Fairy to the handsome young man. "You must be a confrere! Do you possess the magic root that makes it possible to go through walls?"

"Madam," he answered, "I'm the elevator attendant, and I don't have a magic root. Like all service staff, I have roots nowhere!"

Having come to amaze, the Fairy was left dumbfounded. She was shown to her apartment. Night had fallen, and the thaumaturge was preparing to polish Aladdin's lamp, which requires a magic ceremony that is rather complicated. The chambermaid turned a switch, which made blinding light suddenly burst forth. The Fairy ran into the neighboring apartment where the sorcerer was settling himself in. "My friend," she murmured, "This city is full of fairies, charmers, and magicians. Lights go on by themselves, people fly in clouds, and carts operate without horses. I feel ill at ease."

"You miss your forest already. What did I tell you?"

He was interrupted by a shout from the Fairy, who was pointing at the window.

A luminous image had just appeared across the street on level with the third floor. The image wavered at first, then came to life; the characters it contained were suddenly animated by a singular and agitated activity, moved about in all directions for a few minutes, and then the image disappeared. Another one soon replaced it, with characters equally animated. And another after that.

"That's extraordinary!" said the Fairy, who was unfamiliar with cinematography.

"Indeed," agreed the Genie. "I don't know how they managed to pull off a spell like that. As soon as I get back and have cleared my head, I'm going to try it out myself."

They went down to the lobby, which was empty at that time of day. As the Fairy was looking for some magazines to read, she bumped against a case topped by some kind of copper vase that looked to be the bell of a hunting horn. Thereupon a mocking voice roared in a nasal tone, "'The Breton Bagpipe,' a new love song, performed by Dranem at the Eldorado."* He began to sing, *"The pain is craaazy . . ."*

The Fairy was seized by an indescribable terror: "Genie! Help! There's an evil spirit in this room that's made itself invisible to taunt us. Can you hear him?" The Genie then uttered the word that makes spirits adopt a visible form. But the voice continued nonetheless to sing that the pain was crazy, and so on and so forth. Finally a bellboy who had been drawn by the commotion came in and declared, as he carried off the box: "You can't run the phonograph without authorization, you might damage it!"

The surprises were not over for the poor Fairy. Having witnessed the cashier conversing with a small wooden console, she decided to imitate her: she brought the ebonite disks to her ears and began to yell numbers at the console while saying, "Hello! Hello!" After a few seconds, a distant voice, rather harsh, rang in her ears: "You imbecile, give us a break! You've been bothering us for over an hour, stupid idiot." In order to escape this tirade, she ran out into the street, as if she had heard the voice of the devil.

The Genie had a hard time finding her. When he finally did, she was standing, enraptured, watching a poorly dressed man as he manipulated strange little beings on the sidewalk. These dwarves were endowed with an intermittent existence, going back

---

* Dranem (Charles Armand Ménard, 1869–1935), was a French comic singer, star of café-concerts (including the Eldorado) and the stage. The song in question, "Le Biniou," originated in Brittany and dates to the mid-nineteenth century. It was recorded and popularized by the tenor Albert Alvarez (1861–1933) at the turn of the twentieth century.

and forth, and then stopping. The man then took them in his hands and brought them back to life with the aid of a string. The Fairy looked in vain for the spell that held sway over these small gnomes, when a cruel soldier armed with a small white club rushed at the poorly dressed magician and said, "You know very well that it's against the law to sell toys by the roadway. Keep it moving!"

The Genie and his companion saw still more curious objects in various stores: a piano that played by itself, a tin-plated bird that sang better than a natural bird, and some kind of transparent plate on which appeared the skeletons of people who passed before it. And they saw strange maxims suddenly appear on palace marquees, just like the famous "Mene, Mene, Tekel, Upharsin,"* such as "Drink Dubonnet!" or "I only smoke Gauloises!"

"The truth is," said the old Genie, "that the people of this country live in a state of enchantment. We wouldn't be able to surprise them."

"I'm beginning to see this," said the Fairy.

The last blow was struck when they saw, in a music hall, a man in a frock coat execute a thousand marvels. He made various objects disappear, such as small balls, playing cards, hats; and he made others appear: aquariums, bouquets, cascades of ribbons. He made it rain dollars onstage and, finally, he made himself disappear.

"We really are weaklings!" confessed the miracle professionals. "This man is more gifted than we are. He knows secrets that we don't possess."

---

* Biblical reference to the words King Belshazzar saw written on a palace wall by a disembodied hand.

"There's nothing more to do here. Let's go home."

In the middle of the boulevard, surrounded by a crowd of on-lookers, they unfolded their magic carpet, climbed aboard, and rose up in the sky—not fast enough, however, for the miffed Fairy to miss an advertisement light up in bright letters, which read "Get eternal youth with Z cream . . ."

On their way back to their ancient forest, the two divine tourists resolved never again to go off in search of adventure. They will remain in their realm until the end of time. But they are now diminished and more unhappy than before, because they have understood that mankind has succeeded in conquering supreme magic, and that there is no longer a place for fairies in the modern world.

Les Belles Histoires, 1908

ANATOLE FRANCE

The Seven Wives of Bluebeard

(based on authentic documents)

I

The strangest, most varied, and most erroneous opinions have been expressed with regard to the famous individual commonly known as Bluebeard.* None is perhaps less tenable than the suggestion that this gentleman was a personification of the Sun. For this is what a certain school of comparative mythology set itself to do, some forty years ago. It informed the world that the seven wives of Bluebeard were the Dawns, and that his two brothers-in-law were the morning and the evening Twilight, identifying them with the Dioscuri, who delivered Helen when she was rapt away by Theseus.† We must remind those readers who may feel tempted to believe this that in 1817 a learned librarian of Agen,

---

* The translation of the tale is by D. B. Stewart, modified.
† France is likely referring to Hyacinthe Husson's *La Chaîne traditionnelle: contes et légendes au point de vue mythique* (1874), which interpreted fairy tales with Max Müller's Indo-European theory of folklore. After its heyday in the mid- to late nineteenth century, it was later abandoned by folklorists.

Jean-Baptiste Pérès, demonstrated, in a highly specious manner, that Napoleon had never existed, and that the story of this supposed great captain was nothing but a solar myth.* Despite the most ingenious diversions of the wits, we cannot possibly doubt that Bluebeard and Napoleon did both actually exist.

A hypothesis no better founded is the one identifying Bluebeard with the Marshal de Rais, who was strangled by the arm of the law above the bridges of Nantes on the 26th of October, 1440.† Without inquiring, with M. Salomon Reinach, whether the Marshal committed the crimes for which he was condemned, or whether his wealth, coveted by a greedy prince, did not in some degree contribute to his undoing,‡ there is nothing in his life that resembles what we find in Bluebeard's; this alone is enough to prevent our confusing them or merging the two individuals into one.

Charles Perrault, who, about 1660, had the merit of composing the first biography of this lord, justly remarkable for having married seven wives, portrayed him as an accomplished villain and the most perfect model of cruelty that ever trod the earth. But it is permissible to doubt, if not his sincerity, at least the correctness of his information. He may, perhaps, have been prejudiced against his hero. He would not have been the first poet or historian who liked to cast a shadow over his portraits. If we have

---

* Pérès (1752–1840) was the anonymous author of a satirical pamphlet, "Comme quoi Napoléon n'a jamais existé ou Grand erratum, source d'un nombre infini d'errata à corriger dans l'histoire du XIXᵉ siècle" (1827).

† Gilles de Rais (ca. 1405–40), powerful baron and knight condemned and hanged for murdering a great number of children.

‡ Salomon Reinach (1858–1932), French archaeologist and historian of religion who posited the theory that Gilles de Rais was not guilty of the crimes imputed to him (*Cultes, mythes et religions*, 1905).

a flattering portrait of Titus, it would seem, in contrast, that Tacitus has sullied that of Tiberius. Macbeth, whom legend and Shakespeare accuse of crimes, was in reality a just and wise King. He never treacherously murdered the old King, Duncan, who in fact was defeated in a great battle while still young and found dead the following day at a spot called the Armorer's Shop. Duncan had slain several of the kinsfolk of Gruoch, the wife of Macbeth. Macbeth made Scotland prosperous: he encouraged trade and was regarded as the defender of the middle classes, the true King of the townsmen. The nobles of the clans never forgave him for defeating Duncan or for protecting the artisans. They destroyed him and dishonored his memory. Once he was dead, the good King Macbeth was known only by the statements of his enemies. The genius of Shakespeare imposed these lies upon the human consciousness. I had long suspected that Bluebeard was the victim of a similar fatality. All the circumstances of his life, as I found them related, were far from satisfying my mind, and from gratifying that craving for logic and lucidity by which I am incessantly consumed. On reflection, I perceived that they involved insurmountable difficulties. There was so great a desire to make me believe in the man's cruelty that it could not fail to make me doubt it.

These presentiments did not mislead me. My intuition, which had its origin in a certain knowledge of human nature, was soon to be changed into certainty, based upon irrefutable proofs.

In the house of a stonecutter in St. Jean-des-Bois, I found several papers relating to Bluebeard, including his defense and an anonymous complaint against his murderers, which was never pursued, for reasons unbeknownst to me. These papers confirmed my belief that he was good and unfortunate, and that his memory has been overwhelmed by unworthy slanders. From that time forth, I regarded it as my duty to write his true history, without permitting myself any illusion as to the success of such an undertaking. I am well aware that this attempt at rehabilitation is destined to fall into silence and oblivion. How can the cold, naked truth fight against the glittering enchantments of falsehood?

II

Somewhere about 1650 there lived on his estate, between Compiègne and Pierrefonds, a wealthy noble named Bernard de Montragoux, whose ancestors had held the most important posts in the kingdom. But he dwelt far from the court, in that peaceful obscurity which then veiled all save that on which the King bestowed his glance. His castle of Guillettes abounded in valuable furniture, gold and silver ware, tapestry and embroideries, which he kept in coffers. Not that he hid his treasures for fear of damaging them by use; he was, on the contrary, generous and magnificent. But in those days, in the country, the nobles willingly led a very simple life, feeding their people at their own table, and dancing on Sundays with the girls of the village.

On certain occasions, however, they gave splendid parties, which contrasted with the dullness of everyday life. So it was necessary that they should hold a good deal of handsome furniture and beautiful tapestries in reserve. This was the case with Monsieur de Montragoux.

His castle had all the severity of the Gothic period during which it was built. From without it looked wild and gloomy enough, with the stumps of its great towers, which had been destroyed at the time of the monarchy's troubles, in the reign of the

Figure 11

late King Louis. Within it offered a much pleasanter prospect. The rooms were decorated in the Italian taste, as was the great gallery on the ground floor, loaded with embossed decorations in high relief, pictures, and gilding.

At one end of this gallery there was a closet usually known as "the little cabinet." This is the only name by which Charles Perrault refers to it. It is as well to note that it was also called the "cabinet of the unfortunate princesses," because a Florentine painter had portrayed on the walls the tragic stories of Dirce, daughter of the Sun, bound by the sons of Antiope to the horns of a bull, Niobe weeping on Mount Sipylus for her children, pierced by the divine arrows, and Procris inviting to her bosom the javelin of Cephalus. These figures had a look of life about them, and the porphyry tiles with which the floor was covered seemed dyed in the blood of these unhappy women. One of the doors of the cabinet opened onto the moat, which contained no water.

The stables formed a sumptuous building, situated at some distance from the castle. They contained stalls for sixty horses, and coach-houses for twelve gilded coaches. But what made Guillettes so bewitching a residence were the woods and canals surrounding it, in which one could devote oneself to the pleasures of angling and hunting.

Many of the dwellers in that countryside knew Monsieur de Montragoux only by the name of Bluebeard, for this was the only name that the common people gave him. And in truth his beard was blue, but it was blue only because it was black, and it was because it was so black that it was blue. Monsieur de Montragoux must not be imagined as having the monstrous aspect of the threefold Typhon one sees in Athens, laughing in his triple indigo beard. We shall get much nearer the reality by comparing the lord of Guillettes to those actors or priests whose freshly shaven cheeks have a bluish gloss.

Monsieur de Montragoux did not wear a pointed beard like his grandfather at the court of King Henry II; nor did he wear it like a fan, as did his great-grandfather who was killed at the Battle of

Marignan. Like Monsieur de Turenne, he had only a slight moustache and a chin-tuft, and his cheeks had a bluish look. Whatever may have been said of him, this good gentleman was by no means disfigured, nor did he inspire any fear on that account. He only looked the more virile, and if it made him appear a little fierce, it did not have the effect of making women dislike him. Bernard de Montragoux was a very fine man, tall, broad across the shoulders, moderately stout, and well favored; albeit of a rustic habit, smacking of the woods rather than of drawing rooms and assemblies. Still, it is true that he did not please the ladies as much as he should have pleased them, built and wealthy as he was. Shyness was the reason: shyness, not his beard. Women exercised an invincible attraction for him, and at the same time inspired him with an insuperable fear. He feared them as much as he loved them. This was the origin and initial cause of all his misfortunes. Seeing a lady for the first time, he would have died rather than speak to her, and however much attracted he may have been, he stood before her in gloomy silence. His feelings revealed themselves only through his eyes, which he rolled in a terrible manner. This timidity exposed him to every kind of misfortune, and, above all, it prevented his forming a becoming connection with modest and reserved women; and betrayed him, defenseless, to the attempts of the most impudent and audacious. This was his life's misfortune.

Left an orphan from his early youth, and having rejected, owing to this sort of bashfulness and fear, which he was unable to overcome, the very advantageous and honorable alliances that had presented themselves, he married a Mademoiselle Colette Passage, who had recently settled down in that part of the country, after amassing a little money by making a bear dance through the towns and villages of the kingdom. He loved her with all his soul. And to do her justice, there was something pleasing about her. She was a fine woman with an ample bosom, and a complexion that was still sufficiently fresh, although a little sunburned by the open air. She felt great joy and surprise upon becoming a lady of quality. Her heart, which was not bad, was touched by the kindness of a husband in such a high position, and with such a stout, powerful body, who was to her the most obedient of servants and devoted of lovers. But after a few months she grew weary because she could no longer go to and fro on the face of the earth. In the midst of wealth, overwhelmed with love and care, she could find no greater pleasure than that of going to see the companion of her wandering life, in the cellar where he languished with a chain round his neck and a ring through his nose, and kissing him on the eyes and weeping. Seeing her full of care, Monsieur de Montragoux himself became careworn, and this only added to his companion's melancholy. The consideration and forethought that he lavished on her turned the poor woman's head. One morning, when he awoke, Monsieur de Montragoux found Colette no longer at his side. In vain he searched for her throughout the castle.

The door of the cabinet of the unfortunate princesses was open. It was through this door that she had gone to reach the open country with her bear. The sorrow of Bluebeard was painful to behold. In spite of the innumerable messengers sent forth in search of her, no news was ever received of Colette Passage.

Monsieur de Montragoux was still mourning her when he happened to dance, at the fair of Guillettes, with Jeanne de La Cloche, daughter of the Police Lieutenant of Compiègne, who inspired him with love. He asked for her hand, which he was immediately granted. She loved wine and drank it to excess. So much did this taste increase that after a few months she looked like a leather bottle with a round red face on top of it. The worst of it was that this leather bottle would run mad, incessantly rolling about the reception rooms and the staircases, crying, swearing, and hiccoughing; vomiting wine and insults at everything that got in her way. Monsieur de Montragoux was dazed with disgust and horror. But he quite suddenly recovered his courage, and set himself, with as much firmness as patience, to cure his wife of so disgusting a vice. He employed every possible means: prayers, protestations, supplications, and threats. All was useless. He forbade her wine from his cellar: she got it from outside, and was more abominably drunk than ever.

To deprive her of her taste for a beverage that she loved too well, he put valerian in the bottles. She thought he was trying to poison her, sprang upon him, and drove three inches of a kitchen knife into his belly. He expected to die of it, but he did not abandon his habitual kindness.

"She is more to be pitied than blamed," he said.

One day, when he had forgotten to close the door of the cabinet of the unfortunate princesses, Jeanne de La Cloche entered it, quite out of her mind as usual, and seeing the figures on the walls in postures of affliction, ready to give up the ghost, she mistook them for living women, and fled terror-stricken into the country, screaming murder. Hearing Bluebeard calling her and running after her, she threw herself, mad with terror, into a pond, where she drowned. It is difficult to believe, yet certain, that her husband, so compassionate was his soul, was much afflicted by her death.

Six weeks after the accident he quietly married Gigonne, the daughter of his steward, Traignel. She wore wooden shoes and smelt of onions. She was a fine-looking enough girl, except that she squinted with one eye and limped with one foot. As soon as she was married, this goose keeper was bitten by foolish ambition and dreamt of nothing but further greatness and splendor. She was not satisfied that her brocade dresses were rich enough, her pearl necklaces beautiful enough, her rubies big enough, her coaches sufficiently gilded, her lakes, woods, and lands sufficiently vast. Bluebeard, who was never particularly ambitious, trembled at the haughty humor of his spouse. In his straightforward simplicity, he did not know whether the mistake lay in thinking magnificently like his wife or modestly as he himself did; he accused himself of a mediocrity of mind that thwarted the noble desires of his consort. Full of uncertainty, he would sometimes exhort her to taste with moderation the good things of this world, while at others he roused himself to pursue fortune along the verge of precipitous heights. He was prudent, but conjugal affection led him beyond the reach of prudence. Gigonne thought of nothing but cutting a figure in the world, being received at court, and becoming the King's mistress. Unable to achieve this goal, she withered away with spite and contracted a jaundice, of which she died. Bluebeard, full of lamentation, built her a magnificent tomb.

This worthy lord, overwhelmed by constant domestic adversity, would perhaps have not chosen another wife if he himself had not been chosen by Mademoiselle Blanche de Gibeaumex, the daughter of a cavalry officer who had but one ear; he used to relate that he had lost the other in the King's service. She was full of intelligence, which she employed in deceiving her husband. She betrayed him with every man of quality in the neighborhood. She was so dexterous that she deceived him in his own castle, almost under his very eyes, without his perceiving it. Poor Bluebeard assuredly suspected something, but he could not say what. Unfortunately for her, while she gave her whole mind to tricking her husband, she was not sufficiently careful in deceiving her lovers; by which I mean that she betrayed them, one for another. One day she was surprised in the cabinet of the unfortunate princesses, in the company of a gentleman whom she loved, by a gentleman whom she had loved, and the latter, in a transport of jealousy, ran her through with his sword. A few hours later the unfortunate lady was found dead there by one of the castle servants, and the fear inspired by the room increased.

Poor Bluebeard, learning at one blow of his ample dishonor and the tragic death of his wife, did not console himself for the latter misfortune by any consideration of the former. He had loved Blanche de Gibeaumex with a strange ardor, more dearly than he had loved Jeanne de La Cloche, Gigonne Traignel, or even Colette Passage. On learning that she had consistently betrayed him, and that now she would never betray him again, he experienced a grief and a mental perturbation that, far from being appeased, daily increased in violence. So intolerable were his sufferings that he contracted a malady that threatened to take his life.

The physicians, having employed various medicines without success, advised him that the only remedy proper to his complaint was to take a young wife. He then thought of his young cousin, Angèle de la Garandine, whose hand he believed would be willingly granted him, as she had no property. What encouraged him to take her as wife was the fact that she was reputed to be simple and ignorant of the world. Having been deceived by a woman of intelligence, he felt more comfortable with a fool. He married Mademoiselle de la Garandine and quickly perceived the falsity of his calculations. Angèle was kind, Angèle was good, and Angèle loved him; she had not, in herself, any leanings toward evil, but the least astute person could quickly lead her astray at any moment. It was enough to tell her: "Do this or the bogeyman will get you; come in here or the werewolf will eat you" or "Shut your eyes, and take this drop of medicine," and the innocent girl would straightway do so, at the will of the scoundrels who wanted of her that which it was very natural to want of her, for she was pretty. Monsieur de Montragoux, injured and betrayed by this innocent girl, as much as and more than he had been by Blanche de Gibeaumex, had the additional pain of knowing it, for Angèle was too candid to conceal anything from him. She used to tell him: "Sire, someone told me this; someone did that to me; someone took such and such from me; I saw this; I felt that." And by her ingenuousness she caused her lord to suffer torments beyond imagination. He endured them stoically. Still, he finally had to tell the simple creature that she was a goose, and to box her ears. This was the beginning of his reputation for cruelty, which was not fated to be diminished. A mendicant monk, who was passing Guillettes while Monsieur de Montragoux was out shooting woodcock, found Madame Angèle sewing a doll's petticoat. This worthy friar, discovering that she was as foolish as she was beautiful, took her away on his donkey, having persuaded her that the Angel Gabriel was waiting in a thicket to give her a pair of pearl garters. It is believed that she was eaten by a wolf, for she was never seen again.

After such a disastrous experience, how was it that Bluebeard could make up his mind to contract yet another union? It would be impossible to understand, were we not well aware of the power that a fine pair of eyes exerts over a generous heart.

The honest gentleman met, at a neighboring château that he was in the habit of frequenting, a young orphan of quality named Alix de Pontalcin, who, having been robbed of all her property by a greedy trustee, thought only of entering a convent. Officious friends intervened to alter her resolution and persuade her to accept the hand of Monsieur de Montragoux. Her beauty was perfect. Bluebeard, determined to enjoy infinite happiness in her arms, was once more deluded in his hopes. This time he experienced a disappointment to which, given his temperament, he was bound to be more susceptible than all the afflictions he had suffered in his previous marriages. Alix de Pontalcin obstinately refused to give actuality to the union to which she had nevertheless consented.

In vain did Monsieur de Montragoux press her to become his wife; she resisted his prayers, tears, and objurgations; she refused her husband's lightest caresses, and rushed off to shut herself in the cabinet of the unfortunate princesses, where she remained, alone and intractable, for whole nights at a time.

The cause of a resistance so contrary to laws both human and divine was never known; it was attributed to Monsieur de Montragoux's blue beard, but our previous remarks on the subject of his beard render such a supposition improbable. In any case, it is a difficult subject to discuss. The unhappy husband underwent the cruelest suffering. In order to put it out of his mind, he hunted with desperation, exhausting horses, hounds, and huntsmen. But when he returned home, exhausted and worn out, the mere sight of Mademoiselle de Pontalcin was enough to revive his energies and his torments. Finally, unable to endure the situation any longer, he applied to Rome for the annulment of a marriage that was no more than an illusion; and in consideration of a handsome present to the Holy Father, he obtained it in accordance with canon law. If Monsieur de Montragoux dismissed Mademoiselle de Pontalcin with all the marks of respect due to a woman, and without breaking his cane across her back, it was because he had a valiant soul, a great heart, and was master of himself as well as of Guillettes. But he swore that, for the future, no female would enter his apartments. Happy would he have been had he held his oath to the end!

III

Some years had elapsed since Monsieur de Montragoux had rid himself of his sixth wife, and only a confused recollection remained in the countryside of the domestic calamities that had befallen this worthy lord's house. Nobody knew what had become of his wives, and hair-raising tales were told in the village at night; some believed them, others did not. About this time, a widow past the prime of life, Dame Sidonie de Lespoisse, came to settle with her children in the manor of La Motte-Giron, about two leagues, as the crow flies, from the castle of Guillettes. Whence she came, or who her husband had been, not a soul knew. Some believed, because they had heard it said, that he had held certain posts in Savoy or Spain; others said that he had died in the Indies; many had the idea that the widow was possessed of immense estates, while others doubted it strongly. However, she lived in a notable style, and invited all the nobility of the countryside to La Motte-Giron. She had two daughters, of whom the elder, Anne, on the verge of becoming an old maid, was a very astute person: Jeanne, the younger, ripe for marriage, concealed a precocious knowledge of the world under an appearance of simplicity. Lady de Lespoisse had also two sons, of twenty and twenty-two years of age; very fine well-made young fellows, of whom one was a Dragoon and the other a Musketeer. I may add, having seen his commission, that he was a Black Musketeer. When on foot, this was not apparent, for the Black Musketeers were distinguished from the Gray not by the color of their uniform, but by the hides of their horses. All alike wore blue surcoats laced with gold. As for the Dragoons, they were to be recognized by a kind of fur bonnet, of which the tail fell gallantly over the ear. The Dragoons had the reputation of being scamps, a scapegrace crowd, witness the song:

> *Mama, here the dragoons come,*
> *Save us!*

But you might have searched in vain through His Majesty's two regiments of Dragoons for a bigger rake, a more accomplished sponger, or a viler rogue than Cosme de Lespoisse. Compared to him, his brother was an honest lad. A drunkard and a gambler, Pierre de Lespoisse pleased the ladies and won at cards; these were the only ways of gaining a living he knew.

Their mother, Dame de Lespoisse, was making a splash at Motte-Giron only in order to deceive her neighbors. As a matter of fact, she had nothing and was in debt for everything, down to her false teeth. Her clothes and furniture, her coach, her horses, and her servants had all been lent by Parisian moneylenders, who threatened to take them all back if she did not presently marry one of her daughters to some rich nobleman. The respectable Sidonie expected to find herself at any moment naked in an empty house. In a hurry to find a son-in-law, she had at once cast her eye upon Monsieur de Montragoux, whom she summed up as being simpleminded, easy to deceive, extremely mild, and quick to fall in love under his rude and bashful exterior. Her two daughters entered into her plans, and at every encounter, they riddled poor Bluebeard with looks that pierced him to the depths of his heart. He soon fell victim to the potent charms of the two demoiselles de Lespoisse. Forgetting his oath, he thought only of marrying one or the other, for he found them equally beautiful. After some delay, caused less by hesitation than timidity, he went to Motte-Giron in great state, and made his petition to the Dame de Lespoisse, leaving to her the choice of which daughter she would give him. Madame Sidonie obligingly replied that she held him in high esteem, and that she authorized him to pay his court to whichever of the ladies he should prefer.

"Learn to please, monsieur," she said. "I shall be the first to applaud your success."

In order better to make their acquaintance, Bluebeard invited Anne and Jeanne de Lespoisse, along with their mother, brothers, and a multitude of ladies and gentlemen, to pass a fortnight at the castle of Guillettes. There was a succession of excursions, hunting and fishing parties, dances and festivities, dinners and entertainment of every sort. A young lord, the Chevalier de la Merlus, whom the ladies Lespoisse had brought with them, organized the hunts. Bluebeard had the best hounds and the largest turnout in the countryside. The ladies rivaled the ardor of the gentlemen in hunting the deer. They did not always chase the animal down, but the hunters and huntresses wandered away in couples, found one another, and again wandered off into the woods. For choice, the Chevalier de la Merlus would lose himself with Jeanne de Lespoisse, and both would return to the castle at night, full of their adventures and pleased with their day's sport.

After a few days' observation, the good lord of Montragoux felt a decided preference for Jeanne over her elder sister, as she was fresher, which is not saying that she was less experienced. He let his preference show: there was no reason to conceal it, for it was a befitting preference; moreover, he was a straightforward man. He courted the young lady as best he could, speaking little for want of practice; but he gazed at her with his rolling eyes, emitting from the depths of his bowels sighs that could have overthrown an oak tree. Sometimes he would burst out laughing, whereupon the crockery trembled and the windows rattled. Alone of all the party, he failed to remark the assiduous attentions of the Chevalier de la Merlus to Madame de Lespoisse's younger daughter, or if he did he saw no harm in them. His experience of women was not sufficient to make him suspicious, and he was trusting when he loved. My grandmother used to say that in life experience is worthless, and that one remains the same as when one began. I believe she was right, and the true story that I am now recounting is not of a nature to prove her wrong.

Bluebeard displayed an unusual magnificence in these festivities. When night arrived, the lawns surrounding the castle were lit by a thousand torches, and tables served by menservants and maids dressed as fauns and dryads groaned under all the tastiest things that the countryside and the forest produced. Musicians provided a continual succession of lovely symphonies. Toward the end of the meal the schoolmaster and schoolmistress, followed by the boys and girls of the village, appeared before the guests and read a complimentary address to the lord of Montragoux and his friends. An astrologer in a pointed cap approached the ladies and foretold future love affairs from the lines of their hands. Bluebeard ordered drink for all his vassals, and he himself distributed bread and meat to the poor families.

At ten o'clock, to avoid the evening chill, the company retired to the apartments, lit by a multitude of candles, and there tables were prepared for every sort of game: lansquenet, billiards, reversi, bagatelle, pigeon-holes, turnstile, porch, beast, hoca, brelan, chess, backgammon, dice, basset, and calbas. Bluebeard was uniformly unfortunate in these various games, at which he lost large sums every night. He could console himself for his continuous run of bad luck by watching the three Lespoisse ladies win a great deal of money. Jeanne, the younger, who often backed the game of the Chevalier de la Merlus, heaped up mountains of gold. Madame de Lespoisse's two sons also did very well at reversi and basset; their luck was invariably best at the more hazardous games. The play went on until late into the night. No one slept during these marvelous festivities, and as the earliest biographer of Bluebeard has said: "They spent the whole night in playing tricks on one another." These hours were the most delightful of the whole twenty-four; for then, under cover of jesting, and taking advantage of the darkness, those who felt drawn toward one another would hide together in the depths of some alcove. The Chevelier de la Merlus would disguise himself at one time as a devil, at another as a ghost or a werewolf in order to frighten the sleepers, but he always ended up slipping into the room of Mademoiselle Jeanne de Lespoisse. The good lord of Montragoux was not overlooked in these games. The two sons of Madame de Lespoisse put irritant powder in his bed, and burned substances that emitted a disgusting smell in his room. Or they would arrange a jug of water over his door so that the worthy lord could not open it without the water falling upon his head. In short, they played on him all sorts of practical jokes, to the diversion of the whole company, and Bluebeard bore them with his natural good humor.

He made his request, to which Madame de Lespoisse acceded, although, as she said, it wrung her heart to think of giving her girls in marriage.

The marriage was celebrated at Motte-Giron with extraordinary magnificence. Demoiselle Jeanne, amazingly beautiful, was dressed entirely in point de France lace, her head covered with a thousand ringlets. Her sister Anne wore a dress of green velvet, embroidered with gold. Their mother's dress was of golden tissue, trimmed with black chenille, adorned with pearls and diamonds. Monsieur de Montragoux wore all his great diamonds on a suit of black velvet. He looked very fine, his expression of timidity and innocence contrasting strongly with his blue chin and massive build. The bride's brothers were of course handsomely arrayed, but the Chevalier de la Merlus, in a suit of rose velvet trimmed with pearls, shone with unparalleled splendor.

Immediately after the ceremony, the Jews who had hired out to the bride's family and her lover all these fine clothes and rich jewels resumed possession of them and posted back to Paris with them.

IV

For a month Monsieur de Montragoux was the happiest of men. He adored his wife and regarded her as an angel of purity. She was something quite different, but far shrewder men than poor

Bluebeard might have been deceived as he was, for she was a person of great cunning and astuteness, and allowed herself submissively to be ruled by her mother, who was the cleverest devil in the whole kingdom of France. She established herself at Guillettes with her eldest daughter Anne, her two sons, Pierre and Cosme, and the Chevalier de la Merlus, who kept as close to Madame de Montragoux as if he had been her shadow. Her good husband was a little annoyed at this; he would have liked to keep his wife always to himself, but he did not take exception to the affection she felt for this young gentleman, as she had told him that he was her foster brother.

Charles Perrault relates that a month after having contracted this union, Bluebeard was compelled to make a journey of six weeks' duration on some important business. He does not seem to be aware of the reasons for this journey, and it has been suspected that it was an artifice, which the jealous husband resorted to, according to custom, in order to surprise his wife. The truth is quite otherwise. Monsieur de Montragoux went to Le Perche to receive the inheritance of his cousin of Outarde, who had been killed gloriously by a cannonball at the Battle of the Dunes, while casting dice upon a drum.

Before leaving, Monsieur de Montragoux begged his wife to indulge in every possible distraction during his absence.

"Invite all your friends, Madame," he said, "go riding with them, amuse yourselves, and have a pleasant time."

He handed over to her all the keys of the house, thus indicating that in his absence she was the sole and sovereign mistress of the entire domain of Guillettes.

"This," he said, "is the key of the two great wardrobes, this of the gold and silver not in daily use, this of the strongboxes that contain my gold and silver, this of the caskets where my jewels are kept, and this is a passkey into all the rooms. As for this little key, it opens the cabinet at the end of the gallery on the ground floor; open everything, and go where you will."

Charles Perrault claims that Monsieur de Montragoux added:

"But I forbid you to enter the little cabinet, and I forbid you so expressly that if you do enter it, I cannot say to what lengths my anger will go."

In placing these words on record, the historian of Bluebeard has committed the error of adopting, without verification, the version concocted after the event by the ladies Lespoisse. Monsieur de Montragoux expressed himself very differently. When he handed his wife the key of the little cabinet, which was none other than the cabinet of the unfortunate princesses to which we have already frequently alluded, he expressed the desire that his beloved Jeanne not enter that part of the house he regarded as fatal to his domestic happiness. It was through this room, indeed, that his first wife, and the best of all of them, had fled, when she ran away with her bear; here Blanche de Gibeaumex had repeatedly betrayed him with various gentlemen; and lastly, the porphyry pavement was stained by the blood of a beloved criminal. Was not this enough to make Monsieur de Montragoux connect the idea of this room with cruel memories and fateful forebodings?

The words that he addressed to Jeanne de Lespoisse convey the desires and impressions that were troubling his mind. They were actually as follows:

"Madame, nothing of mine is hidden from you, and I would feel that I was doing you an injury if I failed to hand over all the keys of a dwelling belonging to you. You may therefore enter this little cabinet, as you may enter all the other rooms of the house; but if you will take my advice, you will do nothing of the kind, to oblige me, and in consideration of the painful ideas that, for me, are connected with this room, and the forebodings of evil that these ideas, despite myself, call up into my mind. I should be inconsolable were any mischance to befall you, or were I to bring misfortune upon you. You will, Madame, forgive these fears, which are happily unfounded, as being only the outcome of my anxious affection and my watchful love."

With these words the good lord embraced his wife and posted off to Le Perche.

"Friends and neighbors," says Charles Perrault, "did not wait to be asked to visit the young bride; so full were they of impatience to see all the wealth of her house. They proceeded at once to inspect all the rooms, cabinets, and wardrobes, each of which was richer and more beautiful than the last; and there was no end to their envy and their praise of their friend's good fortune."

All the historians who have dealt with this subject have added that Madame de Montragoux took no pleasure at the sight of all these riches, by reason of her impatience to open the little cabinet. This is perfectly correct, and as Perrault has said: "So urgent was her curiosity that, without considering that it was unmannerly to leave her guests, she went down to it by a little secret staircase, and in such a hurry that two or three times she thought she would break her neck." The fact is beyond question. But what no one has told us is that the reason why she was so anxious to reach this apartment was that the Chevalier de la Merlus was awaiting her there.

Since she had come to make her home in the castle of Guillettes, she had met this young gentleman in the cabinet every day,

and oftener twice a day than once, without wearying of rendez-
vous so unseemly in a young married woman. It is impossible to
misconstrue the nature of the ties connecting Jeanne with the
Chevalier: they were anything but respectable, anything but
chaste. Alas, had Madame de Montragoux merely betrayed her
husband's honor, she would no doubt have incurred the blame of
posterity; but the most austere of moralists might have found
excuses for her. He might allege, in favor of so young a woman,
the laxity of the morals of the period, the examples of the city and
the court, the too certain effects of a poor upbringing, and the
advice of an immoral mother, for Madame Sidonie de Lespoisse
countenanced her daughter's intrigues. The wise might have for-
given her a fault too amiable to merit their severity; her errors
would have seemed too common to be crimes, and the world
would simply have considered that she was behaving like other
people. But Jeanne de Lespoisse, not content with betraying her
husband's honor, did not hesitate to attempt his life.

It was in the little cabinet, otherwise known as the cabinet of
the unfortunate princesses, that Jeanne de Lespoisse, Dame de
Montragoux, in concert with the Chevalier de la Merlus, plotted
the death of a kind and faithful husband. She declared later that,
on entering the room, she saw hanging there the bodies of six
murdered women whose congealed blood covered the tiles, and
that recognizing in these unhappy women the first six wives of
Bluebeard, she foresaw the fate that also awaited her. She must,
in this case, have mistaken the paintings on the walls for muti-
lated corpses, and her hallucinations must be compared with
those of Lady Macbeth. But it is extremely probable that Jeanne
imagined this horrible sight in order to relate it afterwards, justi-
fying her husband's murderers by slandering their victim.

The death of Monsieur de Montragoux was decided upon. Certain letters that lie before me compel the belief that Madame Sidonie de Lespoisse had her part in the plot. As for her elder daughter, she may be described as the soul of the conspiracy. Anne de Lespoisse was the wickedest of the whole family. She was a stranger to sensual weakness, remaining chaste in the midst of the profligacy of the house. It was not a case of refusing pleasures that she thought unworthy of her; the truth was that she took pleasure only in cruelty. She engaged her two brothers, Cosme and Pierre, in the enterprise by promising them the command of a regiment.

V

It now rests with us to trace, with the aid of authentic documents and reliable evidence, the most atrocious, treacherous, and cowardly domestic crime of which the record has come down to us. The murder whose circumstances we are about to relate can be compared only to that committed on the night of the 9th of March, 1449, against the person of Guillaume de Flavy by his young and slender wife Blanche d'Overbreuc, the bastard d'Orbandas, and the barber Jean Bocquillon.*

They stifled Guillaume with a pillow, battered him pitilessly with a club, and bled him at the throat like a calf. Blanche d'Overbreuc proved that her husband planned to have her drowned, while Jeanne de Lespoisse betrayed a loving husband to a gang of unspeakable scoundrels. We will record the facts with

---

* Flavy's murder by his wife and two accomplices is recounted in Pierre Champion's *Guillaume de Flavy, capitaine de Compiègne; contribution à l'histoire de Jeanne d'Arc* (1906).

all possible restraint. Bluebeard returned rather earlier than expected. This gave rise to the quite mistaken idea that, gripped by the blackest jealousy, he wanted to surprise his wife. On the contrary, he was full of joy and confidence and, if he thought of giving her a surprise, it was an agreeable one. His kindness and tenderness, and his joyous, peaceable air would have softened the most savage hearts. The Chevalier de la Merlus and the whole execrable Lespoisse brood saw therein nothing but an additional facility for taking his life and acquiring his wealth, still further increased by his new inheritance.

His young wife met him with a smiling face, allowing herself to be embraced and led to the conjugal chamber, where she did everything to please the good man. The following morning she returned the bunch of keys he had confided to her care. But the key to the cabinet of the unfortunate princesses, commonly called the little cabinet, was missing. Bluebeard gently demanded its delivery, and after putting him off for a time on various pretexts Jeanne returned it to him.

There now arises a problem that cannot be solved without leaving the limited domain of history to enter the indeterminate regions of philosophy.

Charles Perrault specifically states that the key of the little cabinet was a fairy key; that is to say, it was magical, enchanted, endowed with properties contrary to the laws of nature, at all events, as we conceive them. We have no proof to the contrary. This is a fitting moment to recall the precept of my illustrious master, Monsieur du Clos des Lunes, a member of the Institute: "When the supernatural makes its appearance, it must not be rejected by the historian." I shall therefore content myself with recalling, as regards this key, the unanimous opinion of all the old biographers of Bluebeard: they all affirm that it was a fairy key. This is a point of great importance. Moreover, this key is not the only object created by human industry that has proved to be endowed with marvelous properties. Tradition abounds with examples of enchanted swords. Arthur's was a magic sword. And so was that of Joan of Arc, on the undeniable authority of Jean Chartier; and the proof afforded by that illustrious chronicler is that when the blade was broken, the two pieces refused to be welded together again despite all the efforts of the most competent armorers. Victor Hugo speaks in one of his poems of those "magic stairways still obscured below."

Many authors even admit that there are fairy men who can turn themselves into wolves. We shall not undertake to combat such a firm and constant belief, and we shall not pretend to decide whether the key of the little cabinet was or was not enchanted, for our reserve does not imply that we are in any uncertainty, and therein resides its merit. But where we find ourselves in our proper domain, or to be more precise within our own jurisdiction, where we once more become judges of facts, and writers of circumstances, is where we read that the key was flecked with blood. The authority of the texts does not so far impress us as to compel us to believe this. It was not flecked with blood. Blood had flowed in the little cabinet, but at a time already remote. Whether the key had been washed or whether it had dried, it was impossible that it should be so stained. What, in her agitation, the criminal wife mistook for a bloodstain on the iron was the reflection of the sky still empurpled by the roses of dawn.

Monsieur de Montragoux, on seeing the key, perceived nonetheless that his wife had entered the little cabinet. He noticed that it now appeared cleaner and brighter than when he had given it to her, and was of opinion that this polish could come only from use.

This produced a painful impression upon him, and he said to his wife, with a mournful smile:

"My darling, you have been into the little cabinet. May there result no grievous outcome for either of us! From that room emanates a malign influence from which I would have protected you. If you in turn should become subjected to it, I should never get over it. Forgive me; when we love we are superstitious."

On these words, although Bluebeard cannot have frightened her, for his words and demeanor expressed only love and melancholy, the young lady of Montragoux began shrieking at the top of her voice: "Help! Help! he's killing me!" This was the signal agreed upon. On hearing it, the Chevalier de la Merlus and the two sons of Madame de Lespoisse planned to throw themselves upon Bluebeard and run him through with their swords.

But the Chevalier, whom Jeanne had hidden in an armoire in the room, appeared alone. Monsieur de Montragoux, seeing him leap forth sword in hand, placed himself on guard. Jeanne fled terror-stricken and met her sister Anne in the gallery. She was not, as has been related, on a tower, for all the towers had been destroyed by order of Cardinal Richelieu. Anne was striving to embolden her two brothers, who, pale and quaking, dared not risk so great a stake. Jeanne hastily implored them: "Quick, quick, brothers, save my lover!" Pierre and Cosme then rushed at Bluebeard. They found him, having disarmed the Chevalier de la Merlus, holding him down with his knee; they treacherously ran their swords through his body from behind and continued to strike at him long after he had breathed his last.

Bluebeard had no heirs. His wife remained mistress of his property. She used a part of it to provide a dowry for her sister Anne, another part to buy captains' commissions for her two brothers, and the rest to marry the Chevalier de la Merlus, who became a very respectable man as soon as he was wealthy.

The Story of the Duchess of Cicogne and of Monsieur de Boulingrin

I

The story of Sleeping Beauty is well known; we have excellent accounts of it, both in prose and in verse. * I shall not undertake to relate it again; but, having become acquainted with several unpublished memoirs of the time, I discovered some anecdotes relating to King Cloche and Queen Satine, whose daughter it was that slept a hundred years, and also to several members of the Court who shared the Princess's sleep. I propose to communicate to the public such portions of these revelations as have seemed to me most interesting.

After several years of marriage, Queen Satine gave the King, her husband, a daughter who received the name of Paule-Marie-Aurore. The baptismal festivities were planned by the Duc des Hoisons, grand master of the ceremonies, in accordance with a formulary dating from the emperor Honorius, which was so mildewed and so nibbled by rats that it was impossible to decipher any of it.

---

* The translation of the tale is by D. B. Stewart, modified.

There were still fairies in those days, and those who had titles used to go to Court. Seven of them were invited to be godmothers: Queen Titania, Queen Mab, the wise Vivien, trained by Merlin in the arts of enchantment, Melusina, whose history was written by Jean d'Arras and who became a serpent every Saturday (but the baptism was on a Sunday), Urgèle, White Anna of Brittany, and Mourgue who led Ogier the Dane into the country of Avalon.

They appeared at the castle in robes of the color of time, of the sun, of the moon, and of the nymphs, all glittering with diamonds and pearls. As all were taking their places at table, an old fairy called Alcuine, who had not been invited, was seen to enter.

"Pray do not be annoyed, Madame," said the King, "that you were not of those invited to this festivity; it was believed that you were either dead or enchanted."

Since the fairies grew old, there is no doubt that they used to die. They all died in time, and everybody knows that Melusina became a kitchen wench in Hell. By means of enchantment they could be imprisoned in a magic circle, a tree, a bush, or a stone, or changed into a statue, a hind, a doe, a footstool, a ring, or a slipper. But in fact it was not because they thought her dead or enchanted that they had not invited the fairy Alcuine; it was because her presence at the banquet had been regarded as contrary to etiquette. Madame de Maintenon was able to state without the least exaggeration that "there are no austerities in the convents like those to which Court etiquette subjects the great."* In accordance with his sovereign's royal wish the Duc des Hoisons had not invited the fairy Alcuine, because she had one quartering of

---

* Françoise d'Aubigné, marquise de Maintenon (1635–1719), second wife of Louis XIV.

nobility too few to be admitted to Court. When the Ministers of State represented that it was of the utmost importance to humor this powerful and vindictive fairy, who would become a dangerous enemy if excluded from the festivities, the King replied in peremptory tones that she could not be invited, as she was not qualified by birth.

This unhappy monarch, even more than his predecessors, was a slave to etiquette. His obstinacy in subordinating the greatest interests and most urgent duties to the smallest exigencies of an obsolete ceremonial had more than once caused serious loss to the monarchy, and had involved the realm in formidable perils. Of all these perils and losses, those to which Cloche had exposed his house by refusing to stretch a point of etiquette in favor of a fairy, without birth, yet formidable and illustrious, were by no means the hardest to foresee, nor was it least urgent to avert them.

The aged Alcuine, enraged by the contempt to which she had been subjected, bestowed upon the Princess Aurore a disastrous gift. At fifteen years of age, beautiful as the day, this royal child was to die of a fatal wound, caused by a spindle, an innocent weapon in the hands of mortal women, but a terrible one when the three spinstress Sisters twist and coil thereon the thread of our destinies and the strings of our hearts.

The seven godmothers could modify, but could not annul Alcuine's decree, and thus the fate of the Princess was determined. "Aurore will prick her hand with a spindle; she will not die of it, but will fall into a sleep of a hundred years, from which the son of a king will come to arouse her."

II

Anxiously the King and Queen consulted, in respect of the decree pronounced upon the Princess in her cradle, all persons of learning and judgment, notably Monsieur Gerberoy, perpetual secretary of the Academy of Sciences, and Dr. Gastinel, the Queen's accoucheur. "Monsieur Gerberoy," Satine inquired, "can one really sleep a hundred years?" "Madame," answered the Academician, "we have examples of sleep, more or less prolonged, some of which I can relate to Your Majesty. Epimenides of Cnossos was born of the loves of a mortal and a nymph. While yet a child he was sent by Dosiades, his father, to watch the flocks in the mountains. When the warmth of midday enveloped the earth, he laid himself down in a cool, dark cave, and there he fell into a slumber that lasted for fifty-seven years. He studied the virtues of the plants, and died, according to some, at the age of a hundred and fifty-four years; according to others at the age of two hundred and ninety-eight.

"The story of the Seven Sleepers of Ephesus is related by Theodore and Rufinus, in a manuscript sealed with two silver seals. Briefly expounded, these are the principal facts. In the year 25 of our Lord, seven of the officers of the emperor Decius, who had embraced the Christian religion, distributed their goods to the poor, retired to Mount Celion, and there all seven fell asleep in a cave. During the reign of Theodore, the Bishop of Ephesus found them there, blooming like roses. They had slept for one hundred and forty-four years.

"Frederick Barbarossa is still asleep. In the crypt beneath a ruined castle, in the midst of a dense forest, he is seated before a table round which his beard has twisted seven times. He will awake to drive away the crows that croak around the mountain.

"These, Madame, are the greatest sleepers of whom History has kept a record."

"They are all exceptions," answered the Queen. "You, Monsieur Gastinel, who practice medicine, have you ever seen people sleep a hundred years?"

"No, Madame," replied the accoucheur, "I have not exactly seen any such, nor do I ever expect to do so; but I have seen some curious cases of lethargy, which, if you desire, I will bring to Your Majesty's notice.

"Ten years ago a demoiselle Jeanne Caillou, being admitted to the Hôtel-Dieu, there slept for six consecutive years. I myself observed the girl Léonide Montauciel, who fell asleep on Easter Day in the year '61, and did not awake until Easter Day of the following year."

"Monsieur Gastinel," demanded the King, "can the point of a spindle cause a wound that will send one to sleep for a hundred years?"

"Sire, it is not probable," answered Monsieur Gastinel, "but in the domain of pathology, we can never say with certainty, 'This will or will not happen.'"

"One might mention Brunhild," said Monsieur Gerberoy, "who was pricked by a thorn, fell asleep, and was awakened by Sigurd."

"There was also Guenillon," said the Duchess of Cicogne, first lady-in-waiting to the Queen. And she hummed:

> She was sent to the wood
> To gather some nuts,

The bush was too high,
The maid was too small.

The bush was too high,
The maid was too small,
She pricked her poor hand
With a very sharp thorn.

She pricked her poor hand
With a very sharp thorn,
From the pain in her finger
The maid fell asleep.

"What are you thinking of, Cicogne?" said the Queen. "You are singing."

"Your Majesty will forgive me," replied the Duchess. "It was to ward off the bad luck."

The King issued an edict, whereby all persons were forbidden under pain of death to spin with spindles, or even to have spindles in their possession. All obeyed. They still used to say in the country districts: "The spindles must follow the mattock," but it was only by force of habit. The spindles had disappeared.

III

Monsieur de La Rochecoupée, the Prime Minister who, under the feeble King Cloche, governed the kingdom, respected popular beliefs, as all great statesmen respect them. Caesar was Pontifex Maximus, and Napoleon had himself crowned by the Pope. Monsieur de La Rochecoupée admitted the power of the fairies.

He was by no means skeptical, by no means incredulous. He did not suggest that the prediction of the seven godmothers was false. But, being helpless, he did not allow it to disturb him. His temperament was such that he did not worry about evils which he was impotent to remedy. In any case, so far as could be judged, the occurrence foretold was not imminent. Monsieur de La Rochecoupée viewed events as a statesman, and statesmen never look beyond the present moment. I am speaking of the shrewdest and most farsighted. After all, supposing one day the King's daughter did fall asleep for a hundred years, it was, in his eyes, purely a family matter, seeing that women were excluded from the throne by the Salic Law.

He had, as he said, plenty of other fish to fry. Bankruptcy, hideous bankruptcy was ever present, threatening to consume the wealth and the honor of the nation. Famine was raging in the kingdom, and millions of unfortunate wretches were eating plaster instead of bread. That year the opera ball was more brilliant and the masques finer than ever.

The peasantry, artisans, and shopkeepers, and the girls of the theater, vied with one another in grieving over the fatal curse inflicted by Alcuine upon the innocent Princess. The lords of the Court, on the contrary, and the princes of the blood royal, appeared very indifferent to it. And there were on all hands men of business and students of science who did not believe in the award of the fairies, for the very good reason that they did not believe in fairies.

Such a one was Monsieur Boulingrin, Secretary of State for the Treasury. Those who ask how it was possible that he should not believe in them since he had seen them are unaware of the lengths to which skepticism can go in an argumentative mind.

Nourished on Lucretius, imbued with the doctrines of Epicurus and Gassendi, he often provoked Monsieur de La Rochecoupée by the display of a cold disbelief in fairies.

The Prime Minister would say to him: "If not for your own sake, be a believer for that of the public. Seriously, my dear Boulingrin, there are moments when I wonder which of us two is the more credulous in respect of fairies. I never think of them, and you are always talking of them."

Monsieur de Boulingrin dearly loved the Duchess of Cicogne, wife of the ambassador to Vienna, first lady-in-waiting to the Queen, who belonged to the highest aristocracy of the realm; a witty woman, somewhat lean, and a trifle close, who was losing her income, her estates, and her very chemise at faro. She showed much kindness to Monsieur de Boulingrin, lending herself to an intercourse for which she had no temperamental inclination, but which she thought suitable to her rank, and useful to her interests. Their intrigue was conducted with an art that revealed their good taste, and the elegance of the prevailing morality; the connection was openly avowed, and thereby stripped of all base hypocrisy; but it was at the same time so reserved in appearance that even the severest critics saw no cause for censure in it.

During the time that the Duchess yearly spent on her estate, Monsieur de Boulingrin used to stay in an old pigeon-house, separated from his friend's château by a sunken road, which skirted a marsh, where by night the frogs among the reeds tuned their diligent voices.

Now, one evening when the last rays of the setting sun were dyeing the stagnant water with the hue of blood, the Secretary of State for the Treasury saw at the crossroads three young fairies who were dancing in a circle and singing:

Three girls in a field:
My heart takes flight, takes flight;
My heart takes flight at your mercy.

They enclosed him within their circle, and their light and airy forms sped swiftly about him. Their faces, in the twilight, were dim and transparent; their tresses shone like the will-o'-the-wisp. They repeated:

"Three girls in a field!" until, dazed and ready to fall, he begged for mercy.

Then said the most beautiful, opening the circle:

"Sisters, give leave to Monsieur de Boulingrin to pass, that he may go to the castle and kiss his ladylove."

He went on without having recognized the fairies, the mistresses of men's destinies, and a little farther on he met three old beggar women, who were walking bowed low over their sticks; their faces were like three apples roasted in the cinders. From their rags protruded bones that had more dirt than flesh upon them. Their naked feet ended in fleshless toes of immoderate length, like the bones of an oxtail.

As soon as they saw him approaching, they smiled upon him and threw him kisses; they stopped him on his way, calling him their darling, their love, their pet, and covered him with caresses that he was powerless to evade, for the moment he made a movement to escape, they dug into his flesh the sharp claws at the tips of their fingers.

"Isn't he handsome? Isn't he lovely?" they sighed.

For some time they raved on, begging him to love them. Then, seeing they could not rouse his senses, which were frozen with horror, they covered him with abuse, hammered him with their staves, threw him on the ground, and trod him underfoot. Then, when he was crushed, broken, aching, and crippled in every limb, the youngest, who was at least eighty years of age, squatted upon him and treated him in a manner too infamous to describe. He was almost suffocated; immediately afterwards the other two, taking the place of the first, treated the unfortunate gentleman in the same way.

Finally all three made off, saluting him with: "Good night, Endymion!" "To our next meeting, Adonis!" "Good-bye, beautiful Narcissus!" and left him swooning.

When he came back to his senses, a toad near him was whistling deliciously like a flute, and a cloud of mosquitoes was dancing before the moon. He rose with great difficulty and limpingly pursued his journey.

Once again Monsieur de Boulingrin had failed to recognize the fairies, mistresses of the destinies of men.

The Duchess of Cicogne awaited him impatiently.

"You come very late, my friend," she said.

He answered, as he kissed her fingers, that it was very kind of her to reproach him. His excuse was that he had been somewhat unwell.

"Boulingrin," she said, "sit down there."

And she confided to him that she would be very happy to accept from the royal treasury a present of two thousand crowns, as a fitting compensation for the unkindness of fate, faro having for the last six months been terribly against her.

Informed that the matter was urgent, Boulingrin wrote immediately to Monsieur de La Rochecoupée to ask for the necessary sum of money.

"La Rochecoupée will be delighted to obtain it for you," he

said. "He is a helpful person and takes pleasure in serving his friends. I may add that in him one perceives greater talents than are commonly seen in the favorites of Princes. He has taste, and a head for business; but he is lacking in philosophy. He believes in fairies, relying on his senses."

"Boulingrin," said the Duchess, "you stink like a tomcat."

IV

Seventeen years, day by day, had elapsed since the fairies' decree. The Princess was as beautiful as a star. The King, Queen, and Court were in residence at the rural palace of Eaux-Perdues. Need I relate what happened then? It is well known how the Princess Aurore, wandering one day through the castle, came to the top of a keep, where, in a garret, she found a dear old woman, all alone, plying her distaff. She had never heard of the King's regulations, forbidding the use of spindles.

"What are you doing, my good woman?" asked the Princess.

"I am spinning, my dear child," replied the old woman, who did not recognize her.

"Ah, how pretty it looks," replied the Princess. "How do you do it? Give it to me, that I may see if I can do it as well."

No sooner had she picked up the spindle, than she pricked her hand with it, and fell swooning (*Contes de Perrault*, édition André Lefèvre, pp. 86–108).* King Cloche, when he heard that the fairies' decree had been accomplished, ordered that the sleeping Princess be placed in the Blue Chamber, on a bed of azure embroi-

---

* France includes references such as these to Lefèvre's scholarly edition of Perrault (Paris: Lemerre, 1875) in order rather ironically to bolster his own erudite affirmation of Perrault's faulty telling of the Sleeping Beauty tale.

dered with silver. Shocked, and full of consternation, the courtiers made ready to weep, practiced sighing, and assumed an expression of deep affliction. Intrigues were formed in every direction; it was reported that the King had discharged his Ministers. The blackest calumnies were hatched. It was said that the Duc de La Rochecoupée had concocted a draught to send the Princess to sleep, and that Monsieur de Boulingrin was his accomplice.

The Duchess of Cicogne climbed the secret staircase to the chambers of her old friend, whom she found in his nightcap, smiling, for he was reading *The King of Garbe's Fiancée.*

Cicogne told him the news, and how the Princess was lying on a blue bed in a state of lethargy.

The Secretary of State listened attentively.

"You do not believe, I hope, my dear friend, that the fairies have anything to do with it?" he said.

For he did not believe in fairies, although three of them, ancient and venerable, had overpowered him with their love and their staves, and had drenched him to the skin in a disgusting liquid, in order to prove their existence to him. The defect of the experimental method pursued by these ladies is that the experiment was addressed to the senses, whose testimony one can always challenge.

"The fairies have had everything to do with it!" cried the Duchess. "The Princess's accident may have the most unfortunate results for you and for me. People will not fail to attribute it to the incapacity of the Ministers, and possibly to their malevolence. Can one tell how far calumny may reach? You are already accused of niggardliness. According to what is being said, you refused, on my advice, to pay for warders for the young and unfortunate Princess. Worse than that, there are rumors of black magic, of casting spells. The storm has got to be faced. Show yourself, or you are lost!"

"Calumny," said Boulingrin, "is the curse of this world. It has killed the greatest of men. Whoever honestly serves his King must make up his mind to pay tribute to that crawling, flying horror."

"Boulingrin," said Cicogne, "get dressed." And she snatched off his nightcap and threw it down by the bedside.

A few minutes later they were in the antechamber of the apartment in which Aurore was sleeping, and seating themselves on a bench they waited to be introduced.

Now at the news that the decree of the Fates had been accomplished, the fairy Vivien, one of the Princess's godmothers, repaired in great haste to Eaux-Perdues, and in order that when she awoke her goddaughter should have a Court, she touched everyone in the castle with her ring. "Governesses, maids of honor, women of the bedchamber, noblemen, officers, grooms of the chamber, cooks, scullions, messengers, guards, beadles, pages, and footmen; she also touched the horses in the stables, the grooms, the great mastiffs in the yard, and little Pouffe, the Princess's lapdog, which lay near her upon her bed. The very spits in front of the fire, loaded with pheasants and partridges, went to sleep" (*Contes de Perrault*, édition André Lefèvre, p. 87).

Meanwhile, Cicogne and Boulingrin waited side by side upon their bench.

"Boulingrin," whispered the Duchess in her old friend's ear, "does it not seem to you that there is something suspicious in this business? Don't you suspect an intrigue on the part of the King's brothers to get the poor man to abdicate? He is well known as a good father. They may well have wished to throw him into despair."

"It is possible," answered the Secretary of State. "In any case the fairies have nothing whatever to do with the matter. Only old countrywomen can still believe these cock-and-bull stories."

"Be quiet, Boulingrin," said the Duchess. "There is nothing so hateful as a skeptic. He is an impertinent person who laughs at our simplicity. I detest strong-minded people; I believe what I ought to believe; but in this particular case, I suspect a dark intrigue."

At the moment when Cicogne spoke these words, the fairy Vivien touched them both with her ring, and sent them to sleep like the rest.

V

In a quarter of an hour there grew all round about the park such an immense quantity of trees, large and small, with thorns and briars interlaced, that neither man nor beast could pass; so that only the tops of the castle towers could be seen, and these only from a long way off (*Contes de Perrault*, pp. 87–88). Once, twice, thrice, fifty, sixty, eighty, ninety, and a hundred times did Urania close the circle of Time: the Sleeping Beauty and her Court, with Boulingrin beside the Duchess on the bench in the antechamber, still slept on.

Whether one regard Time as a mode of the unique substance, whether it be defined as one of the forms of the conscious ego, or an abstract phase of the immediate externality, or whether one regard it purely as a law, a relation resulting from the progression of Reality, we can affirm that one hundred years is a certain space of time.

VI

Everyone knows the end of the enchantment, and how, after a hundred terrestrial cycles, a prince favored by the fairies penetrated the enchanted wood, and reached the bed where slept the Princess. He was a little German princeling, with a pretty moustache, and rounded hips. As soon as she woke up, she fell, or rather rose so much in love, that she followed him to his little principality in such a hurry that she never said a word to the people of her household, who had slept with her for a hundred years.

Her first lady-in-waiting was quite touched thereby, and exclaimed with admiration: "I recognize the blood of my kings." Boulingrin woke up beside the Duchess de Cicogne at the same time as the Princess and all her household. As he rubbed his eyes, his mistress said: "Boulingrin, you have been asleep." "Not at all, dear lady, not at all." He spoke in good faith. Having slept without dreaming for a hundred years, he did not know that he had been asleep.

"I have been so little asleep," he said, "that I can repeat what you said a minute ago."

"Well, what did I say?"

"You said, 'I suspect a dark intrigue.'"

As soon as it awoke, the whole of the little Court was discharged; every one had to fend for himself as best he could.

Boulingrin and Cicogne hired from the castle steward an old seventeenth-century trap drawn by an animal that was already very aged before it went to sleep for a hundred years, and drove to the station of Eaux-Perdues, where they caught a train that, in two hours, deposited them in the capital of the country. Great was their surprise at all that they saw and heard. But by the end of a quarter of an hour they had exhausted their astonishment, and nothing surprised them any more. As for themselves, nobody showed the slightest interest in them. Their story was perfectly incomprehensible, and awakened no curiosity, for our minds are not interested in anything that is too obvious, or too difficult to follow.

As one may well believe, Boulingrin had not the remotest idea what had happened to him. But when the Duchess said that it was not natural, he answered:

"Dear lady, allow me to observe that you have been badly trained in physics. Nothing exists that is not according to Nature."

There remained to them neither friends, relations, nor property. They could not identify the position of their house. With the little money they had, they bought a guitar, and sang in the streets. By this means they earned enough to support themselves. At night Cicogne staked at manille, in the inns, the coppers that had been thrown her during the day, while Boulingrin, with a bowl of warm wine in front of him, explained to the company that it was ridiculous to believe in fairies.

Les Sept Femmes de la Barbe-Bleue
et autres contes merveilleux, 1909

EMILE BERGERAT

The 28-Kilometer Boots
For Octave Mirbeau

My dear Mirbeau, do you believe in dreams?* I mean in the meta-
physical sense of the word? You undoubtedly hold the key to one
I had last night, since you are its cause, if not its focus.

I had just finished your latest book, *La 628-E8*, and like many
others got swept up in its belligerent verve, which, in your quality
as drum major in the battle for modernism, is your trademark.

In your new guise as philosophical motorist, dressed in bear-
skin and helmeted like a deep-sea astronaut, you inspired in me a
jealousy that even our old friendship failed to calm. Your sixty
kilometers per hour kept me awake at night. I had to get myself
one or else lose my senses, which means, as you know, the strait-
jacket. I sold everything and pawned the rest. It cost thirty-two
thousand francs, and at that price it was a bargain. I bought it
without even haggling, to hell with the consequences.

---

* The tale's dedicatee is a French decadent writer (1848–1917) and author of *La 628-E8*
(1907), a novel of international travel from the perspective of a speeding car. Friend of
Bergerat.

Figure 12

"Here's the thing," I said to the genial automaker, "I need it to be vertiginous, Mirbeau be damned. Is it vertiginous?"

"It's guaranteed for a death race," he replied.

"That's not good enough. I need to be able to climb to the summit of the Brocken* in ten minutes, like Faust on Walpurgis Night."

"With or without Mephistopheles, as you prefer."

"It's a deal then."

And I left.

"Bon voyage, poet!" he cried after me, and it was well said, but I was already speeding toward the ends of the earth, without knowing where I was going, of course. You just go! That's the thrill, at least according to the experts, when they fess up to it.

---

* Highest peak in northern Germany, linked by Goethe in *Faust* to the revelry of witches.

I wasn't yet traveling much faster than chickens fleeing the coop and was just leaving the city gates when I saw in the blink of an eye the fleeting silhouette of a giant of a man who was polishing his boots on the tollhouse bench.[*]

This would have assuredly been a banal sight if the man hadn't thrown me a sidelong glance from under puffy eyelids, whose erubescence I took for a bad omen. The boots he was polishing looked enormous, ancient, and quite similar to those worn by stagecoach postilions who sleep upright on their horses, from one post house to the next, held by the weight of their bodies in equilibrium. I accelerated my vertiginous automobile as the road opened before me, broad, airy, and inviting.

I hadn't devoured more than twelve kilometers before the booted man, his legs striding aloft, passed over my head and disappeared into the horizon. Was I already feverish with the fever that comes from the sport of speed? No, my pulse was normal. Then who was this gymnasiarch[†] bounding lightly in such boots over a car nearly careening out of control? A caricature of a cloud, no doubt, formed and carried by the wind.

And yet, oddly, sixteen kilometers farther on, I found him standing erect before me, perched on a milliary distance marker. With bloodshot eyes he peered into a deep wood, scrutinizing the road that disappeared into it. From the sniffling of his hairy nostrils and the slaver of his lolling tongue, it was obvious to me that he was on the scent of some prey in the forest, and to catch

---

[*]   Allusion to the ogre in Perrault's "Le Petit Poucet." This tale is inspired by the last portion of the tale, when the ogre chases Petit Poucet (who ends up outsmarting him).
[†]   Person responsible for training athletes in gymnasia in ancient Greece.

up with him I stepped on the gas as he stretched out his huge legs and, poof! disappeared beyond the timberline.

As full of faith in my invincible automobile as Elijah* in his prophetic mantle, I sped off under the green shadows of the oak trees, hot on the heels of the winged-booted man. I swore that I would not allow science—and what a science this is, my dear Octave, that can reduce distance to a hypothesis!—to be trounced by some spectral vision, the stuff of fairy tales. We'll see if a pair of boots, ordinary, outmoded boots, can triumph over a thirty-two-thousand-franc machine, guaranteed diabolical and signed by a mechanic who makes Archimedes† and Vaucanson‡ look like puppet makers. So I opened up the throttle, and she went so fast that I nearly ran over a young boy holding two little girls by the hand, who I imagined were picking violets in a meadow for the Feast of Mother Goose.

I stopped abruptly as you do when you're just learning how to drive. The boy asked me to take him and his sisters in my vertiginous machine to save them from a bad man who wanted to gobble them up alive—without salt or pepper, he added laughing. So I piled them into the back of the car and took off again at 70 kph. The pediphagist§ was waiting for me at the edge of the forest. "Humph! humph!" he snorted. "I smell fresh meat in your motorcar." It was no time to dawdle—you don't joke around with ogres. The chase began, a dreadful chase that, in my dream, was like a battle between the ideal and the real or, if you prefer, between the

---

* Biblical prophet (book of Kings).

† Ancient Greek mathematician and inventor.

‡ Jacques de Vaucanson (1709–82), French inventor of automata.

§ *Puérophage* (neologism): child eater.

old-fashioned and the new. Don't forget that my manufacturer had flung the all-too-fitting barb of *poet* at me.

However quickly my vertiginous, limitless, death-defying auto gained speed, this child-eating Polyphemus* went faster thanks to his boots, since all he had to do was spread his legs to cover seven leagues in a single stride. I was sure we were going to succumb, just as reason succumbs to madness, when the boy remarked that this span of twenty-eight kilometers was unwavering, that the enemy could neither increase it nor reduce it.

"It's always seven leagues, never more, never less. So all you have to do is slow down or speed up to stay either behind or ahead of his magic stride."

Thus spoke the malicious Little Thumbling, and to hear him I thought I was listening to David calculate the trajectory between his slingshot and Goliath's forehead.

And so with my hand on the wheel, which was as compliant and as sensitive as a watch spring, I followed his advice to vary my speed, and was thus able to evade the Polyphemus, who kept landing a league either behind or ahead of us.

Thus, on this fantastical chase, we arrived in some barren and sandy region, sown with golden-flowered gorse, beyond which appeared a blue sea. Judging from the familiar sound, like the ripping of a great canvas, we were only about two leagues away from its precipice. I was about to begin braking so as not to hurtle into it when the child cried out,

"Go ahead and slow down. He's done for!"

And indeed, with his geometric stride, the imbecilic ogre's legs

---

* Man-eating giant in Greek mythology.

spread wide and he landed in the rushing waters. Owing to our own momentum, we weren't able to stop before reaching the water's edge.

Would you believe, my dear Mirbeau, that our good pediphagist could swim like Neptune himself? He had removed his boots so he could reach a boulder, which formed a small island, where he figured he could save himself, and they washed up on shore. This was a truly strange dream!

My Little Thumbling, who was crazy with joy at seeing the boots bobbing along like seaweed, threw himself out of the car and, followed by his two small sisters who still clung to their bouquets of violets, ran to retrieve them on the strand. Then he put them on. I told you that they were immense, but they shrank to the size of his small feet. Polyphemus was raging on his islet. With the boots on his feet, the happy little thief took one of his florists under each arm, the brunette to his left and the blonde to his right, and with a twenty-eight-kilometer stride, the ingrate fled back to Mother Goose.

As you can well imagine, I ran the "Vertiginous" at death-race speed to catch up with him, but, alas, I didn't know where Mother Goose lived.

And then I woke up.

Are you adept at oneiromancy? What does this dream mean? Perhaps poets have something to do with the invention of the thrill of speed, perhaps good old Perrault deserves some of the credit for it. Can your 628-E8 travel seven leagues in a second? There are boots that can, my dear Octave, and old boots at that.

(Dessin de Marcel Capy.)

L'OGRE ALLEMAND ET LE PETIT POUCET FRANÇAIS

Figure 13: The German ogre and French Little Thumbling

Cinderella Arrives by Automobile

Now I'm really starting to worry: I had another dream last night. There must be an automaker somewhere who's hypnotizing me. After all, I'm not a professional, it's not like I'm obsessed. What's happening to me?

I told you my dream about the seven-league boots and the child-eating ogre chasing me, whom I evaded thanks to a prodigious car, French in mark, called the "Vertiginous." Well, last night it came back to haunt me. This despite having returned home escargotically* in an omnibus.

As I was drifting off to sleep or, to put it technically (since I'm being analytical), in the hypnagogic state, I found myself in some kind of manor house, part château, part farm, of the sort still found in Brittany. It was near sunset, with daylight disappearing under the neighboring woods. And yet the sun still illuminated, almost irradiated a superb carriageway that, as level as a straight-edged ruler, passed by the entrance to the dwelling.

A vast and stately fireplace opened into a central common room, which was adorned with finely crafted old furniture, chests, armoires, tall chairs, a sideboard, bread bin, and gleaming copper service. Its mantelpiece was crested by a coat of arms, and its forged-iron firedogs had uprights that rose like floor lamps. The fireplace was symmetrically equipped with pewter dishes and hunting rifles, whose verdigris vivified the dwelling's bronzed atmosphere.

Four people were sitting around an oblong table: a gentleman, his lady, their two daughters, all in gala dress. They were eating a

---

* *Escargotiquement* (neologism): slowly like a snail.

strange meal, which consisted of an oversized pumpkin placed in the middle of the table, in which they took turns immersing their spoons with mechanical gestures. This pumpkin was the only dish on the table. They emptied it in silence, as they would a pot of jam, without eating into its vermilioned rind, which was chastely veiled in lace. And with each bit of sorbet consumed, they spat out the seed, which was fought over by a swarm of rats stationed by their motionless feet.

In the hearth boiled a cooking pot full of pure water. At its edge a cat, whose tail was drawn across its paws like a foot warmer, was looking at these rats without seeing them, and listened to them without hearing, because it was deaf and blind, as old as Methuselah, and as hairless as a muff trampled under a farandole.

At that moment, my hypnagogic hallucination settled into a pure dream and, with all my senses unhinged, I saw myself sitting on a stool by the fireplace next to yet another, third, daughter, hidden until then in the shadows, who was stirring the ashes with a hairpin in search of a potato.

"Are you hungry?" I asked her.

"Always," she replied. "I have been for sixteen years."

This was her age.

"What is your name?"

She pointed at the cinders.

A horn blast suddenly resounded outside, and three white hackneys followed by a palfrey in a silver harness emerged from the woods, which were darkened to a purple haze, and appeared at the threshold of the room. Dressed for court, the father, mother, and two daughters mounted the horses. They took the path as straight as a ruler and headed off to the King's ball.

The girl named for the cinders watched them as they left and then began to cry. I have never seen anything as lovely in the midst of ugliness, nor so ugly in the midst of such beauty, as this little servant girl. Her tears revealed her heart to me, and I understood that she loved the King. I had slipped into a state of somnambulism, and my perceptions were clairvoyant.

"You are a learned man," she said. "Won't you do something for me?"

"Not learned," I smiled, "but a poet who is at your service. What is it you desire?"

"To go to the royal ball and arrive before them."

"Before whom?"

"My evil sisters and my cruel stepmother."

Who can explain why I then asked this absurd question: "Cinderella, do you have pink feet?" I firmly believe that madness infiltrates dreams. She did not respond, but instead ran toward the cooking pot, removed its cover, and jumped into the boiling water. I cried out in fright, but her face, transfigured by suffering, gleamed like the face of a martyr. Oh, yes! She loved the King! I quickly removed her and placed her on the stool. On her feet were shoes of crystal that were so small, so tiny in their diamond-like sheath, that the Empress of China would have died of jealousy, I assure you. Two tea roses in two Venetian glasses!

"It's time to keep your promise, poet," she cried, pouting like a spoiled child.

So I took out my all-purpose talisman, which I keep with me at all times. I then made a connection—hello! hello! (don't forget that it's a dream)—with the omnipotents you know well—or rather, you don't know. I went over to the pumpkin and tossed off the rhymes necessary for any incantation worthy of its salt.

The cucurbit turned into an automobile.

It was once again the "Vertiginous," that chef d'oeuvre of French mechanics, and the latest word in earthly locomotion.

"Here's your carriage, my little Cinderella. I offer it to you on behalf of all poets, great or minor, dead or alive, in honor of your love. The *malle des Indes*, today known as the Orient Express, travels no faster than a tortoise next to this lightning flash on wheels. Even if your sisters and stepmother have already arrived in the courtyard of the royal palace, you will get to the ball before them.

"Alas! I cannot dance with him wearing these rags!"

And she displayed the tattered clothes that hung on her body. But all of a sudden the old furniture became the accomplices of poets: chests and armoires opened all at once and threw at her pink and charming feet innumerable pieces of a pentacentennial wardrobe, in which all the fashions of our mothers, grandmothers, great-grandmothers and beyond were represented. The coquettish girl wanted only lace. So they all came alive: Mechlin lace, Valenciennes lace, point de Venise (not to be confused with point d'Alençon), English lace made in Brussels, Auvergne lace made in Le Puy-en-Velay, not to mention Spanish lace. They all sewed themselves together around the girl, dressing her in an arachnoid dress in which her virginal young body appeared most chastely in its triumphant nudity.

As for me, I had already assumed my position as driver, hand on the wheel like a captain at the rudder.

"Let's go, Cinderella! To the King's ball!"

In my currently sad state of wakefulness it's impossible for me to recall why all the rats, who had been transformed into cyclists, were running all around, in front of and behind us, in the wake of the "Vertiginous." Suffice it to say that this was the case. The old deaf and blind cat was the only one to remain behind, next to the pot simmering by the fire. In my opinion he was philosophizing about the meaning of our adventure, although not in the least surprised by it because he knew well that gods are little concerned by the limitations of speed and will happily supply fairy cars in exchange for a couple of good rhymes (and rightly so, if they can shoe Mercury with winged sandals fast enough to cross the seven heavens in less time than it takes me to write this).

She married the King, she is queen, and she presently holds us in disdain. She invites only pedantic scholars to her court. And yet not one of them has explained scientifically to her how she managed to acquire glass slippers by plunging her feet in boiling water. What's more, in their ignorance of matters of love, they speak of fur rather than glass slippers.* Cinderella's slipper made of *fur*! What imbeciles!

Such was my dream.

Contes de Caliban, 1909

---

* Pun in French: *pantoufles de verre* (glass), *de vair* (fur used in heraldry). Reference to nineteenth-century controversy over the composition of Cinderella's slipper, begun with Balzac. Balzac wrote: "The word *vair* has become so obscure in the past hundred years that Cinderella's famous slipper, doubtless of miniver [*menu vair*], is now presented as made of glass [*verre*] in countless editions of Perrault's tales." See Delarue, "À propos de la pantoufle de Cendrillon."

GUILLAUME APOLLINAIRE

Cinderella Continued, or the Rat and the Six Lizards

It has not been stated what became of Cinderella's coach and team when, after the second ball at court, having heard the first stroke of midnight and having lost her squirrel-fur slipper, she did not find them waiting at the gate of the royal palace.*

The fairy—Cinderella's fairy godmother—was not so cruel as to turn the great hulking coachman (who had such fine mustachios) back into a rat, or the six footmen in lace-bedizened coats back into lizards, and since she had done them the honor of letting them remain men, by the same token she let the hollowed-out pumpkin remain a beautiful gilded coach and the six mice remain six fine, dappled mouse-gray horses.

But at the first stroke of midnight the great hulking coachman took it into his head that he would do better out of selling the coach and horse than skimping along on his wages, year in and year out, and that the six footmen, thoroughgoing idlers, would be only too glad to form a band—of which he would be the chief—which would prey upon travelers on the great highways.

---

* The translation of the tale is by Iain White.

Giddyap, then! Coach and team smartly set off before Cinderella reached the palace gate. He halted only at an inn, where, whilst nibbling at a turkey flanked by a pair of fattened pullets and gulping down brimming tankards of wine, the noble band sold the horses and the carriage to the innkeeper—who offered them *pistoles* enough. In this way they changed their clothes and armed themselves. The great hulking coachman, whose name was Sminthe, adopted a special disguise. His mustachios having been shaved off, he dressed as a woman and put on a green satin skirt, a dress *à l'ange*, and a cape. In that garb he was in a position to direct his six rascally companions without risk to himself. Things being arranged to the satisfaction of both parties, they bade the innkeeper farewell and quit Paris to, as the saying has it, *live in clover, wandering the roads*.

We shall not follow them in their exploits on the highways, about the fairs, and in the castles, where the band managed so well that, in a mere seven years, they could return to Paris, where they lived off the fat of the land.

During the time he had lived in female dress, Sminthe had taken to a stay-at-home way of life, which led him to give due thought to the brilliant operations he had had carried out by the six brigands-footmen-lizards; he had also learned to read and had amassed a quantity of books, among which were the *Révélations de Sainte Brigitte*, the *Alphabet de l'imperfection et malice des femmes*, the *Centuries* of Nostradamus, the *Prédictions de l'enchanteur Merlin*, and a good few more singular works of a like sort. He acquired a taste for learning, and after the band had gone into retirement, Sminthe spent a good deal of his time in his library, reading and meditating on the power of the fairies, on the vanity that is intelligence or human cunning, and on the foundations of true happiness. And seeing him always immured in his book-filled room, his six acolytes (who among themselves called him not Sminthe but Lerat, because of his origins, or rather because of what they knew of them, for unawares they paid homage to that animal, as do savages who honor their totems and the animals therein depicted) came in the end to call him Lerat de Bibliothèque;* the name stuck, and it was under that name that he was known in the Rue de Bussy, where he lived and compiled numerous works, which have not been published but which have been preserved in manuscript in Oxford.

Such time as remained to him he devoted to the education of his six scoundrels, each of whom made his way in the world—the first as a painter who executed marvelous likenesses of innkeepers' lovely wives, the second as a poet who composed songs which the third set to music and gave life to on the lute whilst the fourth danced perfect sarabands in which he assumed a thousand refined and droll attitudes. The fifth became an excellent sculptor and fashioned gracious statues in lard for pork butchers' shop-windows, and the sixth an unrivaled architect, endlessly building castles in Spain.

Since they were always seen together—although nobody had any inkling of what they had been—they were called "*les Arts*" for between them, they represented the six: Poetry, Painting, Sculpture, Architecture, Music and the Dance. And here we may admiringly note how shrewd is popular etymology—*les Arts* having been *lézards*.

Sminthe or Lerat de Bibliotheque died in the odor of sanctity, and four of his companions likewise died in their beds. Lacerte

* Homonym of "le rat de bibliothèque," French expression for bookworm. France similarly plays on the homophony of "les Arts" (the arts) and "lézards" (lizards).

Figure 14: Cinderella

the poet and Armonidor the musician outlived them and conducted their affairs so maladroitly that they were constrained, in order to make a living, to live once more on their wits. One night, having forced an entry to the Palais Royal, they carried off a casket. They opened it on their return home and found therein only a pair of white and gray fur slippers. They were Queen Cinderella's squirrel-fur slippers, and at the very moment they were despairing of profiting by their find, the officers of the watch (who had made out their tracks) came upon the scene, arrested them, and marched them off to the Grand Châtelet.

The crime was so grave and so well attested that they were beyond hope of avoiding execution.

They opted to cast dice to decide which should take all the blame on himself and exonerate the other.

The loser—Armonidor—was as good as his word and saved his confederate by declaring that he had suggested they take a walk and that his friend knew nothing of his intentions.

Thus Lacerte returned home and composed his friends' epitaphs; but a month later he died, for his art did not make him a living and he was eaten up with weariness.

As for the little squirrel-fur slippers, the vagaries of time brought it about that they are now to be found in the museum of Pittsburgh in Pennsylvania, where they are catalogued as: *Pin Trays (first half of the nineteenth century)*, although they are authentically of the seventeenth century; nonetheless, this description leads one to believe that they were in fact used as pin trays in the period indicated by the antiquaries of Pittsburgh.

However, one is at a loss to explain how it was that Cinderella's little squirrel-fur slippers found their way to America.

1919

CLAUDE CAHUN

Cinderella, the Humble
and Haughty Child

She dropped one of her glass slippers,
and the prince picked it up very carefully.
—Perrault

My father got remarried, which overjoyed me. I'd always dreamt of having an evil stepmother. The heavens granted me even more, giving me two stepsisters. They were deliciously cruel. I especially liked the older one, who despised me so much it thrilled me. Seeing me always seated in the fireplace's cinders, whose heat penetrated me delectably (sometimes even burning me), with her sweet, familiar voice, didn't she call me *Cinderass*? Never was a word so sweet to my ears.

Unfortunately, they were pretty girls, suitable for marriage. They soon left us, leaving me with my parents who, devoted to one another, regarded the world with a drunken tenderness. And I too was enveloped by their splendid, universal indifference. I would do anything to avoid such a marriage . . . But how would I, since I was of an amorous mind, and so submissive?

Furthermore, I felt my pleasure diminish each day, and my ecstasy wane. I understood why (for lack of anything better, I had given myself to solitary reveries and reflected a lot): such delights fade with habit. At present, I was too downcast, too humiliated, to experience the joy of daily humiliation. I had to climb back onto the bank, onto a tall bank, to dive back into the infinite sea of human voluptuousness. A princess, ah! *If I were a queen!* . . . To wed, publicly, the least of my vassals, to get him to force me to abdicate, to abuse me, to prefer the whores of his village to me! *Can one make such fantasies come true?*

My very wise godmother, Madame Fairy, to whom I confessed my desires, came to my rescue. She knew our Prince very well (long ago, she had even attended his baptism) and revealed to me the *curious particularities* by which he could be seduced:

He had a passion for women's shoes. Touching them, kissing them, letting himself be walked on with their charming heels (pointed heels with a scarlet tint so they looked as if they were splattered with blood)—these were the simple pleasures he'd been looking for since he was a child. The ladies at court could not satisfy him. Awkward and timid, lest they wound the heir to the throne, they wear house slippers. And fearing he would lower himself to kiss their feet, they raise them, with all the signs of respect, to his mouth, which is august, but bitter, unyielding to smiles . . . What this royal lover needs is a haughty and dominating mistress, with hard heels and no pity, the one I could be—me, the one who understands!

"Godmother, you are demanding a terrible sacrifice of me! This man is the opposite of the one my heart desires."

"I know, my dear. But it's for a purpose. *Every sacrifice has its own reward.* By playing your role, you will experience an excitement more profound than any of the all-too-common ones you've known until now. My blasé Cinderella, listen to me: the sharpest pain on earth (for you, the greatest pleasure) is to go against one's instinct, to violate it and to chasten it time and again . . ."

Convinced by my good godmother, I accepted her presents— three pairs of cinder-gray horses, a carriage, a driver, and six lackeys; clothes of velour and gold; and cute *vair* slippers (he adores fur) that she entrusted to me just for him . . .

She advised me to be proud and fierce, mysterious to perfection, and to flee at the stroke of midnight—and to do so the second night, in the process losing my little left slipper (but in full light and under the eyes of the Prince who would follow me).

(My feet are small and compact, and sort of stunted—since I have the habit of binding them in a vise of stiff cloth laced firmly in the Chinese fashion. This exquisite and most effective torture fills me with utter satisfaction . . .)

I obeyed. Yesterday, I saw the Prince, who disturbed me greatly. Alas! I guess his thoughts all too well! And I noticed many essential details . . . *He blushed at the mention of boots. He blushes,* he told me naively, *if he walks in front of a display of shoes, which seems to him to be the worst inconvenience;* but a display of flesh does not affect his modest and tolerant soul. He is astonished that games so foolish and even a bit repugnant can be pleasing.

I agree with him. And perhaps I would truly love him if he occasionally wanted to switch roles . . . I can't entertain the thought for a second, for if I were to ruin his illusions, he would send his cricket back home all too quickly! I'll have to deceive him to the grave.

The important thing is being a Princess. When I'm a Princess, with the help of my godmother, I'll be able to get the lowliest of my valets to beat me.

Then, I'll once again put on my scullery maid dress, precious rags the color and odor of cinders, in which I'll secretly bury my crazed head every day. I'll go out at night. I'll meet passersby (there's no lack of poor or ugly, even dishonest people). And the better I play my role for the dear Prince, the more marvelously intense the contrast of these humiliating contacts will be for me.

ca. 1925

Bibliography

Primary Sources

Adelswärd-Fersen, Jacques d'. *Ébauches et débauches*. Paris: Vanier, 1901.

Apollinaire, Guillaume. "La Suite de Cendrillon, ou Le Rat et les six lézards." *La Baïonnette* 185 (16 January 1919): 42. "Cinderella Continued, or the Rat and the Six Lizards," translated by Iain White in *Spells of Enchantment*. Ed. Jack Zipes. New York: Viking, 1991. 606–8.

Arène, Paul. *Les Ogresses*. Paris: Charpentier, 1891.

Baïonnette, La. 185 (16 January 1919). Issue entitled *À la Perrault: écrits nouveaux sur vieux thèmes*.

Baudelaire, Charles. *Le Spleen de Paris* (1869). *Œuvres complètes*, vol. 1. Ed. Claude Pichois. Paris: Gallimard, "Bibliothèque de la Pléiade," 1975.

Bergerat, Emile. *Contes de Caliban*. Paris: Charpentier, 1909.

Cahun, Claude. *Héroïnes*. Ed. François Leperlier. Paris: Mille et une nuits, 2006.

Daudet, Alphonse. *Contes du lundi* (1873). *Œuvres*, vol. 1. Ed. Roger Ripoll. Paris: Gallimard, "Bibliothèque de la Pléiade," 2001.

France, Anatole. *Les Sept Femmes de la Barbe-Bleue et autres contes merveilleux* (1909). *Œuvres*, vol. 4. Ed. Marie-Claire Bancquart. Paris: Gallimard, "Bibliothèque de la Pléiade," 1994. *The Seven Wives of Bluebeard and Other Marvelous Tales*. Translated by D. B. Stewart. London: John Lane Company, 1920.

Lemaître, Jules. *Dix contes*. Paris: Lecène et Oudin, 1890.

———. *En marge des vieux livres*. Paris: Société française d'imprimerie et de librairie, 1906.

——. *La Vieillesse d'Hélène: nouveaux contes en marge*. Paris: Calmann-Lévy, 1914.

Lorrain, Jean. *Princesses d'ivoire et d'ivresse* (1902). Ed. Jean de Palacio. Paris: Séguier, "Bibliothèque décadente," 1993.

——. "The Princess Mandosiane." *The Parisian* 7.3 (September 1899): 230–34.

Mendès, Catulle. *Les Contes du rouet*. Paris: Frinzine et compagnie, 1885.

——. *Les Oiseaux bleus* (1888). Ed. Jean de Palacio. Paris: Séguier "Bibliothèque décadente," 1993.

——. *La Princesse nue*. Paris: Ollendorff, 1890.

Mockel, Albert. *Contes pour les enfants d'hier*. Paris: Mercure de France, 1908.

Perrault, Charles. *Les Contes de Perrault*. Dessins par Gustave Doré. Paris: Hetzel, 1867.

Rachilde. *Contes et nouvelles*. Paris: Mercure de France, 1900.

Régnier, Henri de. *La Canne de jaspe*. Paris: Mercure de France, 1897.

Ricard, Jules. *Acheteuses de rêves*. Paris: Calmann-Lévy, 1894.

Schwob, Marcel. *Le Livre de Monelle* (1894). *Cœur double; Le Livre de Monelle*. Ed. Jean-Pierre Bertrand. Paris: Flammarion, 2008.

Veber, Pierre. *Les Belles Histoires*. Paris: Stock, 1908.

Vivien, Renée. *La Dame à la louve* (1904). Ed. Martine Reid. Paris: Gallimard, 2007.

Willy. *Une Passade*. Paris: Flammarion, 1894.

Secondary Sources

Baycroft, Timothy, and David Hopkin, eds. *Folklore and Nationalism in the Long Nineteenth Century*. Leiden: Brill, 2012.

Byrne, Joseph. *Encyclopedia of Pestilence, Pandemics, and Plagues*. Westport, CT: Greenwood Press, 2008.

Chatelain, Nathalie. "Les Contes de fées en Europe à la fin du XIXe siècle: naissance, essence et déliquescence du conte de fées fin-de-siècle." 2 vols. Diss. Université de Nancy 2, 2005.

——. "Lorsque le titre se fait épitaphe: chronique de la mort annoncée du conte de fée fin-de-siècle." *LHT* 6 (2009). fabula.org. Web. 14 January 2013.

Delarue, Paul. "À propos de la pantoufle de Cendrillon." *Bulletin de la Société française de mythologie*, no. 5, January–March 1951.

Goyau, Lucie Félix. *La Vie et la mort des fees: essai d'histoire littéraire*. Paris: Perrin, 1910.

Hasard, Paul. *The European Mind: The Critical Years, 1680–1715*. New Haven, CT: Yale University Press, 1953.

Hennard Dutheil de la Rochère, Martine, and Véronique Dasen, eds. *Des Fata aux fées: regards croisés de l'antiquité à nos jours*. Lausanne: Université de Lausanne, 2011.

Hopkin, David. *Voices of the People in Nineteenth-Century France*. Cambridge: Cambridge University Press, 2012.

Jullian, Philippe. *Esthètes et magiciens*. Paris: Perrin, 1969.

Laboulaye, Édouard. *Derniers Contes bleus*. Paris: Librairie Furne, Jouvet et Cie, 1884.

Lacassin, Francis, ed. *Si les fées m'étaient contées: 140 contes de fées de Charles Perrault à Jean Cocteau*. Paris: Omnibus, 2003.

Lemire, Charles. *Jules Verne, 1828–1905: l'homme, l'écrivain, le voyageur, le citoyen*. Paris: Berger-Levrault, 1908.

Maugue, Annelise. *L'Identité masculine en crise au tournant du siècle*. Paris: Rivages, 1987.

Palacio, Jean de. *Perversions du merveilleux: Ma Mère l'Oye au tournant du siècle*. Paris: Séguier, 1993.

Péladan, Joséphin. *Comment on devient fée*. Paris: Chamuel, 1893.

Renan, Ernest. *L'Avenir de la science*. Paris: Calmann Lévy, 1890.

Seifert, Lewis C. *Fairy Tales, Sexuality and Gender, 1690–1715: Nostalgic Utopias*. Cambridge: Cambridge University Press, 1996.

Todorov, Tzvetan. *Introduction à la littérature fantastique*. Paris, Seuil, 1970.

Viegnes, Michel. "La Force au féminin dans le conte merveilleux fin-de-siècle." Hennard 321–336.

Zipes, Jack. *Spells of Enchantment*. New York: Viking, 1991.

Biographical Notes

Jacques d'Adelswärd-Fersen (1880–1923): novelist and poet, editor of the short-lived literary journal *Akademos: revue mensuelle d'art libre et de critique* (1909), one of the first French reviews having gay content. Wealthy aristocratic dandy who scandalized Parisian high society. His "Sleeping Beauty" is included in his collection of poetry and prose pieces, *Ébauches et débauches* (1901).

Guillaume Apollinaire (Guillaume Albert Wladimir Alexandre Apollinaire Kostrowitzky, 1880–1918): born in Rome, of Polish ancestry. Important presurrealist writer, notably of poetry, including the collections *Le Bestiaire* (1911), *Alcools* (1913), and *Calligrammes* (1918). Apollinaire had close ties to cubist artists and exhibits an important visual element in his poetry. "Cinderella Continued" was published posthumously in an issue, devoted to Perrault, of the satirical wartime journal *La Baïonnette*.

Paul Arène (1843–96): author of novels, plays, and tales; Provençal poet; journalist. Arène collaborated with Alphonse Daudet and associated with writers François Coppée, Catulle Mendès, and Octave Mirbeau, among others. His tale "The Ogresses" is drawn from the 1891 collection bearing the same name.

Charles Baudelaire (1821–67): poet, author of *Les Fleurs du mal* (1857) and the groundbreaking collection of prose poetry, *Le Spleen de Paris* (1869), which includes his tale "Fairies' Gifts." A translator of Edgar Allan Poe, Baudelaire, through his own work, greatly influenced decadent writers at the end of the century.

Emile Bergerat (1845–1923): poet, essayist (for *Le Figaro*, among other publications), dramaturge. Member of the Académie Goncourt and son-in-law of the influential writer Théophile Gautier. He sometimes wrote under the name Caliban (character from *The Tempest*, Prospero's half-human slave); the tales included here were published in his *Contes de Caliban* (1909).

Claude Cahun (Lucy Schwob, 1894–1954): artist, photographer, and surrealist writer who wrote under several pseudonyms. Cahun was one of the few women to be accepted by surrealists. Niece of symbolist novelist Marcel Schwob. Leftist activist and Resistance fighter during the German occupation. Her personal androgyny, sexual nonconformity, and Judaism are apparent in her work. *Héroïnes*, texts on Eve, Delilah, Judith, and Sappho, was published in the *Mercure de France* (1925). While unpublished during her lifetime, "Cinderella, the Humble and Haughty Child" has appeared in modern editions of *Héroïnes*.

Alphonse Daudet (1840–97): realist novelist and author of short stories. He wrote both regional fiction about Provence, including *Lettres de mon moulin* (1869), and novels of Parisian manners. "Fairies of France" is drawn from his *Contes du lundi* (1873), whose other tales also deal with the Franco-Prussian War.

Anatole France (1844–1924): prolific author and critic, highly regarded during his lifetime, France was a member of the Académie française and a Nobel laureate (1921). *Les Sept Femmes de la Barbe-Bleue et autres contes merveilleux* was published in 1909.

Jules Lemaître (1853–1914): writer, primarily of plays, and theater critic, member of the Académie française. Rightist and anti-Dreyfusard. Author of several collections of tales, including *Dix contes* (1890), *En marge des vieux livres* (1906), and *La Vieillesse d'Hélène* (1914).

Jean Lorrain (Paul Duval, 1855–1906): prolific decadent writer and journalist. Author of early homoerotic novel *Monsieur de Phocas* (1901). The tales included here were first published in *Princesses d'ivoire et d'ivresse* (1902). He also wrote fantastic tales, notably *Contes d'un buveur d'éther* (1895).

Catulle Mendès (1841–1909): prolific writer and critic who traversed many genres, from Parnassian poetry to decadent-flavored novels. Like Bergerat, he was Théophile Gautier's son-in-law. A copious producer of tales, he left dozens of volumes of various tones, some naive and others racy, Parisian tales of manners as well as fairy tales. Those included here were first published in *Les Contes du rouet* (1885), *Les Oiseaux bleus* (1888), and *La Princesse nue* (1890).

Albert Mockel (1866–1945): Belgian symbolist poet and literary critic. Author of books on Stéphane Mallarmé and Émile Verhaeren. He wrote one collection of tales, *Contes pour les enfants d'hier* (1908).

Rachilde (Marguerite Eymery, 1860–1953): decadent novelist and literary critic for *Mercure de France*, who first gained notoriety with *Monsieur Vénus* (1884). Subsequent novels, such as *La Marquise de Sade* (1887) and *Madame Adonis* (1888), frequently pushed representations of gender and sexuality to new arenas. Her short stories include *Contes et nouvelles* (1900) and *La Découverte de l'Amérique* (1919).

Henri de Régnier (1864–1936): an influential symbolist poet, Régnier also wrote many novels and tales, and was literary critic for *Le Figaro*. He was elected to the Académie française in 1911. His collections of tales include *Contes à soi-même* (1894) and *La Canne de jaspe* (1897).

Jules Ricard (1848–1903): fin de siècle novelist and playwright. His *Acheteuses de rêves* (1894) contains five "Contes de la fée Morgane."

Marcel Schwob (1867–1905): important French symbolist writer from a family of writers (including niece Claude Cahun). In addition to writing many short stories, he was a journalist, biographer, literary critic, and translator. His hybrid collection, *Le Livre de Monelle* (1894), contains reimagined fairy tales recounted by Monelle's sisters.

Pierre Veber (1869–1942): prolific playwright and theater critic who also wrote novels and tales. "The Last Fairy" is collected in *Les Belles Histoires* (1908).

Renée Vivien (Pauline Mary Tarn, 1877–1909): London-born daughter of wealthy Anglo-American parents who emigrated to Paris when she reached her majority, Vivien was a prolific writer who wrote primarily in French. She became acquainted with literary figures such as Pierre Louÿs and was for a time attached to Natalie Clifford Barney's circle, which has come to be known as Sappho 1900. While primarily a poet, she also translated Sappho's fragments and wrote a novella, *Une Femme m'apparut* (1904), as well as the collection of stories *La Dame à la louve* (1904), which includes "Prince Charming."

Willy (Henry Gauthier-Villars, 1859–1931): prolific journalist, music critic, and novelist. A very visible presence in Paris during the Belle Époque, he is primarily known today as the first husband of a young Colette, whose *Claudine* novels he signed with his own name. "Fairy Tales for the Disillusioned" numbers among the stories of *Une Passade* (1894).